Ghosts

Strange Tales of the Unnatural,

The Uncanny and

The Unaccountable

Aakenbaaken & Kent   New York

Ghosts

Copyright 2012, all rights reserved.

No part of this book may be used or reproduced in any manner whatsoever without written permission except in the case of brief quotations for use in articles and reviews.

Aakenbaaken & Kent   New York, NY 10003

akeditor@inbox.com

This is a work of fiction. Names, characters, places and incidents are either the product of the authors' imaginations or are used fictitiously. Any resemblance of the fictional characters to actual persons living or dead is entirely coincidental.

The cover image was designed by Kelly Matherly and incorporated into the complete cover by Reese-Winslow Design (www.reese-winslow.com).

ISBN: 978-1-938436-07-9

ACKNOWLEDGEMENTS

We wish to thank Lynne Gregg and Julian Kindred for their endeavors in assembling this anthology of ghost stories written by the Houston Writers Guild. Lynne has been with us since the beginning, and Julian arrived recently, but their talents appear to be limitless.

We also wish to thank the members who wrote the various stories, whose names you will find on the Table of Contents page. Without complaint, they wrote and rewrote their stories in order to satisfy the editors and produce publishable products.

Our thanks also go to Stephanie Jaye Evans, who took time out from book signings of her debut novel, *Faithful Unto Death*, to write us a ghost story for our anthology. A writer whose next book, *Safe From Harm*, you will eagerly await.

And to Joe Lanza, legal eagle extraordinaire, who took time out from the courtroom to create the unbeatable stories contained in this book. Look for Bishop and Ceré in a soon to be published novel of their own!

Especially, we wish to thank Chris Rogers, who has been a stalwart member for the last fifteen years, giving of herself without hesitation or measure, both in teaching us the writing process and helping us refine and edit our manuscripts.

If you would like to keep up with the Houston Writers Guild, go to our webpage www.houstonwritersguild.org or send an email to info@houstonwritersguild.org

Table of Contents

Clothes Make the Magic	Chris Rogers	9
Miracle Baby	Stephanie Jaye Evans	25
Unforsaken Love	Kelly Matherly	43
The Stall	Julian Kindred	45
Bloody Mary	Joseph L. Lanza	49
The Man in the Fedora	Ann Conti	63
The Name	Sandra DiGiovanni	69
Transparent Bob	Joe Lanza	85
Ashes	Lynne Gregg	97
The Jumbie House	Pamela Fagan Hutchins	107
The Stop	E.L. Russell	115
X Marks the Spot	Ann Conti	121
The Ghost in my iPad	Enid Russell	125
The Ghost of the Bar-B-Bar	Thomas J. Dowling	137
My Francine	Shawn Caldwell	143
A Silent Graveyard	Frank Carden	155
A New Caretaker	Ginger Fisher	157
Secret Playroom	Karen Alterisio Nelson	165
Swirlship	Joseph Lanza	175
You're D-dead, Bob	J. Dennis Papp	181
Havelock Cemetery	Joe Lanza	193
Live on Stage	Chris Rogers	197

Clothes Make the Magic
by
Chris Rogers

The trunks arrived at the theater while Elsa was pouring her third cup of Wakeup Wallop tea.

"To Ms. Elsavere Maxine Lord," she read on the delivery ticket. It was from an estate executor, the estate of "Albert and Rosalyn Tremont."

Thrilled, dismayed, Elsa felt both, like push-pull on her brain cells. The Tremonts were the most famous couple in Chicory, Texas, actors who'd toured the world, leaving audiences enchanted in town after town, country after country. Far and wide the Tremonts were known, at least by older generations. Any acting group would be delighted to own their personal costumes and props.

Would the Chicory Lord Theater appreciate the publicity such a bequest was certain to create? Like Santa appreciated hot cocoa and cookies on his long, cold delivery route.

As a cofounder determined to make their tiny theater a shining star on the Texas arts-and-entertainment map, Elsa felt her heart champing wildly: *O-pen, o-pen, open those treasure chests!*

But storage was going to be a problem.

A bulky, unwieldy, elephant-sized problem. She read the delivery ticket again.

"Wait," she told the young men wheeling in two more trunks. "Is this right? You have twenty-two trunks to deliver?"

The taller, white-haired man, with a bushy white moustache and the bearing of a "Mover in Charge," glanced out the door, where a red and green commercial cargo van sat parked at the curb.

"Let's see ..." He looked toward the stairs, up which he and his helper had wrestled the four chests already unloaded. "Twenty-two in all, so that'd make sixteen, plus these two, still to come in."

"Oh, my. We simply don't have the room." Again she studied the ticket. "Were your instructions to deliver them to the theater, specifically? Or to me?"

"Well...," A finger aside his nose, he frowned in concentration. "They clearly belong to you, ma'am. That's what the attorney said who handled the estate. This was the address on the delivery bill, but you can take them anywhere you want."

"I see."

Her garage would surely hold them all, if she left her car in the driveway. Sun, hail, bird droppings ... she grimaced. Yet, there simply wasn't room here.

"I live two streets over. How much extra would you charge to take the remainder of the trunks to my house and unload them there?"

He nodded, clearly thinking hard about it.

"Any stairs to climb at your house?"

"Oh, no. You could back in close to the garage and unload everything."

"No extra charge, then, ma'am." His beaming, chubby-cheeked smile held a sparkle of relief.

Upstairs in the prop-and-wardrobe room, Elsa poured her cold tea into a small planter that held a Christmas cactus to give it a morning wakeup, then lifted the cactus out of the Styrofoam cooler that kept it dark for twelve hours a day. She examined the bright pink buds that graced it.

"What do you think, will we have blossoms for the holiday this year? Yes, Orson, I hear you shifting around in your urn and watching over my shoulder." She carried the cactus to the hall window, and set it in the filtered light of the sill, as near to its native rainforest conditions as she could provide. The plant was older than Elsa, passed down from Orson's grandmother.

Her husband didn't answer, of course, but she knew he was watching the plant's progression from the shelf where she had set his urn on her arrival this morning. Christmas Eve would mark the second anniversary of Orson's death, yet she could hear his cheerful, husky voice as clearly at times as if he, rather than merely a pot of ashes, were sitting above the makeup table. He never answered inane questions, however, reserving his remarks for juicier exchanges.

"Dress rehearsal tonight," she reminded him. A local playwright had adapted a delightful play from the ever popular but boringly stale "A Christmas Carol." Their new version, "Christmas with Dickens," was set in small-town Texas, just after World War II ended, and the script was quite a treat. The acting, however, had yet to come together, and opening night was only two days hence.

Elsa loved acting, as did Orson, and in the first year after he passed on, thrusting herself into various characters' skins seemed the only thing holding her own fragile self together. Tonight, though, she was directing. When this year's fall season started, the Chicory Lord's tenth anniversary, everyone with directing experience was otherwise occupied, so she stepped in. Her first time behind the curtain, rather than center stage, she'd watched the eager and talented woman who took her place shine in the role like never before, and realized there came a time to move back and give newcomers the limelight.

Fifty six seemed awfully young, though, to be outdated like a can of soup.

"Eeny, meeny, miney, moe..." She approached the first of the four trunks. "Orson, you know I'm hoping to find magic in one of these chests. The theater's wardrobe allowance has gotten pitifully small since you left. Our leading man, in particular, could use a bit more panache to make his role come alive."

She pried open the brass latches with surprising ease, considering how long the chest had probably been stored. Or had the aging performers sorted through the contents on occasion, reminiscing with the memories they evoked? As soon as Elsa swung the lid up, a strong odor of cedar emerged.

"Thank goodness the clothes were properly preserved. No moth holes or bug juice."

"They'll need airing," Orson cautioned. "Nothing sours an audience faster than stink in the air."

"Well, of course they will!" Hearing steps approach the doorway, Elsa glanced up. "Megan, come look at this fine suit for Fred."

Scrooge's nephew, Fred, was played by a young man who bagged Elsa's groceries each week. Megan played Anne Priestly, a young reporter who interviews Fred, Bob Cratchit and, later, each of the Christmas ghosts, to find out why Ebenezer suddenly turned his business over to his nephew and vanished.

"Do you think it will fit?" Megan held the pants up in front of her, peering down to check the length. "Charlie's awfully tall."

Elsa wouldn't mention it, but Charlie was the only young man in town tall enough to perform opposite Megan, who stood almost six feet tall in her stockings. A grocery checker at the same store where Charlie worked, they were both taking a year between high school and college to save up tuition.

Ghosts 11

"A nip here, a tuck there. We'll make it fit." Elsa couldn't resist running her fingers over the fine fabric. "This is a suit worthy of a leading man, don't you think?"

"Is there a dress in here for Anne?" Megan laid the pants aside and reached into the trunk with both hands, shoving the clothes this way and that. "Better yet, a pair of women's slacks! Katherine Hepburn would've worn slacks as Anne Priestly."

Before long, the four trunks stood empty, their contents draped four or five deep over every clothing rod, wall hook, and chair back. Purses, shoes, jewelry, and hats crowded the shelves and every surface. Megan had claimed three outfits for her role as Anne, and Elsa had found suitable attire for every cast member. She couldn't wait to explore the other eighteen trunks waiting in her garage.

"Maybe the Tremonts kept set props as well as wardrobe from their plays," Orson mused aloud, fully aware that Megan wouldn't hear him. "Ebenezer's house could use a few pieces more reminiscent of the period than of last week's rummage sales."

"I can get my mom to let the hems out," Megan said.

The girl had no interest in set design or any other part of putting a play together, only in the actors and, in particular, her own costarring role. But she was an energetic actress, and Elsa liked her.

After Megan departed with her bounty, Elsa located a box of hangers and began sorting the pieces by style and gender. Nubby white, rabbit-collared sweater. Ebony tuxedo with scarlet satin cummerbund. Tan sheepskin coat. Multi-colored, demurely cut bathing suit. Black chiffon cocktail dress.

A hanger slipped loose, dropped to the floor, and Elsa found herself admiring the dress in front of the full-length mirror. Fitted bodice, full skirt, it was designed to flip and swirl as a woman walked. Or danced.

"Like Sophia Loren in *Houseboat*. Put it on," Orson coaxed.

Elsa couldn't help noticing that Rosalyn Tremont had worn a ten, exactly her own size. She smiled as she reached down to pick up the hanger, visions of her own youthful performances dancing in her head.

"If I'm not mistaken, Cary Grant sported a gray wool gabardine similar to this one as Roger Thornhill in *North by Northwest*," Elsa told Charlie as he was trying on the suit. "Or maybe when he was John Robie in *To Catch a Thief*. Or both. Cary was fond of gray gabardine."

The pants needed taking in just a smidgeon, but the coat fit Charlie as if tailored for him. He no sooner had buttoned it when Elsa noticed an easy new elegance to his posture. *Clothes make the man*, she'd often quoted. Put a bum in a tuxedo, and he'd try to live up to it every time.

"Cary Grant …?" Charlie's gaze remained locked on his image in the mirror as he squared his shoulders and straightened his tie. "Wasn't he in a lot of those black-and-white oldies my mom watches on cable?"

Struck by sudden *déjà vu*, Elsa realized Charlie's tie-straightening motions were precisely like those Cary Grant had used hundreds of times on screen.

"Cary remained popular long after Technicolor came." She chuckled. "He was known as the most cinematic, debonair and charismatic of all leading men. Did you know that?"

Charlie fell smoothly into a fancy dance step that ended with him facing Elsa in a dramatic little bow. "May I have this dance, madam?"

Before she could answer he'd taken her hand and gently coaxed her from the chair. He twirled her into his arms and into an oh-so-proper waltz, humming as they danced.

"Charlie, if I hadn't personally mourned Cary's passing with a moment of silence in nineteen eighty six, I'd swear I was waltzing with the old charmer himself. Your new suit for this play seems to have magic powers."

"Maybe I should borrow it. I need all the magic I can get to pass my job interview tomorrow. It means more money, and they'll let me work part time once I'm in college."

"I don't know about that, but I wouldn't be surprised if Cary's dashing duds gave you enough gumption to ask Megan out on a proper date."

He lost a step, and their dancing came to a halt as he stumbled over her foot, catching his balance barely in time to avoid falling on his face.

"Sorry, Elsa. I suppose I should read through my lines before rehearsal."

"Charlie O'Connor, that girl is not going to bite your head off. The worst that can happen is she'll say no."

"As long as I don't ask, there's still a chance. But if I ask and she says no, that's the end of it. It's like a door that's open just a crack and you inch it wider little by little, peek in, then maybe slip through the opening. But once it's slammed shut and locked, there's no way in."

Elsa shook her head in exasperation. When Charlie did finally get to Beer n Pizza U, those big city goons were going to hammer him raw.

Ghosts 13

"For such a smart, handsome boy, Charlie, you can be outright dumb. But you're right about preparing for rehearsal. I suggest you go downstairs, find Ms. Megan Gage, and read through your lines together. And send up anybody you see down there who hasn't yet got a new set of clothes."

Beyond the open garage door, in the early afternoon sunlight, a flash of bright orange snagged Elsa's attention. Ms. Ooty Lockett certainly loved her bright colors. Sometimes they seemed to be the only thing holding the skinny slip of a girl together. She looked all of fourteen but was actually knocking on thirty and couldn't put two sentences in a straight line. But she was a talented set designer.

Elsa had phoned Ooty the minute she opened the third trunk and found it filled with Art Deco props. Not exactly post-WWII brick-a-brack, but Scrooge wasn't one to toss out yesterday's furnishings and accessories just because a decade or two had passed. They could be made to work.

Ooty scurried into the garage—she always moved as if escaping a tidal wave. Once inside, she blinked, adjusting to the change in light, and when her gaze fell upon the props Elsa had set out on a folding card table near an open trunk, her pinched face softened in what Elsa took to be awe and delight.

"Ohhhhh, Elsa, it's … I'm … this, I mean it's … how did you …?"

"I believe what you're trying to say, Ooty, is that these things are exactly what you need to make Scrooge's house comfortable for Fred, after he takes charge of his uncle's business, and, at the same time, to spiff up the entire set as authentic 1940s Texas."

"Can I … I mean, can we …, I just can't wait, Elsa, can we …?"

"Yes, of course. We can load up our cars right now and take everything back to the theater."

Ooty picked up a chrome lamp with an amber alabaster shade. As she polished the metal with the hem of her shirt, she looked up at Elsa.

"You … I … this is …." Ooty's lips clamped shut, leaving her clear blue eyes to eloquently express her gratitude.

Waiting for Josh Baker, a.k.a. Texas rancher Bob Cratchit, to finish buttoning his coat, Elsa fingered the excellent silk and wool scarf that would complete his outfit. Such a fine thing the Tremonts had done for their little group. The players had shown a surge of renewed energy for their parts after donning their new clothes. Actors and crew always did their best to pull together whatever was needed for a show, but usually it turned out a mish mash at best.

She looped the red scarf around Josh's neck and stood back to look him over as he turned toward the mirror. Charlie, as Fred, had the starring role, but Josh was by far the best actor of them all. He had the same gangling good looks and shy, humble screen presence that made Jimmy Stewart one of the most beloved actors of Hollywood's golden years.

Ghosts of movies past. Was it a sign of aging, this recent habit of comparing people to stars of the silver screen?

If anyone in their cast had a shot at a film career, though, it was Josh. He was so devoted to acting that he was stealing time from his prelaw studies in Houston to participate in the show.

"Not quite right," he said, studying his image in the glass.

"I think you look appropriately rugged and outdoorsy," Elsa argued.

"A hat. Cratchit would wear a hat."

"Oh! Well, then, I have just the ticket."

From a shelf Elsa snatched a steel-colored cowboy hat with a top-hand crease, the sort a real Texas rancher would wear. Some things never went out of style. Josh studied it for a moment, then nodded approval and set the hat on his head. He repositioned it, tugging the brim a bit lower on his forehead, and with that slight change, his whole body fell into character.

Elsa suddenly needed to sit down. Had she imagined it, or had the boy actually matured a few years in that instant?

"I have a bad feeling about this." Genevieve Wallace handed Elsa a year-end income statement and balance sheet. "Why couldn't we have done a traditional version of a traditional Christmas show? Who's going to turn out for a play written by a Texas nobody which bastardizes the classic work of a beloved author?"

A glance at the bottom line told Elsa all she needed to know. They were broke, as usual. Genevieve wrung her hands in predictable woe at the end of every quarter, but Elsa wasn't going to get her own panties in a bundle over a puny bank balance when they had an entirely unexpected and mortally vital matter to worry about.

"In an exchange of bad news, Genny, I've got you beat." She handed over a letter addressed to "Current Chairman of the Board, Chicory Lord Theater." Elsa was only acting chair, filling in for cofounder Nelson Drake, who, at age

84, had dropped dead on the front row last spring during an excellent performance of "Once upon a Mattress."

Before taking the letter, Genevieve transferred her reading glasses from their perpetual resting spot on her bosom to the bridge of her nose.

"No! Why didn't I learn about this sooner?"

"It was in that pile of mail." Elsa guided her friend to a chair. Nelson Drake had bought this building the year before he passed to avoid this exact situation. "Apparently, Nelson never got around to transferring the deed to the board. Now, his heirs are dumping it as part of liquidating Nelson's estate, and the same developers are offering more than its book value to make sure it doesn't slip away from them again."

"We could pool our resources—I mean all of us, every board member, actor, and all of the families who support us!" Genevieve straightened in her chair. "We can beat the buyers' offer!"

"I'm afraid they have very deep pockets." Elsa poured them each a cup of the Jasmine Soother tea she brewed every afternoon about this time.

"In that case ..." Her friend's jowly mouth drooped at the corners. "I suppose a Texas play about a headstrong young heir taking over his uncle's estate is appropriate for our last hurrah."

Charlie strolled onstage as confidently polished as Cary Grant himself and handsome enough to take a woman's breath, as he very nearly did when Megan dashed on in her role of local news reporter. When Charlie/Fred opened the door to her brisk knock, Anne did a double-take that certainly wasn't part of the script.

"Does she remind you of Katherine Hepburn," Elsa asked Genevieve.

"Not a bit."

"That's what I thought, too."

"Katherine Hepburn would chew Charlie up and spit him into next week." Genevieve's bony elbow poked Elsa's arm. "But she's the spittin' image of Lauren Bacall, and if those two pups don't head off to the soda shop together after rehearsal, I'll buy the pie tonight."

Elsa had to agree. But now Josh was stealing the stage with his Jimmy Stewart "aw, shucks" portrayal of Rancher Cratchit. Elsa was sorry that she and Genevieve were the only two in the audience for the dress rehearsal. She especially wished Charlie's parents could see their son's stellar performance. They rarely attended a show at the Chicory Lord, however, and weren't likely to attend this one. Josh was doomed to practice corporate law as his father and grandfather had done. It might be in his blood, but Elsa knew it wasn't in his heart.

Genevieve, who usually chattered throughout a rehearsal, sat surprisingly quiet. At the emotional climax, Elsa saw her surreptitiously reach for a tissue and dab at her eyes. Would wonders never cease? Possibly not, because when the lights dimmed for the closing of their "bastardized version of a classic," Genevieve applauded like nobody's business.

From the back of the small theater came additional and unexpected applause. Elsa turned to see a strange young woman seated in the back row.

"Now that's just plain sneaky," Genevieve whispered. "Slipping in for the dress to avoid paying for a performance."

As they soon learned, the woman was a freelance reporter from Houston, their nearest metropolis.

"I heard about the impending loss of your historical theater," she confided, glancing about suspiciously. "Your predicament would make a good human interest story."

"Actually, it's only the building that's historical." Elsa liked to keep the facts straight when talking to a reporter. "A number of years ago, this space sat vacant for quite some time, then a few friends with acting experience got the idea of turning it into a theater. Now we sell out for most of our shows."

Must she mention that more than half the tickets were complimentary, usually to aspiring actors or their family members who came to see the show more than once? Surely, that small fact could go unsaid.

"How does it feel to lose this wonderful theater you spent so much time nurturing and that has become such a vibrant part of your community?" the reporter asked.

"It makes *me* feel like fighting!" Genevieve answered, even though the question wasn't directed at her.

"Are you going to oppose the sale?" The reporter jotted something on her note pad, but Elsa had already seen her press a recorder into action.

"The theater isn't being sold," Elsa said calmly but as firmly as possible. "Only the building. Our theater was designed 'in the round,' which means we took a rectangular warehouse space, roughed out a circle in the center, and constructed graduated banquette seating around it. Our acting company can easily move to a new location."

"Do you have a location in mind?"

Ghosts 17

That was the rub, of course. To Elsa's knowledge, no vacant warehouse existed in Chicory or any town nearby.

"We only received notice today," she said, which wasn't exactly a lie. The letter had sat unopened for a day… or so. "The board hasn't met to discuss it."

"Do you perceive a board member coming forward to counter the buyer's offer?"

"You mean like Nelson Drake," Genevieve said. "He rescued us the last time this hap—"

"There's *no one* like Nelson Drake," Elsa said, before Genevieve could go off on a tangent. "He was a loyal and generous gentleman."

"Unlike his heirs?" The reporter directed her question this time at Genevieve.

"Those money-grubbing upstarts! We'll handcuff ourselves clear around the building before we let a developer come in and turn it into another mini-mall."

Seeing that Genevieve had stoked up a full head of steam, Elsa decided to end the interview. She couldn't prevent the reporter from talking to others in the company, but she whisked Genevieve upstairs for a calming cup of Lavender Dreams tea.

After she'd adequately defused Genevieve's fight response, at least for the moment, and had locked up the theater after her friend's departure, Elsa sat upstairs in the wardrobe room, finishing her tea with Orson. Her gaze perused the variety of garments retrieved from the trunks, some elegant, some intentionally tattered.

"The Tremonts played so many roles, and their lives touched so many people …"

"They'll be remembered." Orson sounded testy, for no good reason Elsa could imagine. "What more can an actor expect? You do the job right, you get the applause, and maybe someone will remember you long enough to tell a friend."

"Why do you sound so bitter? Acting was just a bit of fun for you, wasn't it?" Orson was an accountant by day. "That's what you always told me."

"Yes! But it was more than that for you, Max—"

"Max? You haven't called me that in years."

"Not since you took Elsa as your stage name, which I never agreed with, you know."

"Getting back to the Tremonts, what if their possessions have a value beyond what they mean to a small acting company? An Internet auction might—"

"Might what? Bring in enough money to—*what*? Save the theater?"

"It does sound like a tired plot from a dusty old Mickey Rooney - Judy Garland film, doesn't it?" Elsa laughed. *"The show must go on!"*

"Must it?"

Spotting a hint of sparkle on an upper shelf, Elsa brought over a stepstool and pulled down a pair of black sequin evening sandals. She kicked off her sneakers and stepped into them.

"Perfect fit." Orson's voice had softened and picked up a wistful note. "You have the most beautiful feet, my dear."

"They're quite comfortable in these shoes." And wouldn't they go nicely with that black chiffon dress?

Shoving aside a few hangers, she found it and held it up in front of her as she looked in the mirror.

"Lose the black jeans and sweatshirt," she said. "Do something clever with this straggly hair..."

"Max, you always did clean up pretty darn good for opening night."

The next day, after a visit to the salon a block from the theater, Elsa walked in to find Genevieve on the telephone and scribbling frantically.

"Four tickets for Friday night. We'll have them for you at the window. Thank you and Merry Christmas." She keyed the OFF button and looked wide-eyed at Elsa. "We're sold out. A handful of comp seats left for drop-in VIPs. That's it."

"For tomorrow night?" Elsa heard the door open and close downstairs. No rehearsal scheduled, but people were coming to help tidy up.

"And the next night, and the next, including the Sunday matinees. What's come over people?"

"Could it have something to do with that reporter?"

"How could she get a story?"

"The Internet!" Ooty gestured frantically from the doorway. "Web buzz!"

Without waiting for them to respond, Ooty dashed in and scooched Genevieve over so she could reach the keyboard.

Ghosts 19

"The Internet?" Elsa frowned. "It's never worked that well before."

One of the young techs had designed a theater website, and he kept it updated, posting short film clips and casting credits for every performance, plus news of upcoming shows. Elsa had noticed him filming last night during rehearsal ... but the site had never evoked the kind of traffic they'd hoped was possible.

Ooty had gone instead to a Houston television website—and there it was, "Christmas with Dickens," front and center.

"Hundreds," Ooty said. "Thousands. We ... they ..."

"That reporter must have posted her story and linked to our site," Elsa reasoned.

The headline read: *Brilliant Actors Out In the Cold on Christmas?*

"We've gone viral!" Genevieve squealed.

Come opening night, the house was so packed that Elsa, Genevieve, and the third board member, who only showed up for mandatory meetings and free performances, had to stand in the back, which, as Genevieve kept reminding, was three more bodies than the fire code allowed. Elsa saw two firemen in the audience, so she felt safe enough. Several people came who did not look like Chicory residents—not that Elsa knew *everyone* in town, but she prided herself on being a people person.

Just before curtain, she made her usual announcements—refreshments in the lobby, restrooms upstairs and down, many thanks to yada-yada-yada—plus one additional revelation.

"Tonight, we have the privilege of presenting an original play by a local playwright, a story which I know is going to charm your socks off. Austin, would you step out for a moment, please?"

The young man who joined her would win no prizes for looks, but a murmur swept through the audience when they saw him. Austin Lamb was best known for causing trouble. He'd recently served twelve months in a state correctional facility.

"What many of you don't know about Austin Lamb is that he's a self-taught dramatist talented beyond his years. While he was away, we corresponded about his work, and tonight's presentation is a first glimpse at what I believe to be a fresh, innovative take on a favorite Christmas story. In addition to being our writer, Austin also carries one of the minor roles in tonight's production. Help me welcome a man I predict will become a luminary in Chicory's chronicles, Austin Lamb."

The weak applause was precisely what Elsa had expected, but she believed that trotting skeletons out of the closet made them less scary. That Austin had apparently turned his excess energy from troublemaking to writing while he was incarcerated and, in her opinion, deserved his second chance, carried little weight with the townsfolk. She wrapped up her remarks with warm and heartfelt praise for their lamented friend and benefactor, Nelson Drake. Finally, she thanked the audience for attending and added the hackneyed but always useful exit line, "Now on with the show."

This time, they applauded with gusto. The house darkened for the actors to take their places, and thirty seconds later, the show was on.

Ooty's spectacular set created such a magnificent image of 1940s Texas that Elsa found herself sucked right into the scene even though she could recite the dialogue backwards. The characters came instantly alive, so engrossing in their authenticity that Elsa felt every heart in the audience beating in time with the rise and fall of the onstage action. When the lights came up at intermission, she heard a faint moan of disappointment ripple the room before the applause broke out, then a buzz of chatter as people crowded their way to the lobby.

Are we a hit? She didn't want to jinx it by predicting too soon.

Spying the reporter from two nights ago, Elsa attempted to reach her, to thank her for the article, but one person after another stopped her to gush about the play, and when she looked again, the reporter had crossed to the other side of the room and was chatting with another out-of-towner. *Fine, I'll just send her a thank-you note.*

The show ended with a standing ovation, but such overly enthusiastic response might mean that the audience merely wanted to get their butts out of the hard seats. Elsa had learned to rein in her glee until the local critic responded in print and, even more important, the word-of-mouth votes were cast.

Yet this audience seemed genuinely thrilled.

After their last bow, the actors lined up in the lobby to greet their fans. Charlie and Megan stood shoulder to shoulder, Elsa observed, and thought that might be a smear of lipstick at the corner of Charlie's mouth. Astonished to see Josh's parents talking animatedly with their son, approval written on their faces, Elsa strolled closer to eavesdrop. Could that actually be praise coming out of their mouths?

Even the town's "bad seed," Austin Lamb, was receiving handshakes from everyone who passed.

And now Ooty was talking with last night's reporter, and the sophisticated out-of-towner was handing Ooty a business card. *What an amazing night.*

An ebullient feeling of completion overcame Elsa. Truth be told, sell-out performances for the entire run wouldn't save the building from being sold, but look at the pride on the faces of performers and patrons alike. This tiny theater had originated a work by a local talent, had presented it with talented local players, and had thrummed the collective heartstrings of an audience consisting of locals *and* metropolitan visitors. What more could she ask?

"You could take this show on the road," said a handsome baritone voice near Elsa's ear. "I predict that before closing night, at least one critic will call it a 'new classic'."

Turning, she saw that the voice's owner was equally as handsome as his voice, distinctively gray at the temples, and intensely attentive to what she was wearing.

"I hope that means you enjoyed it." He'd sounded sincere enough, but … She offered her hand. "I'm Elsa—"

"Elsa Maxine Lord. Your picture in the playbill gave you away." He placed his hand warmly around hers, arousing a sensual flutter she hadn't felt in quite some time. "I'll bet your friends call you Max."

"Not in a while." But my, didn't it make her feel young.

Cocky attitude, unruly dark hair and small moustache, taunting eyes—like Clark Gable in *The Misfits*. Another ghost of movies past. Orson was a Gable lookalike, too.

"Has anyone told you tonight," he said, without letting go of her hand, "that you look exactly like Sophia Loren?"

"Who *was* that man?" Genevieve asked, when the crowd finally had gone and they sat together over a pot of Wild Orange Blossom tea.

"Hunter Crowe. He's the show manager for a cruise ship out of Galveston."

"And?"

"The ship is being readied for the next cruise, which leaves on Christmas Eve for a holiday excursion, so he has several days free. He read about us online, saw the film clip, and …" Could she really believe he was serious?

"And *what*, Elsa? Stop being obtuse. If I wasn't so happily hitched, that gorgeous hunk of male pulchritude could park his boots under my bed any night."

"It wasn't like that!" But Elsa felt heat rise in her face, the same heat she'd been feeling elsewhere since he held her hand for that all-too-brief moment. "He asked if I'd be willing to fill in for a director that took ill, that's all."

"From the way he was looking at you, that's not all he wanted."

"I don't even know him. And he was a perfect gentleman." He certainly *was* perfect—oh my, she hoped Orson couldn't hear her thoughts.

"A cruise is a darn good place to get better acquainted," Genevieve said.

"Of course I heard," Orson said when they were alone at last. "I hear your waking thoughts every morning, your secret thoughts in the shower—"

"Stop that!" Elsa looked at the business card Hunter Crowe had given her. She couldn't deny wanting to try her hand at directing a play for a wider audience than the Chicory Lord would ever attract, providing she could find a new space.

"You just want to see that young rake again," Orson teased.

Elsa felt a flush of nervous energy, but was it reproach or desire? Desperate to change the subject, she said, "Did you see Josh on stage tonight?"

"If that fellow doesn't become the next Robert Redford, I'll bust my urn."

"You said Brad Pitt would be the next Redford."

"And wasn't he?"

"For a while. The world moves so fast these days."

"Don't let it pass you by, Max."

The light shimmered, and she felt her husband's presence behind her, the familiar brush of his lips on her hair. In these two years since his passing, he'd never appeared to her as more than a voice, yet she could smell the spicy lemon scent of his skin.

"Genevieve thinks we should fight to hang on to the theater."

"A waste of energy. The Chicory Lord was grand in its day, but chasing after the past is not the way to embrace your future."

"I can't leave you, Orson."

Ghosts 23

"Who said anything about leaving me? These old ashes can enjoy a sea voyage."

"You just want to make sure I don't get too close to Mister Hunter Crowe."

The lights shimmered again, and she felt his hands on her shoulders.

"My darling Max." The lights went out completely as he coaxed her out of her chair and into his arms.

This was impossible. It was one thing to pretend you were talking to your dead husband, quite another to believe he had materialized.

His embrace was as warm and firm and loving as ever.

"Christmas Eve will mark the second anniversary of the day I had to leave you. What better way to honor it than to sail together into the future? You will become the dazzling play director you're meant to be."

That *did* sound exciting. "'Christmas with Dickens' did turn out rather well."

"It was brilliant, and not all to the credit of our budding playwright."

"This could be fun. We haven't been on a cruise together since—"

"We shared a glorious past, Max."

In the dark, cuddled in the warm, solid realism of her husband's arms, she could believe they had never parted. "That sounds like a segue, Orson. Are you about to deliver a 'We'll always have Paris' line?"

"After the ship sails on Christmas Eve, you know there'll be a Christmas party. I want to see you dance, Max, in the same dress you're wearing now, with the skirt swirling and flipping flirtatiously around your beautiful legs."

"I suppose you expect me to carry your urn in and set it on the table alongside my champagne glass."

"Works for me."

She could feel the rumble of his laughter. It soothed away the ache that had clutched her heart for two years.

"After the dance, when the ship is well at sea, and a brisk wind is up, carry my urn to the rail on the main deck—"

"No!"

"—and open it. Once I know that you're waltzing bravely into your future, Max—"

"No."

"—you can watch me fly and know that I'm dancing happily with the wind."

She sobbed into the warm fragrance of his shirt and felt at peace and knew that he was right. For each of them, the show must go on.

About Chris Rogers

A native Houstonian, Chris Rogers discovered hidden treasure the first day she rode a bus downtown and stepped into the central library. She read everything in the children and young adult section but especially enjoyed books that fell into a series—*Windy Foot, Nancy Drew, The Hardy Boys.* In the adult section she discovered Perry Mason and Agatha Christie mysteries but also science fiction and fantasy.

Marriage and children got in the way of high school, but she continued reading and eventually took some college courses before becoming a graphic designer. After twenty years in that industry, 12 in her own business, Chris wrote her first novel and fell in love with writing. She folded her business tent, spent the next seven years learning the craft and won third place in a prestigious national short story contest, which opened the door to publishing her Dixie Flannigan suspense series with Bantam Books: *Bitch Factor, Rage Factor,* and *Chill Factor.*

Chris's short stories and essays have appeared in *Alfred Hitchcock Mystery Magazine* and *Writer's Digest,* among others.

Living in Hilltop Lakes, Texas, she continues to write her own stories while also ghostwriting nonfiction projects for clients. Chris returns to Houston frequently to teach writing classes, workshops and seminars.

Miracle Baby
Jackson's Story
by
Stephanie Jaye Evans

There is not one thing in the world I can do to make my parents mad at me. Except die. All they ask of me and of God is for me to stay alive. But there for a while, it looked like we were both going to let them down, and I'm pretty sure God would have gotten the blame, because, like I said, my parents never get mad at me.

I'm a miracle baby. Really, being a miracle baby is no big deal anymore. Two thousand years ago there was only one miracle baby; now they're all over the place. We're the babies who would never have been born thirty years ago. Our mothers waited too late, or their insides were topsy-turvy, or our dads had a low sperm count (I know way more about this than I really want to).But now it seems like medical technology can solve any fertility problem.

The thing about the parents of miracle babies is this: one, they tend to be indulgent (that's why my parents don't get mad at me), two, they're overprotective.

Here's a for instance; I wanted to take judo. This was three years ago so I was just twelve then, but I wasn't little or anything, I was big for my age; I'm still a pretty big guy. Grant, he's my friend and we've gone to school together forever, he was taking judo, so I wanted to take it too. My dad would get off early from work and sit outside the window of my judo school with all the other parents and watch me in my white *gi* with the white belt. Sensei wouldn't let the parents sit inside because he says they're a distraction. He meant for him, not us. He says parents in Sugar Land always try to teach his classes for him. Sensei put park benches on the sidewalk outside of the storefront and that's where parents had to stay. Even in the heat. The Smoothie King next door loved the policy.

Anyway, Dad would sit outside and watch me make my holds and throws, going "Ha!" the way sensei taught me and Dad loved it. Then the day came when sensei set me against an opponent, my age and size, but a couple of belts more advanced than me. In the first three seconds he threw me over his shoulder and I landed with a thud that knocked my breath out. It took me a second before I could breathe but I jumped up and I was going back for more, when *bam, bam, bam*! Dad was banging on the window and waving at me to come out. He walked right in, which, like I said, is against policy, and stopped the whole class.

Sensei and the other kids and all the parents were looking at us. Sensei was trying to explain that no one had ever been injured in one of his classes, and he'd been teaching for more than twenty years, and I was telling Dad, "Dad! Look, I'm not hurt! I'm not made of glass!" But my dad kept shaking his head no, no, no as he gathered up my street clothes and duffle and hustled me out. And even though judo is all about learning to protect yourself, that was the end of judo. So you see what I mean about being overprotected.

It didn't take too many episodes like that for me to figure out that any activity where I might, just conceivably, get hurt, would make my parents nervous. So I had to keep away from anything that looked dangerous.

Or make sure my parents never knew about it.

So you'll understand why I had to be so cagey the Sunday my church youth group announced that summer camp this year would include a three day survival trek for all the high schoolers.

There wouldn't be any problem getting permission to go to the two week summer camp our church sponsored. Camp suited my parents to a T. The camp is in the Texas Hill Country, which is not too far away from where we live, not by Texas standards, anyway. If you go in a car, it takes maybe four hours. If you go in the church bus, it's more like six hours because Sara has to make like thirty potty breaks, and we pull over for lunch at a roadside park and we definitely have to stop at the jerky stand where they have at least twelve different kinds of jerky, including venison jerky and turkey jerky and the only thing better than saying "turkey jerky" is eating it.

What my parents liked about camp was there would be daily Bible studies, swimming, hiking, guys raiding the girl's cabin and stealing all the panties, girls raiding the guy's cabin and doing semaphores with our boxers – what my parents would consider "good, clean, SAFE fun" – but nothing dangerous. The survival trek? There was no way on this earth or the next that I was going to get them to agree to the survival trek.

It's only because we had a new youth minister that I was able to pull it off at all. The guy we used to have, Jason, went back to school to get his masters. Jason knows my parents, and he knows that they're kind of weird about me. He doesn't agree with them, and he told them so right up front. Jason thinks every kid, and especially a guy, has to take some risks in life.

Even if Jason disagreed with Mom and Dad, he wouldn't ever go against them. So if Jason had still been youth minister, he would have taken a second look when I turned in my signed permission form, including the second form for the survival trek. He would have called up my mom and dad to make sure they understood exactly what the trek entailed, and that would have been that.

The new youth minister, Gregory, came from someplace up north. Texas was all new to him. The survival trek had been Gregory's idea. Where he used to live, he was an assistant guide on these survival treks, so he knew all about them. He didn't know anything about the whole "miracle baby" problem I had with my parents and he didn't think a thing of it when I turned in my permission form. He gave me a smack on the back of the head and said, "Great, Jacko! It's gonna be super!" and added my form to the stack he already had.

I didn't forge Mom's signature. It would make me nervous to forge a signature on a paper from church. What I did is wait until she was completely involved in her work.

That was easy because Mom is a painter. I want to say she's an artist; her paintings hang in rich people's homes all over America. She advertises in The New Yorker magazine and in Texas Monthly twice a year, "Fine Portraits for your Home or Office" and that brings in enough commissions to keep her busy. Usually she paints people's kids. They come to her studio in the back of the house and she talks to them, and poses them and takes a bunch of pictures and makes some sketches. No matter what they're wearing when they come to her studio, in their portraits the girls are all wearing long, floaty, white dresses and the guys are wearing open-necked white and jeans. She tells the clients it's important to keep the painting's focus on the kid. She told me it takes too long to paint the elaborate outfits kids show up in. Whatever, the parents are always happy and they're the ones who pay.

I used to tell friends she was an artist, but she'd shake her head. "An artist paints what he sees, his own vision. I paint other people's vision. I get paid to paint what other people want to see."

I got all distracted there, and off-topic, but the point is, my mom gets so involved in her work when she's painting, that I once threw a lit firecracker in the toilet and shut the lid and she didn't know—and I mean, it made a very impressive *boom!*—until I went tearing down to her studio because the toilet bowl had cracked and there was water pouring all over everywhere — do *not* try this at home.

So when I had to get that permission slip signed for the survival trek, I knew I was going to have to catch Mom in the middle of a portrait if I wanted to go. And I did want to go.

What I did was I filled out every blank on the forms, except for the signatures. Then I highlighted the two places you needed to sign. I came into Mom's studio while she was working on a picture of two girls. She had a brush in each hand and one between her teeth, made her look like a pirate. I slipped the brush out of her right hand (she paints with both hands, but she only writes with her right) and replaced it with a pen. I said, "Mom, sign where it's yellow, I need it for camp" and she did. It was that easy.

Camp was great. The Texas Hill Country is pretty and the air is a lot dryer; the temperature might be as hot as Sugar Land, but it doesn't feel as hot. That's good when you're spending most your time outside. It will be no surprise to you that the Hill Country is not flat, like Sugar Land and all the rest of east Texas, but all rolling hills. It's not lush and green like where I live, either. Green stuff is a lot more sparse in the Hill Country, and it's grey green and blue green and brown green. The trees are scrubby and close to the ground. There's limestone outcroppings and springs and rivers (great for tubing) and waterfalls, not waterfalls like Niagara, these are gradual waterfalls; the water sheets down over layer after layer of limestone. Think of a long, shallow staircase with the stairs only an inch or so high, and you kind of get the picture. And it smells spicy, like Colorado, juniper and cedar.

I had fun at camp, I always do. Yeah, but what I was really looking forward to was that survival trek.

All the kids were going on the trek, I mean everybody in the ninth grade and over. Do you realize that if my parents had their way, I would have been stuck for three days at the base camp with the middle schoolers and the parent chaperones?

We all packed backpacks with water bottles, tarps and bed rolls, Swiss Army knives, stuff like that, the essentials.

"Ladies," Gregory said, "no makeup, shampoo, etcetera, just the essentials."

I heard Sara say "Those are the essentials." I was pretty sure she'd brought along a hair dryer and flat iron, too; her backpack looked that heavy. Turned out I was wrong, though. All the guys had to carry bags of freeze-dried foods, because even though the idea was to live off the land, I don't think Gregory wanted to be stuck in the middle of nowhere with twenty-three hungry teenagers; we might eat him.

Everybody had to leave their cell phones and Walkmans at base camp. Gregory was the only one who carried a cell phone and that was just for emergencies. Not that we were planning on having any.

The church bus dropped us off at our starting point at dawn on the fourth day of camp. We had Krispy Kreme doughnuts for breakfast and even the skinny girls crammed. It was going to be a long time before our next civilized meal.

Okay, it was hot, the sun was too bright and the sticker burrs got caught in my shoe laces and I didn't care. I had a great time. Matt and Charlie and I were horsing around. We didn't spend much time on the trail since we kept getting shoved off the trail and we kept pantsing Charlie which didn't take much because he wears his pants so low on his butt and every time we pulled his pants down you could see his hula girl boxers and the girls would scream and Gregory would say, "Guys, guys, let's remember we have ladies with us."

Gregory was a good guide, funny and interesting and he knew a lot of stuff about how to construct a fishing line, and how to tell if a plant was edible. He was surprised at how different the plants were. He probably should have boned up on the west Texas region; surviving out here is probably way different from up in Washington State. He would have been in big trouble if we hadn't had luck in the fishing.

We cleaned, gutted and grilled the fish on mesquite branches. We stewed dandelion leaves, too. Gregory said if the leaves had been young, we could have eaten them like salad. I don't know about that, but stewed, they looked and smelled disgusting, and nobody would even try them except Gregory, and he didn't eat much.

If it had been a few months later, we could have gathered pecans, there are tons of pecans in the Hill Country, and even raw pecans taste good. This early in the summer, though, the pecans are big, hard and green. If you manage to get into one, the green juice will dye your fingers dark brown and the meat of the nut will be too bitter to eat.

We did find blackberries. They're sweet and juicy, good to eat. You have to find a lot of them to make a dent in your appetite.

Gregory chose a camp site close to the river in the shade of a clump of trees. It was like a little canyon there and the shade from the trees and the bluffs made it cooler. I know this sounds like hindsight, but I remember having a moment when I looked up at the bluffs around us and thought there was a reason why we should be camping up there instead of down here by the river. That thought stayed in my brain about a quarter second before I was off messing with Charlie and Matt, splashing across the river (it was only thigh deep at its deepest) and throwing mud.

We had more fish for dinner; Gregory broke down and cooked some of those freeze-dried Noodles Alfredo; we ate them up, I'll tell you for sure. Then Sara hauled her backpack into the circle around the fire and dumped out two dozen Hershey bars with almonds (so, you see, she hadn't packed a hair dryer after all). We knew it was cheating, but we didn't care, we all had one, even Gregory, and the candy put everyone in a more satisfied mood and we thought Sara was the best thing on earth.

The night had cooled things off; the stars were so much clearer than they are near Houston, and we all sang and no one felt self-conscious or anything. Gregory led a prayer. After that he took a stick and drew a line down the middle of the camp site and said "Girls this side, guys that side, I sleep in the middle and I will tear the leg off anyone who tries to cross over. I mean it." It was a survival trek, but it was still church camp.

We all went to bed; maybe I should say to sleeping bags. Everybody lay on top of theirs; it was so warm outside, it's not like you needed to cover up. I have a thing about spiders. The thought of spiders walking over my bare skin while I was asleep — well, I went ahead and got inside my sleeping bag and I must have fallen asleep right away.

I was dreaming that my mom was calling my name, she was saying, "Jackson, Jackson! Would you wake up? Geez, that kid sleeps like a rock." That was weird, because Mom doesn't talk that way. The weirdness woke me right up. I was completely awake at once, my eyes looking up at a black sky with thousands of diamond bright stars you can never see in Sugar Land. I knew I wasn't dreaming anymore, but I could still hear that voice, and another voice, too.

"Go down and get him, he's never going to wake up in time."

"Youuuuuu go down and get him, there's spiders down near the river."

"Spiders! I don't think we need to be worried about spiders right now, just..."

I got out of my sleeping bag and walked a little ways off from Gregory and the kids. I looked up to where the voices were coming from, up on the bluff. There were two girls standing there. Wearing full, white dresses. In the Hill Country. The moon was bright and about three quarters full, so I could see right away I didn't know them. They weren't with the church group. They weren't anyone I ever remembered seeing. I was thinking I *must* have seen them somewhere because something about them was familiar. Two girls, standing side by side on top of the bluff.

"There he is. Hey Jackson! Get your fanny up here!"

"Oh, my gosh. Fanny? Did you say fanny?"

"He's just fifteen, you want him to hear me say ass?"

"He just did."

"Jackson, call it whatever you want to, get it up here really, really quickly."

I said, "Do I know you?" I knew I didn't.

"Jackson, this isn't a good time to make introductions. We know you, okay?"

"I'm Annie Laurie, call me Annie, and this is Rosie. But Rosie is right, move your buns, boy."

I was climbing while they fussed at me. It wasn't hard to find handholds on the limestone, even in the dark. The girl who said she was Annie reached a hand out when I got near the top and pulled me on up.

Rosie said, "Right. Jackson, you're safe now, you might want to holler at your friends to get out before it hits."

Can you imagine how weird all this was? I'm standing on top of the bluffs in the middle of the night with two strange girls I'm pretty sure I've never seen before, they're dressed like they come from the 1800s and they're acting like they've known me all my life. The moon was nearly full and the stars were really bright; I mean, we're out in the middle of nowhere, probably three miles or so from the nearest road, so part of my brain is thinking, "Where did they come from?" and the other part of my brain is trying to puzzle out what they were saying.

"Before it hits?" I shook my head like that would make things clearer.

Annie put an arm around Rosie's shoulder and leaned close to her ear. "Shouldn't he be able to hear it by now?"

Then I did hear it.

In that one instant I knew. I knew what that roar was, I knew why we shouldn't have camped on the shores of the river and I knew I had to get the hell down there and wake everybody up and I was halfway down the bluffs, yelling my head off, "Get up! Get up! Climb! Climb! Climb!" when the flood hit. One second I was scrambling down, still a couple of feet off the ground, next I was underwater, moving fast, head over heels, water in my eyes, my ears, my nose. The noise was terrific, a jumble of underwater sounds I couldn't make sense of. I slammed against a rock outcrop; I tried to hold onto the slimy smooth surface; the water tore me away. Someone bumped into me, snatched hold of my jeans, then they were gone. I surfaced and took a long, grateful lungful of air before I was dragged down again but I'd had time to glimpse a tree down river. The tree was in the middle of the river now, though that scrubby little tree had been as high and dry as me a few minutes ago.

I struggled back to the surface. I didn't swim, you couldn't swim in that, but I tried to aim myself towards the tree and as I swept past I grabbed hold of the trunk with both arms and the force of the water almost yanked my arms out of socket trying to wrench me loose but I held on.

I was battered by all the broken-off limbs and branches in the water. I tried to shield behind the tree but it wasn't any protection. A dead cow went swirling by, its eye open. Its sharp hooves barely missed me. My face was scratched and I felt like I was getting beaten to death but I couldn't drag myself any further out. I couldn't reach the branches above me. I tried, but I couldn't reach and I couldn't hold on with only one arm for more than a second, the current was so strong and water was pouring over my face and I could only get my face free every minute or so to gulp some air and I thought

I might drown right there, holding on to the trunk but not able to keep my face far enough out of the water. I heard, "Give me your hand, Jacksie."

Rosie was in the branches above me. She wasn't there before and then there she was. Annie was there, too, both of them holding a hand out to me. Beneath the leaves of the tree, in the darkness, I couldn't see them clearly as they leaned over me, just the pale ovals of their faces, their dark eyes and their long dark hair falling forward. I kept one arm around the trunk, reached up and they grabbed hold of my arm with their strong, warm hands. I tried to climb some, but my legs were weighed down by my wet jeans and my leg hurt like fire when I tried to brace against the tree. Mainly they hauled me out and up without my help until I could lean my stomach over the lowest branch. They must have been strong because I was bigger than them, and my wet clothes made me heavier. I rested, I think a long time; it's hard to tell. Rosie and Annie both kept a hand on my back. They must have thought I would pitch back in.

When I had my breath back (and after I ralphed the portion of river I'd swallowed, gross when you think about the dead cow), I pulled myself the rest of the way up. It was hard. My leg hurt when I bent it. It hurt when I didn't bend it. Finally I got to where I could straddle the branch, my back against the trunk. I'd lost my shoes in the river, never even felt them come off. My wet jeans and tee shirt made me clammy and chilled. My leg was killing me. I rested my head in my hand (keeping tight hold of a branch with the other), tried to wipe the water out of my eyes, tilted my head and whacked the water out of my ears. All I could hear was the roaring of the river, that same river I'd waded in just a few hours ago.

But that was before the flood. The flash flood. That's what we call them in Texas. They don't happen where I live. The Houston area floods, sure, but it's not a surprise, you know it's coming because it's been raining for forty days and forty nights and the ground can't take another drop. The TV weatherman stands out in the rain with a ruler, measuring how much higher up his leg the water has risen. "Yup. It's coming up, neighbors! Better get ready!" There's no surprise about it.

In land like the Hill Country in west Texas, you might not have rain for months. Then the heavens open up. The earth is packed hard and dry, so it can't absorb the water fast enough, besides, there's a lot of shale and limestone, and that doesn't absorb water, it channels water.

All that water has to have someplace to go; it seeks the lowest level, the creek beds and river beds. Then the water goes rushing down the channel, uprooting bushes and picking up stones, for miles and miles, all the way downriver to some point on the map that hasn't had a drop of rain. Hasn't even seen a cloud. A wall of water pours down river to some point where twenty-three kids and a youth minister who didn't know any better have set up camp for the night next to the river and below the bluffs.

It took me a little bit to realize those two girls were patting me, and rubbing my back and making encouraging noises. I could barely hear them over the roaring, grumbling river. The way they were acting, it reminded me of my mother—I couldn't think of my mom, not now. It was very dark out; the moon gave some light but my Timex Indiglo, the one that glows in the dark, doesn't glow if the crystal is broken, so I couldn't tell what time it was. You'd think the wind would have been whipping around, and there would be thunder and lightning, but there wasn't. The storm had happened miles and miles upstream from us; we never got a drop of rain. Above me, I saw a still, calm, clear night, below me, an ugly, surging, angry river. And the river was still rising.

"Where's everyone else?" I had to yell to be heard over the river, "Are they all okay?" I knew that was a stupid question; I knew everyone else was not okay. Matt and Charlie, Taylor and Walker, Sara and Lauren…

Rosie was on a branch close to me, her slim, dry back pressing against me. I think she was trying to keep me warm. I felt her give a small shrug.

"We don't know, Jacksie," she shook her head and her hair brushed across my neck, "We only came for you."

I shoved back from her so fast I nearly shoved myself back into the river. You can't go that far when you're on a branch. Annie grabbed my shoulder to steady me.

I looked up at her. She was squatting on a branch a little higher than mine, one pale arm around the trunk, the other stretched out to hang on to me, her white skirts bunched around her.

"Why did you come for me?" I said, "Who are you? Why didn't you wake up everybody?"

Annie let go of my shoulder and pointed to my ankle. "I think you're bleeding. I'm pretty sure." She carefully sat down on her branch and braced her bare, pink feet against the branch I was sitting on. She reached over and with both hands stripped off my wet sock and dropped it into the river. There was no splash when it hit. The river was in such an uproar it swallowed the sock without ever noticing. There was a long red gash right over the bone of my ankle. I could see the white edges of the puckered skin and the slow welling of red blood that fell in drops to the river below. Annie's fingers were pressing all up and down my foot and ankle; she laced her fingers through my toes and levered my foot back and forth like she thought she was a doctor in the ER. I yanked my foot away.

"Who are you?"

"Put your foot in my lap and let me see if I can tie up your ankle and stop the bleeding."

Rosie leaned across me. "You have something to tie it up with? I'll tear off one of these sashes if you need it."

"No, I've got this." Annie pulled a square of blue from a pocket in her skirt and rolled it to make a bandage. The handkerchief had a border of pink and green embroidered flowers. It looked like one of those vintage ones my mom collects. I couldn't think about my mom. I could feel my mother's terror and grief for a minute but I shook the vision off. I had to stay alive. My parents needed me.

Rosie had inched over on her bottom and was practically sitting in my lap. The arm that held on to the trunk was so close to my face that I could smell her clean, warm skin. She pointed to the handkerchief Annie was rolling into a bandage.

"Where do you think she came up with that, anyway? I mean, the handkerchief."

"Artists," said Annie and they laughed together; a low throaty chuckle that reminded me of my dad's laugh. When Dad heard about this, he'd be out here with helicopters and boats and...when he heard.

Annie patted her lap, "Come on, Jacksie, stick your old stinky foot up here. Let me see what I can do."

I did. I don't know why, except that I was bleeding.

Annie patted my foot dry with the tail of her shirt. "Whoo, boy! Don't you ever cut your toenails? Rosie, look at this foot, I think this boy is half alien, how do they keep him in shoes with toenails like that?"

Rosie leaned over to get a good look at my toenails. Her hair smelled like lemons. "Nasty! Jackson, cut your toenails, you'll lose five pounds and never miss it."

Ghosts 37

My toenails weren't great, I don't get pedicures or anything, but they weren't as bad as they were making out.

Very deftly, like a boy scout working on his first aid badge, Annie tied my ankle up with that fancy blue handkerchief. She leaned way over, took one end in her teeth and one in her free hand and tightened the knot. I could hear the handkerchief tear and when she pulled away, one corner of the pretty handkerchief was torn.

Rosie said, "I could have helped you with that, you know."

"It's done. Doesn't matter." She patted her first aid job with satisfaction. She lifted my foot up with one hand, and smoothed her skirt over her legs, then gently set my foot back on her lap. On her clean, white, dry skirt.

My stomach did a slow turn inside me.

"Annie, why isn't there any blood on your skirt?"

Her skirt was as pure white as it had been when I first saw her standing on the bluffs.

"And how come your skirt is dry? You and Rosie are both dry. How come?"

Annie didn't look at me, just sat there with her long legs stretched out, toes clinching on the branch I sat on, her hands softly kneading the bottom of my foot. She turned to Rosie, "Which is better, do you think, 'how come' or 'why is it that? Shouldn't it be, 'Why is it that your skirt is dry?'"

Rosie put on a school teacher voice and looked down her short nose. "There's no question but that your version is the more correct, but I can't help but think the vernacular 'how come' is effective and communicates the intended meaning and has the added virtue of not sounding so pedantic."

"Pedantic! That's worse than 'fanny'."

I'd drawn my foot away and I did some shifting, trying to get my leg more comfortable. My leg was really hurting. Not the leg with the cut ankle; that wasn't so bad. My other leg. I was insecurely positioned and I couldn't move much with the girls sitting so close to me.

"Why is it that?" I asked.

They kept talking.

I made a throat clearing noise this time. I was shivering so it didn't come out right. It was kind of a strangled sound.

"Why, Annie, is it that you and Rosie are bone dry, even where I should have messed you up? How did you get into this tree before me, and how did you get into it dry? And please tell me," I took a deep breath; I was starting to shake hard, "would you please tell me who you are and…" I tried to get it just right. "Why is it that you know me?"

They stopped talking and looked at me. They looked at each other. Rosie looked down and gave a jump.

"Let's move on up, ya'll, everybody move up one."

She was right. We needed to climb and climb fast. The river was higher, it didn't seem as turbulent, but it looked fast and black and dangerous and it was definitely deeper. Annie and Rosie were climbing easily, their clean, white skirts floating out, getting in my face and smelling like bleach and Dad's pressed shirts. I wasn't doing so good. I was aching all over—I'd gotten banged and beaten up during that time I spent in the river. And my leg hurt so bad I was clenching my teeth in spite of them chattering

It hurt a lot more when I put my weight on it. I stopped and stood on the other foot. I tried to roll up my jeans to see where it was hurting so much but my wet jeans were stiff and thick. I could only get them up a few inches. My hands were scraped and bloody, and the river grit in my jeans rubbed the sore places. In fact, the grit in my jeans was rubbing all sorts of sore places. I didn't feel good. I gave up on looking at my leg and kept climbing. My teeth were chattering so hard it gave me a headache.

We moved as high as we were going to be able to. The thin branches above wouldn't be able to support us. I had my sore leg straight along the length of the limb, trying not to move it, and the leg with the cut ankle dangling down for balance. The dark water wasn't more than four feet below us, just two feet under my foot, and I started thinking that there was a very real possibility that I might die out here huddled together with these two strange girls on either side. They were perched as close to me as they could get, their arms around me, their hands trying to rub some warmth into my skin. They didn't seem to be afraid for themselves at all, just anxious about me. I pressed my hands against my jaw to get my teeth to stop and tried again to get some answers.

"Did my mother send you?" Where did that asinine question come from?

They looked at me, eyebrows up.

Rosie said, her voice slow and thoughtful, "Well, you know, maybe she did. What do you think, Annie?"

Annie frowned and shook her head, "I don't know; I don't know how these things work. It's a nice idea, though, isn't it? I like that. I like thinking that."

"Yeah," Rosie said. It came out as a sigh, "Yeah, me, too."

"Why just me? Why not wake everyone?" I felt like crying. I never cry.

Rosie's eyes were cast down. The sun wasn't up yet, there was just that bare lightening, a rim of pink on the horizon and with the light, I could see that Rosie's hair wasn't dark, the way it had looked in the dark of the night, it was a fair brown, long and wavy. Her lashes were thick and long, but they were fair, too. She didn't wear any makeup. She looked older than me, in spite of no makeup.

Annie put a hand on my knee. I put my hand over hers. My hand was thicker and brown, my fingers an inch or more longer. Her hand was soft and white. I don't know why I put my hand on hers. It was really stupid. But it felt good. It felt comforting and kind of, I don't know, this sounds so stupid, but it felt kind of loving, not in a girlfriend way, more like… I don't know.

"They couldn't hear us, Jackson," Annie said, "You could. We did what we could."

"Anyway," Rosie looked at me directly now, "You woke them up, and since we woke you up, in a way we did wake everyone up."

"That's right! We did!"

This was clearly a cheering thought and they smiled at each other. I noticed Rosie had a space between her two front teeth. I do, too. It looked cute on her.

I said, "Were we in time? Did we wake them up in time?"

They got quiet.

I hadn't made sense out of any of this, and they wouldn't answer my questions and my leg was hurting more and more, not the one with the cut ankle, the other one, and the river was still rising, and I didn't think I had the strength to climb anymore even if there had been more tree to climb, which, like I said, there wasn't, and I was thinking about Sara, how she had brought candy bars for every one of us, carried them the whole way on the hike, and it was a long hike and I was thinking about what a nice thing that was to do, and how funny she could be.

I dreamed Mom was in trouble, she was in some kind of danger, and she was calling to me. She was saying, "Help me! Isn't there anyone else besides me? Please, God, let there be someone else!"

I started to jump up to help her, only half awake and I found myself hanging from my armpits fifteen feet over the river. A river that had returned to its normal level, no more than knee deep. I'd been tied to the tree or I would have fallen that fifteen feet. I'm not used to sleeping in trees.

I was full awake now, I can tell you, and someone was still calling, only it wasn't my mom. It took me some doing to get back on my perch, my leg hurt so much I could feel it along the back of my skull.

As soon as I could, I yelled back "I'm here! Who is it?" It came out more like a croak than a yell and I had to bite my tongue to bring some spit to my mouth. I yelled again. "Who is it?"

"Oh Jackson, is it you? It's me, it's Sara, oh, are you okay? Can you see anyone else?"

I looked around. Who I didn't see were Annie and Rosie. Not a trace. I saw broken tree branches and slick mud sheets on the shore. I saw one turquoise hiking boot and a broken Styrofoam cooler. I saw Gregory floating face down, caught in a dam of fallen branches and leaves.

I said, "Not really."

That was the longest day of my life.

I wrestled with the cords tying me to the tree until I realized I still had my Swiss Army knife in my pocket. Cut myself loose and held the cord up in the air to see it better. Not a cord, two white sashes tied together. Pretty resourceful, Annie and Rosie.

I had made my way down to the lowest branches, being careful with that leg, when I heard someone come splashing up the river singing "We're Marching to Zion" at the top of his lungs. It was Matt and that was a beautiful sound. I don't care if he is tone-deaf.

Matt and I got Gregory out of the river. Matt took his shirt off and covered Gregory's face. Matt said, "Oh, God" and I knew he meant that as a prayer.

We got Sara down from the tree she'd clung to all night. We didn't tell her about Gregory. The three of us started upriver. I had my arm around Matt's shoulder, to take the weight off that bad leg—just so you know, it turns out I had a broken leg, so I wasn't being a baby or anything.

Sara was on my other side, pretending she was helping to support me. She's so much shorter than me, I'd have had to walk on my knees to actually put any weight on her. Sara was all scratched up and she'd lost one contact so she had taken out the other to keep it safe and she'd put it under her tongue so it wouldn't dry out, only she'd swallowed it, so she was squinting. Her

Ghosts 41

curly brown hair was so tangled she couldn't get her fingers through it, much less a comb, not that she had a comb.

We were singing old Beatles songs—we've been hearing them from the cradle; we knew them all. When we'd come to the end of a verse, Sara would kick her leg up through the water and make a big splash. We didn't get any dryer as we went along.

The only other kids we came across were John and Nancy. They've been going together since 5th grade. They were seniors, and still together. They were sitting on the sand next to the now tame river. John had Nancy cradled in his arms. Her right arm was bent in a place an arm isn't supposed to bend. He was rocking her back and forth, her head leaning against his chest, her eyes closed, he was saying "Tell me the story about the crazy cat that bit your brother. I love that story." I've heard that story and it is funny, but I think John was trying to keep her mind off her arm. Nancy opened her eyes a slit when she heard us, and she gave us one of her big toothy grins. She closed her eyes again, and John told us to go on and find some help. I bet he marries that girl someday.

We didn't find help, help found us. We told the rescue guys about John and Nancy and we told them about Gregory. Sara cried and cried when she heard. Some big old guy my granddad's age picked her right up off her feet and carried her all the way to the bus they brought out to pick us up. He was saying, "Don't cry now, baby girl, don't cry." That made her cry harder.

The bus was nearly full already, there was an old couple, he looked like Willy Nelson only his braid was shorter, and a lone hiker, and eighteen teenagers from my youth group. Except for Gregory, we had all made it. Then I cried.

I didn't tell anyone about Rosie and Annie. It's not like I thought I'd imagined them, but I couldn't explain them either.

When I got to the hospital — I told you I broke my leg — and the nurse started cutting my clothes off me, I let out a holler.

"Did I hurt you, sweetheart?"

"No, but, you see that cloth around my ankle, would you please not cut that off? Is there any way you could untie it?"

Well she did, and that was going above and beyond—it took her a long time, the handkerchief was rank with blood and river water.

She put it in a box labeled 'personal effects'.

I'm not going to put you through a description of what it was like when my parents got hold of me. Let's just say I don't think I'll be joining the military. I can't see my mother like that again. Not ever.

But I didn't get in trouble; they weren't mad at me. I didn't die, did I?

A week or so after I'd gotten home, I used my crutches and hobbled into Mom's studio. She keeps a couch in there because I like to watch her paint. It makes me peaceful inside. She was standing in front of her canvas and I asked her if she could work from the side so I could watch. She does that for me sometimes.

Mom stepped aside and my heart stopped dead inside my chest. It must have showed.

"What is it?" she said, "You don't like it? What?"

"I like it fine." I said.

You know, of course. You've probably known all along. It was Rosie and Annie.

Instead of the hazy blue background Mom usually painted, she had painted them standing together in a garden. Annie had an arm around Rosie's waist; Rosie's arm was around Annie's shoulder. Just like when I saw them, they're wearing those white dresses, tight on top and flaring into full, soft skirts. They don't have that shimmery perfect look Mom usually paints. They look like real girls. They look as though they've been sharing some inside joke, and you walked out into the garden to join them. They look happy to see you, like maybe they'll share the joke with you, too. That's how it seemed to me. My eyes were stinging.

"Who is that, Mom?"

"Oh," she was a little flustered. "They're not anyone you've met, Jackson."

"What's their names?"

Her voice was soft and sad. "That's Barbara Rose and Annie Laurie."

Barbara Rose. Rosie. And Annie.

"Who are they? I never saw them come to the house."

"Oh, Jackson." Mom sighed and put down her paint brush. She pulled the barrette out of her hair, shook her hair out and then pulled her hair back and clasped it with the barrette. She sat down next to me so she wasn't looking in my eyes. I noticed for the first time that Mom's eyelashes are thick and long, and very fair.

"You're going to think I'm a stupid old woman," she said.

Ghosts 43

"Tell me anyway."

"You know Dad and I had trouble having kids. I didn't have trouble getting pregnant, I had trouble staying pregnant. Twice, before you, I got pregnant. I couldn't keep the pregnancies. I lost the babies."

"They were girls?"

"Beautiful little girls. So tiny. I held them each for a long time. After Rosie, We didn't think we had the courage to try again." She sniffed and wiped her nose with her sleeve.

"Barbara Rose and Annie Laurie."

She nodded and pointed to the portrait. "They'd be about that old if they'd lived. Barbara Rose, three years older than you, Annie Laurie, two."

"Doesn't look like your usual portrait. They look…real."

Mom looked at the painting with me. She was smiling a sad smile.

"Yes. My vision this time."

I've never told my parents. Once I said something funny and Dad laughed and I wanted to say, "They laugh the same as you do, Dad, only in a girl way." But I didn't.

So, what do you think? Did my sister's ghosts save me? Or did my mother create those two girls out of the strength of her own imagination?

I'll tell you what, if she did, then my mom is wrong, she is an artist.

Anytime I start feeling that the whole episode is too unreal to believe, I get that handkerchief out of my top drawer where I keep it hidden at the back. It's stained and it's torn on one corner, but it's clean and pressed. I did that on my own.

I get that handkerchief out and I go down to my parent's bedroom where Dad hung the portrait of Rosie and Annie. I look into my sisters' faces. I look at the pocket on Annie's shirt. Peeping out you can see the corner of a pale blue handkerchief, embroidered around the border with pink and green flowers. The corner is torn.

About Stephanie Jaye Evans

Stephanie Jaye Evans is a fifth generation Texan. She received her B.A. from Abilene Christian University and won a University-wide writing contest with a piece that contained the word 'breast', quite an accomplishment at a Church of Christ university. After a lifetime of raising sons who raised hell, she attended Rice University's Master of Liberal Studies Program and wrote a mystery as her capstone project. That mystery, *Faithful Unto Death*, won the 2010 William F. Deeck-Malice Domestic Grant for Unpublished Writers. *Faithful Unto Death—A Sugar Land Mystery*, published by Berkley Prime Crime, came out in June 2012. The second in the series, *Safe From Harm*, will be out in March 2013. She is currently at work on the third novel in her Sugar Land Mystery series. Stephanie lives in Sugar Land, Texas with her longsuffering husband and two badly-behaved pugs, Tommy and Mr. Wiggles.

Unforsaken Love
by
Kelly Matherly

Sharp pointy hats slayed the brisk night air with pierced pleasure,
As the witches chanted their deadly singsong.
Their body's moved to transparent beats
Deadly claws ripped decayed leaves from the ground.
A man, holding a single rose stood under a willow tree in the distance.
He knew what he wanted,
And he could care less how insalubrious were his actions.
The chanting rose until it reached the tree tops.
Leaves brushed the man's polished wingtip shoes.
A woman formed from the foliage
Heart pounded hard in his chest and his face glowed with pleasure.
A ghost lifted from the ground.
Do you, Victor, take this woman?
Love is unforsaken.

About Kelly Matherly

I minored in English not because I was interested in writing, but because it seemed the appropriate minor for my advertising major and required only three extra classes. I never thought of myself as a writer, mainly because of my dyslexia. One day, after reading a large novel at lightning speed, something weird happened. I started thinking, dreaming and even talking to myself and others in narrative. In order to get the constant narration out of my head, I sat down and wrote my first novel, *Heads Will Roll*.

The Stall
by
Julian Kindred

The red gas light on my dashboard's been on for the past fifteen miles and there's still no sign of a gas station. The clock reads one thirty a.m. I really don't want my car to stall out on the side of the road out here in the middle of nowhere. This shoot I'm driving to might be my last one, and I really can't afford to be late.

It's a porn shoot, Tiffany's Country Girl Lesbian Gang Bang. I'm neither a country girl, nor a lesbian, but my fans don't care. They voted me into the top twenty porn stars in the country this year. My name's not Tiffany either, it's Margaret Carmichael, but no porn star ever uses their real name.

I hope it's my last shoot. After I'm done with it, I'm off to Hollywood. It's swell to know that my porn career's been good for something other than just putting food on the table. Getting into the top twenty got me noticed, and now I'm all set to play the bitchy girlfriend in the upcoming monster movie *Flytrap*. The script's pretty standard. Teenagers go where they shouldn't and some mutated plant monster thing comes and eats them. My character dies about halfway through, but I've never had so many lines to learn before. I go over them again and again in my head to try and pass the drive, hoping to remember the entire script. I'll be naked for most of it, but that's nothing new. At least the sex is almost as fake as porn.

I take a sip of iced coffee from my go-cup, and nearly spill it when I spot some lights up ahead. I'm almost off the freeway exit when I realize it's a tire store. I curse hard and loud, for all the good it does, and find my way back to the freeway. The mile meter shows the light's been on for seventeen miles now.

I take another sip and try to remember my next line. Better to keep my mind busy than to let it wander off. If it does, it might not come back, and I can't lose my mind right now, not with so many big changes coming at me. The line's something stupid about vines and penis size, but I can't recall the specifics.

I see lights up ahead. I slow down, careful to make sure I'm really seeing a gas station this time. There are pumps and a sign that says open. I glance at the red light on the dash. It's good enough for me.

I make a sharp right turn off the exit to pull into the station. When I do, I realize how small and isolated it really is. Only one car is in the parking lot. A minivan. I can make out the inside of it as I drive around to get to the pumps. A bunch of boxes with soda, beer, and junk food is packed inside. The driver must be unloading stuff for the station. Nothing is around but empty road and a forest of trees running parallel to the freeway as far as the lights from the station let me see.

I just want to get my gas and leave as quick as possible. This place has a weird, uncomfortable vibe. It tingles the in middle of my back, like a shiver wants to run up my spine.

I pull up to one of the pumps and get out. The screen that says how much money you're spending reads, "PAY INSIDE." *Great.* I get the pump set up, grab my purse from the front seat and head on in.

Four people are inside. Two Indian men, as in from India, not Native Americans. One's young, a little older than me and dressed in jeans and a sweater, and the other's old, maybe in his fifties or sixties. The older one is rail thin, with a bushy white mustache and a pot belly that makes him look like he's hiding a basketball under his sweater vest and windbreaker. The other two are Mexican and mom and son, or at least I assume they are. The woman's age is hard to tell, but she's got that rounded look to her of someone who was just born overweight and can't get rid of it. Her kid can't be older than seven, thinner than the Indian man, and standing perfectly still as his mom plays at one of a pair of arcade games. Maybe they're those lottery games places like this sometimes have. If they are, they're not the sort I've seen before.

As I walk around to the counter, the mother gives me a glance that makes me feel like I've been splashed with dirty dishwater. Nobody's at the cash register, but the younger Indian guy walks behind the counter a second later and punches a few buttons.

"How can I help you?" he asks, his voice so thick with an accent that for a moment I think he's speaking Spanish. Or maybe I just think that because the Mexican mom keeps tossing me looks.

"Need some gas," I say, pulling out my credit card and handing it over. He nods, and tucks it away while I go back to my car and start gassing up. Where's the car the mom and son used to get here? Maybe it's around back.

The minivan stocked with goods probably belongs to one of the Indian guys. An owl, or some other animal, makes a noise out in the dark, and I decide I'd rather be inside the creepy gas station than outside of it. I should probably use the restroom while I'm here so I don't have to make another stop.

I hurry back inside. The mother's wrapping up her game and doesn't bother looking at me this time, taking her son by the arm and making for the door just after I come in. The Indian guys stop talking as I walk past them. Their strange words hang in the air. Did they think I could understand them?

The bathroom's around the corner but the ladies' room door has an out of order sign on it. I try the handle anyways. It doesn't budge. I glance at the men's room door. It's not like a bunch of people are here. I can hear the two Indian guys speaking again. Neither sounds like they're going anywhere soon. The door swings open when I try the handle, and I walk in.

The place stinks of urine and pieces of toilet paper cling to the wet tile around the urinals. I wrinkle my nose and go to the only stall. The inside is thankfully cleaner than the rest of the men's room. Except for the graffiti on the walls.

I can't help but read them as I go about my business. The biggest one is a stylized logo of Metallica on the door with lightning bolts coming off the 'M' and 'A', but plenty of other things are written on the walls. On my left, someone had decided to match animal names with sexual organs. Pig had an arrow pointing to pussy, cow had one pointing to cock. Even a few limericks and a scratched out phone number with a promise that the owner really was a girl decorated the walls.

Just as I flush the toilet, I hear the door open. Footsteps squelch into the bathroom. I squeeze my eyes shut and take a deep breath.

I open the door and walk right over to the sink to wash my hands. A man is standing at the urinal unzipping his fly. When he sees me he does a double take. He's wearing a red flannel shirt, blue jeans, and matching cowboy boots and hat.

"I'm sorry, ma'am! I meant to go into the men's room," he says, neck and face turning red.

"You're in it," I say. "Not too many urinals in the lady's room."

He sighs in relief but doesn't stop watching me wash my hands. I can't say I blame him for not wanting to go while I'm there, and I'd be lying if I said I wasn't a little grateful for him waiting. I'd seen enough penises to last me a lifetime.

Ghosts 51

I start rinsing away the lather when he says, "Do you know when you're due?"

I stop. "I'm sorry?"

"Your baby. Do you know when are you're due?" he asks again.

I hadn't told anyone I was pregnant. Not my mom who's been so supportive of me. Or my agent, who'd helped get me the *Flytrap* part. Or any of the three men I thought might be the father. Hell, I'd only seen the little positive sign on the home pregnancy test two days ago after throwing up my Cheerios for the third morning in a row.

"August, I think," I say, my voice catches on each word. It's November right now. "How'd you know?"

"Don't know," he says with a shrug. "You planning to keep it?"

"I don't know." I bite my lower lip.

The baby's why I want out of porn. I know several other porn stars that are moms. They did their best for their kids, but that's not what I want. But it was the only job I'd ever been able to hold on to. Movies seemed the next logical step, but did I really have what it took to be more than just Death Fodder Girl Friend or Stand in Number Three?

The man tilts his head. "Yes, you do," he says, voice soft. "You wouldn't be thinking about it so much if you didn't already know."

Grabbing some paper towels I stalk out of the bathroom. I can feel my brow furrowing, like the muscles in my forehead are trying to dig through my skull. Who the hell does that cowboy think he is?

The air clears of the stench of old urine as soon as I'm out of the bathroom. The sudden change makes something shift in my stomach. I turn and run back into the restroom. I ignore the cowboy as I rush into the stall. Falling to my knees, I feel the churning in my stomach build to a burn and move up my throat. I taste the spaghetti I had for dinner, but it's bitter now as it comes up.

My scalp tingles, and I become aware of the cowboy, kneeling beside me holding back my hair. My stomach convulses as the rest of my dinner comes up, sloshing into the toilet. His large hand rubs between my shoulder blades and something taut slackens. "You're going to be okay," he says to me. "Both of you."

I just stay there on the bathroom floor, waiting to puke again. But I don't. The contents of the bowl are a reddish brown. If it weren't for the acidic odor wafting up from the bowl I might be looking at diarrhea. The thought should make my stomach churn all over again, but thankfully it doesn't. There must not be anything left inside of me to be mixed up.

"Thanks," I say. I turn to face the cowboy. He's not there.

The Indian men fall silent again when I walk up a few moments later. I have to remind the younger one he still has my credit card. With both card and receipt in my hand, I walk back to my car. The only other vehicle in the parking lot is that minivan, still full of boxes.

I get in my car, and take off for my last shoot.

About Julian Kindred

Julian Kindred graduated from the University of Texas at Dallas in 2011 and became the President of the Houston Writers Guild in 2012. An avid reader and lover of all things fantasy and paranormal, he recently completed his first novel and is working on his second, with plans for more to come.

Bloody Mary
by
Joseph L. Lanza

"Bloody Mary!"
"Bloody Mary!"
"Bloody Mary!"

In the cramped, darkened bathroom of a ten-year-old recreational vehicle nicknamed the Behemoth, Diana Temple and I waited eagerly. The game was Bloody Mary. The goal was to get a vengeful spirit to appear in the mirror. Which, all things considered, was a magnificently stupid thing to do because, if the urban legend was true, Bloody Mary's ghost would rip off your face. Ranks right up there with dating a known serial killer.

Diana's blue eyes looked into my gray ones, her face a pale oval in the darkness; an angel's face with a devilishly wicked mind. At twelve she's already almost as tall as my four feet eleven inches, but where my hair is long and black cherry red, hers is shoulder length, curly and blond. She's always into mischief and fiercely loyal to her father (and the man I love) Bishop.

Excitement and uneasiness animated her expression as she whispered, "Again?"

I nodded, we chanted.

"Bloody Mary!"
"Bloody Mary!"
"Bloody Mary!"

A wave of dread washed over me. It's a silly high school game, I told myself. What must Bishop be thinking? He was at the table in the kitchenette, absorbed in his writing. Diana looked at me again. I nodded.

"Bloody Mary!"
"Bloody Mary!"
"Bloody Mary!"

Still no action in the old mirror, but we were hopeful. It was a lot like sitting around campfires telling ghost stories.

"Bloody Mary!"
"Bloody Mary!"

"Bloody Mary!"

The mirror glowed, dim, green.

Peachy.

"Awesome," Diana breathed.

We looked at each other, stifled laughs, and turned back to the mirror.

"Bloody Mary!"

"Bloody Mary!"

"Bloody Mary!"

The green grew, its soft radiance emanating from the glass. An eerie light suffused the small room, reflecting off our surprised faces. My flesh began to crawl. Common sense raised its hand and suggested that now would be a good time to stop.

"Bloody Mary!"

"Bloody Mary!"

"Bloody Mary!"

Common sense lost out. Slowly the green light faded, but something started to appear in the mirror. Something indistinct, except for a pair of lips. I saw the lips move. I read lips because I'm partially deaf, and they said, "Ceré Rosas."

My left cheek burned and Diana shrieked. The door flew open, light streamed into the bathroom, and I fell out, bouncing off the door frame, slamming up against the opposite wall. Diana jumped over me and flew out of the Behemoth.

Bishop stood looking down at me.

"What the bloody hell are you . . . dammit Ceré!! You cut yourself!"

He stooped and put his finger to my left cheek. When he pulled it away, I saw blood.

Outside, I heard Diana laughing herself silly. Bishop stuck his head into the bathroom. He looked around, and looked at me again before gazing back into the bathroom.

I felt the blood trickling down my cheek.

"How bad is it?" I asked. My voice was not as steady as I hoped it would be. Bishop stuck his head back into the bathroom, reached in, and came out with a towel.

"One of those scratches is bleeding like a stuck pig."

He quickly wiped my face and pressed the towel against my cheek to stop the bleeding.

"One?" I asked.

"Christ, Ceré," he exclaimed, "what were you doing in there?"

"Playing Bloody Mary," I explained.

"And you cut yourself?"

"Did I?"

My love shook his head. "Probably on the door frame when you fell out."

"I guess so." But my stomach was queasy.

"You must have," Bishop reaffirmed. He pulled the blood-soaked towel away, inspected me, pressed it against my cheek again, and continued, "Mary Worth's ghost did not appear and scratch your face. Mary Worth is an urban legend and usually young girls are the ones playing the game."

"So," I asked, "which version of the legend do you ascribe to?"

Depending on the version of the story you believe, Mary Worth is a witch burned at the stake four hundred years ago, or a beautiful woman horribly disfigured in an auto accident in the modern era. Either way, if her vengeful spirit appears, you're in deep doo-doo.

"Neither," Bishop replied, annoyed, "the game satisfies a craving for excitement by playing around in the dark."

"I can think of other ways to get excited playing around in the dark," I deadpanned. Bishop scowled, and I concluded that it might be unwise to mention those "other ways" in front of a twelve year old. The Behemoth's door was open and I could still hear Diana laughing outside, which meant she could probably hear us inside.

"Ceré!" she called out. "Did Mary get you?" More laughter, but I was beginning to get creeped out. After all, I had scratches on my face that were bleeding. Diana obviously hadn't seen the scratches, and was laughing so much she may not have heard Bishop scolding me.

Bishop pulled the towel away a second time, and examined the gash.

"That's better," he said, extending his hand.

I took it and pulled myself to my feet. Stepping into the bathroom, I examined myself in the mirror. There were two scratches on my cheek below my left eye, one deep and still oozing. An old half-dollar-sized burn scar along my jaw-line marred my appearance and made me feel ugly. It had brothers and sisters on my left arm and shoulder. The blood that had dripped onto and stained my tee shirt looked worse than the actual injury.

I stepped out into the corridor and got a paper towel from the kitchenette. Folding the towel into a small square, I dabbed at the oozing scratch. I've only

Ghosts 57

known Bishop for a short time. We live in the old RV and vagabond around the country in self-imposed isolation. I'm comfortable with that because I'm afraid of people, and the fear is so great, it often robs me of speech. Sign language, lip reading, and pantomime have become the barrier that protects me from social interaction. But with Bishop, speech comes easy, as it does with his daughter. Diana and I had butted heads at first when she joined us for the summer after school was out, but things worked out in the end.

"Hey Ceré!" Diana called out. "Where are you?"

"Coming," I replied.

"Ceré!" Diana exclaimed when I emerged into the sunlight and she saw my face.

"Damn, Ceré," Bishop said, following me out. "You really did a number on yourself."

"What?" I looked around at him, puzzled. Bishop grabbed the back of my tee shirt and pulled it so that I could see the material, stained red. Bishop reached down, touched my back, and showed me the result. More blood on his fingers.

"Bloody hell," Bishop said, disgusted.

"More like Bloody Mary," I replied, laughing. I swatted Bishop with my hand, teasing. "If you hadn't opened the door I wouldn't have fallen out and cut myself."

"If I hadn't opened the door," Bishop said in his most serious voice, "Mary Worth would have sucked you into the mirror with her." Now he was teasing me.

"Is that all the happened Ceré?" Diana asked nervously.

"Just cut myself when I fell through the door," I reassured her.

Bishop smiled, "Ready to head back in?"

I preferred to remain outside, and told Bishop so. We were at a state park capable of accommodating RVs, near Rockport along the Texas coast. Bishop likes privacy, and large trees shaded the Behemoth, screening us from beachgoers and other campers. Grotesque branches, twisted northwest from a near constant southeast wind that blew across the beach, reached for me. Even in the September heat, the breeze felt cool and I dug my stubby toes into a mixture of coastal grass and white sand, hot against the soles of my feet, and smelled the tang of salt air. The sunlight slanting down from the west warmed my skin, the denim in my ragged jeans already burned against my flesh. My jeans are always in a hopeless state of disrepair, and this pair had more holes than most, which was fine because I wore bikini bottoms beneath. Perfect jeans for the beach. Suddenly Mary Worth seemed far, far away.

"Last one in the water buys dinner!" Diana suddenly yelled, running toward the beach, tee shirt and shorts fluttering to the ground. A look of panic transformed Bishop's face until he realized that Diana had been wearing a one-piece beneath her clothes. I used his momentary befuddlement to my advantage. I dropped my jeans and ran, flinging my tee shirt off halfway to the water. Diana was laughing and when I turned around, Bishop was standing at the edge of the water, a bemused smile on his buzzard face. He began to mock-stalk me. I backed up until a wave slapped against my lower back. The cut there stung like the dickens, and I grimaced. Bishop caught the momentary flash of pain on my face.

"Come out of the water now!" he exclaimed.

"I'm fine," I replied, hands and fingers dancing familiar patterns as I signed.

"It needs to be disinfected. Don't you know there are nasty bacteria in the water?"

I rolled my eyes. Spoil-sport. I obliged him, however, and he led me back to the Behemoth and helped me inside. It was as serene and calm as usual. I tested the waters, saying, "Bloody Mary."

Nothing happened.

If anything had been going on, it was over.

"Shower," I said as I started toward the bathroom.

"Soap and water," Bishop scolded, "Clean it good. I'll disinfect it when you come out."

Inside the tiny bathroom I dropped my bikini bottoms and pulled off the top, squeezed into the shower, and turned it on. I slung the wet bikini pieces over the shower curtain rod. As always, the water was a lukewarm feeble stream, but it got the job done. I finished, dried and wrapped a towel around myself, and tapped on the inside of the door.

Bishop thrust a new bikini in and looked me over, obviously enjoying the view. I flashed him for the fun of it. After I had put on the bikini and wrapped my hair in a towel, with one last grimace at the mirror, I stepped out into the hall. Diana came in and slipped into the shower while Bishop disinfected my cuts.

"Ready for some chow?" He asked when Diana finally emerged.

"Yea!" Diana exclaimed, pumping her fist, and I seconded her. I dried and brushed my hair, pulled on another tee and slipped my feet and their stubby toes into a pair of flip-flops. The nice thing about coastal towns is that they don't expect you to dress up when you go to a restaurant. Bikini, tee shirt, and flip-flops are perfectly acceptable attire.

It was growing dark by the time we were seated. We got a nice table by the water and enjoyed the breeze and salty night air. I doodled on a paper napkin while we waited on our food, my mind drifting.

A sharp intake of breath brought me back to reality. I blinked my eyes into Diana's staring ones. Her blues travelled down to the napkin; my grays followed.

A hideously disfigured face stared back at me. A woman's features, contorted by pain and scarring, and eyes that bored straight through me.

I grabbed the napkin, wadded it, and threw it over the rail.

"Dammit, Ceré," Bishop complained. "That could be a five-hundred-dollar fine!"

"I D-O-N-'-T C-A-R-E," my fingers flashed in return, their movements sharp and vigorous. My scowling face underscored the message. Bishop blinked once, but didn't push the issue.

"She drew Mary Worth's face," Diana said, voice subdued.

"She drew what her imagination supplied," he replied, and left it that.

The waitress dropped a pair of beers on the table. The sweat soaked bottles were inviting, and I grabbed mine before Diana could swipe it. Bishop wasn't as quick on the uptake. She swooped down on his longneck and took a swig before handing it back. Exasperation marked his eyes and lips.

We didn't return to the Behemoth until ten-thirty. The southeasterly wind had picked up, gusting strongly now, whistling through the branches of the twisted trees. The Behemoth trembled in its grip as we prepared for bed.

Diana slept on the small couch at the front of the Behemoth, and I shared the bed with Bishop in the back. I slept in a pair of panties and tee shirt, cuddled against Bishop's bare body (he wore only boxers). Sleep came easily but about two in the morning I woke.

I wasn't sure why I woke. I looked around the interior, and listened intently. Nothing but the wind, a subdued symphony of low moans and whistles as it worked its way through the trees and around the body of the Behemoth; the occasional snore from Bishop, a discordant note.

Nature was calling, so I arose and went to the bathroom. I left the door open a crack because I didn't want to turn the lights on and blind myself. A little ambient light filtered in, which was just fine for my night vision.

I finished my business and washed my hands. I looked at myself in the mirror but could hardly see anything in the darkness. I thought about Mary Worth and that stupid game. *Had* I scratched myself? It couldn't be supernatural, although I recalled the hot streak on my face just before I fell out the door. The image of the face I'd drawn on the napkin rose uninvited to my consciousness. The temptation to assert reason over superstition was great, too great. I decided to chant those words as an act of defiance. I whispered them at the mirror.

"Bloody Mary!"

"Bloody Mary!"

"Bloody Mary!"

I waited in the silence.

"What the bloody hell are you doing?" Bishop asked from the left as the door swung open. I shrieked and jumped sideways, slipped, and fell on my bum.

"Dammit, Bishop!" I yelled at him, "What the hell are you doing, scaring the shit out of my like that?"

"I didn't mean to," he said defensively. "But I heard you whispering that stupid phrase."

"Act of defiance," I told him. "Help me up." I extended my hand, and Bishop lifted me. I stumbled out of the bathroom, and gave Diana an apologetic smile. She was sitting straight up on the couch like a ramrod, eyes wide.

"Be with you in a minute," Bishop said, stepping into the bathroom and shutting the door. Maybe Mary Worth would get *him*, I mused. That would teach him.

I slid back beneath the sheets and, a few minutes later, Bishop joined me. "Sorry I scared you," he apologized.

"That's okay," I said, and laughed, "It's kind of funny when you think about it." I snuggled against him and settled down to sleep. Bishop hugged me to him.

And that's when it happened: a hot streak along my back. For some reason, Bishop had scratched me, probably as a prank. He did it too hard.

Ghosts 61

"Shit!" I exclaimed, hitting his shoulder with the palm of my hand as I lifted myself on my other arm. "That isn't funny Bishop!"

Another scratch. "Shit!" I yelled at him. "Dammit, stop it!"

Bishop looked at me in confusion as I began to realize he hadn't scratched me.

Suddenly, his cell phone rang.

Silence descended like a shroud. Phone calls at that time of the morning are never good things.

"Carl," he told me, referring to his older brother as he looked at the caller ID. Bishop flipped the phone open and spoke. As he listened, his face grew grave.

"When did it happen?" He asked, voice low. I heard the buzz of speech coming from his cell phone, but couldn't make out any words. Diana was standing by the bathroom door, watching her father, eyes large.

"Where's he at now?" Bishop listened. "Okay," he said, "We're on our way."

The phone squawked at him some more. Bishop's brows drew together in irritation.

"This isn't the time to discuss that subject!"

"This isn't the time to..." was all I heard the raised voice on the phone say before I couldn't make out any more words. Bishop had turned away from me and was shielding the phone with his hand. I didn't know what the emergency was, but I had a pretty good idea what Bishop and Carl were arguing about, and why Bishop was becoming angry. I hadn't met Bishop's family yet, but the emails I'd been getting from them weren't warm and fuzzy. I'd lived on the street, and that's where Bishop had found me, and they didn't like that fact.

"He's right, Bishop," I said, "This isn't the time to spring me on your family."

"You have to meet them sometime, Ceré."

"Yea," I agreed reluctantly, "But this isn't the time. What's happened?"

Bishop took a breath, started to argue, and conceded the point. He spoke into his phone, "Okay, Carl, you win. I'll check Ceré into a hotel. See you in a couple of hours." He hung up the phone.

"Dad's had a heart attack," Bishop told me and Diana without preamble, "He's in the hospital in Angleton. They don't know how serious yet, but they don't think it's too bad. Mom's hysterical. Diana and I need to go up."

I nodded, and Diana looked like she was about to cry. Small wonder.

"We'll ride up and get you a hotel room, Ceré." Bishop continued.

"Don't fret it, Bishop," I told him, smiling, "I can stay in the Behemoth."

"By yourself?"

"I'm a big girl."

"Are you sure?"

"I'm sure. Keep me posted, okay? I hope he gets well fast."

Nodding, he and Diana quickly grabbed a few items, while I pulled on jeans. I followed them into the darkness as they packed Bishop's old Honda Civic.

The sand was dappled in black and silver as shadows danced across it and when I looked up through the tree branches, I saw small islands of cumulus sailing off to the northwest and, periodically, a three-quarters full moon peeking between them. The wind from the southeast was blowing stiffly now, plastering the tee shirt to my back and flapping the edges of the fabric as I stood watching. The symphony of wind wasn't as pronounced outside, and the whoops and whistles I heard sounded about an octave higher.

Diana gave me a silent hug, and Bishop gave me a final kiss.

"Sure you'll be okay?"

I nodded, "I'll be fine."

"You know where the key is if you want to drive the beast up."

"Thanks, but I think I'll let the beast stay right where it is. Besides, I like the beach."

"Sure?"

I laughed, "Yes, Bishop; quit being so over-protective."

His smile was sheepish and he gave me another kiss before getting into the Civic. I waved to Diana again. She put down the window and teased, "Don't let Mary get you!"

I watched them drive away and realized how lonely I was going to be. I stood for a moment in the darkness and looked around as the sound of the Civic receded. I felt very isolated, despite the knowledge that other campers were nearby, invisible behind the bent and twisted trees.

And I was alone, at about two in the morning. When I stepped up into the Behemoth, the interior was unnaturally quiet. Strange how you notice the silence when you're by yourself, I thought. It's palpable, pressing on your ears like cotton. Absent are all the little noises, Bishop breathing, Diana shifting around on the couch, all the little sounds that register in the background, despite my bad ear, and make me comfortable.

Then I heard the wind whistling and the Behemoth gave another shudder as a particularly strong gust pushed against it. The sound wasn't mournful, but more strident, trilling. My private symphony had resumed.

I gave myself a little shake and made sure the doors were locked and secured. On my way back to bed I came to the open bathroom door. Odd, I thought someone had closed it. I remembered Diana leaning against it. Oh well, I told myself, lots of bustling about, probably Bishop or Diana grabbing a toothbrush or deodorant. Still, it was a little icky.

I clicked on the bathroom light (I admit it, cluck, cluck, cluck) before pushing the door shut, and went back to the bed. The Behemoth looked as lonely as I felt. I got one of Bishop's tee shirts and exchanged it for mine. It smelled like him, and the odor made me feel less abandoned. I wasn't really abandoned, it just felt that way. I lay on Bishop's side of the bed, which was still warm, snuggled under the blankets, and clicked off the lights.

A moment later the bathroom door creaked open. I scowled. Maybe the latch didn't catch all the way. Reluctantly, I got up to close it, stubbing my toe on the bed's baseboard in the darkness.

Darkness.

If the bathroom door was open, it shouldn't be dark. There should be light streaming through it. Cautiously, I approached the bathroom, reached in, and clicked the light back on. I shut the door and returned to the bed. I lay down I turned back towards the bathroom. The door was open, light out, a black oblong in the near darkness. I hadn't even heard a tell-tale creak.

Shit.

I got up again, nervous, and closed the stupid door. I didn't bother with the bathroom light this time since it wasn't going to cooperate. I went back to bed, turned the night table lamp on, and snuggled under the blankets.

I looked at the bathroom door. It stayed closed. I breathed a sigh of relief and turned on my side.

The nightstand light went out. I looked towards the bathroom. The now open door stared at me silently.

Double shit.

I was determined not to be scared and try this one more time. Bishop, I had discovered, was a skeptic about all things unexplainable, and I decided that tonight it would be a good plan to emulate him in that regard.

I got up again and shut the door. Then I found something to prop against it to keep it closed. My backpack, loaded with several large books, worked perfectly. I clicked on both night stand lamps, and rolled back into bed, wrapping the blankets around me. As I did, both lights went out and I saw the door was open.

Triple shit and time for a new plan. My flesh began to crawl. This was not a good development (understatement). Because getting out of bed and running screaming through the park like a soon-to-be-dead extra in a slasher flick probably wasn't a wise choice, I started considering other options. One option was calling Bishop and asking him to come back, but I really didn't want to do that. It was too sensible.

Another option was to sleep outside. That was probably reasonably safe if I didn't object to serving as the main course for a swarm of mosquitoes.

I felt the hot streak of a scratch slash across my back. I sat up and reached around to find out if I was bleeding. Another scratch scored my back.

I was out of the bed and on my way to the main door in a heartbeat. Mosquitoes, here I come. I even had the blood feast laid out for them across my back.

The main door wouldn't open, even though I unlocked and unlatched it. Great. I had one door that wouldn't stay shut and another that wouldn't open. I pushed again, but the door felt as if something was holding it closed.

I came to my knees and cried out in pain as something scored my back again. A cacophony of scratches exploded across my body. No place was sacred, and I frantically tried to shield myself with my hands as my mind became suffused by the pain. It stopped, and I found myself huddled against the main door in the small well formed by a step downward.

I crawled to my feet, my body sticky with blood. When I tried to turn on the lights, nothing happened. I inspected myself by the moonlight that filtered through the windows and saw scratches running down my leg and along my arms, several oozing blood. The back of my tee shirt was wet with blood, and several red blotches marred the front. I lifted the tee shirt and saw scratches across my belly and torso. I reached up and felt more blood on my face.

The room became darker. The Behemoth shuddered as the wind pushed against it again, whistling.

Near panicked I tried once more to open the main door so I could escape. It still wouldn't budge. I crawled over the driver's seat and tried that door, but it wouldn't open either. I was really scared now. I sat on the floor at the front of the RV, back to the driver's seat, and watched the interior of the RV for any sign of movement. Through the small amount of ambient light that filtered through the windows, I saw a dark shape step out of the bathroom and advance.

Mary Worth!

We stared at one another, her leering face a hideous mass of scar tissue, the same face I'd unconsciously drawn earlier, and in the near darkness one thing that stood out was blood where it glistened on her nails. My blood!

She began to walk towards me. I had nowhere to run. Frantically, I looked for some way to defend myself. Nothing came to mind or hand. I turned and kicked the main door. A thousand pin-pricks stabbed my foot and calf in return, and the door didn't budge.

Mary Worth was on me, her long, filthy nails tearing at my face as the pain blinded me. She was solid, her nails scraped my skin raw. I heard myself screaming as I pushed past her and stumbled towards the bedroom. Perhaps I could cover myself with a blanket as protection against her nails. Could ghosts scratch you though a blanket?

The bathroom door gaped, and the thought flashed through my mind that I could use it as a barrier. I jumped in and pulled the door shut behind me, threw the latch. If Mary was in the living area, maybe she couldn't get to me through the door. Right?

Wrong.

The room glowed softly green. Terrified, I looked at the mirror. I saw Mary Worth there, slowly coming towards me, fingers extended like claws, her lips moving, chanting my name. She was going to come out of that mirror and claw me to death. I just knew it!

I threw the lock on the bathroom door and pushed. Now *it* wouldn't open. I tried again, kicked it, threw my body against it, but no luck. I turned back towards the mirror. Mary Worth had almost reached me, any second now.

Blind with fear, I balled my tiny hand into a fist, and slammed it into knuckles first the mirror. Cracks radiated out from where my knuckles hit, and the sliver-sharp edges that defined the cracks sliced into my flesh.

Seven years bad luck, right? Yeah, right, I'd already had so many years of bad luck, I figured Lady Luck owed me, with interest. Busting the mirror was more like a down payment on payback.

I slammed my fist into the mirror again; blood smeared across the cracking glass as my knuckles slipped against the mirrored surface, and I felt the blood between my fingers pooling in my palm. I hit the stupid mirror several more times, spreading the cracks across it until large chunks dropped out, broke into myriad pieces on the plastic counter top, and tumbled to the floor. Somehow I managed to keep from cutting my feet on them.

The room was dark. I saw and heard nothing. Trembling, I flipped the light switch, smudging it with blood. This time the light came on.

I looked at my hand. The backs of my fingers looked like shredded meat and the pain was beginning to numb them as it finally registered on my brain. I pushed open the door and stumbled out of the bathroom towards the kitchenette where I rounded up paper towels and pressed them to my knuckles. Sharp pains jabbed deep into my hand because the paper was pressing slivers of mirror deeper into the wounds. I was weeping from the intensity of the sensation.

And when I turned towards the bedroom, I saw a dark shape, a woman's shape, indistinct, but beyond a doubt in my mind, Bloody Mary, standing there.

"Leave me alone, leave me alone!" Fear tore the words from my throat as the form advanced. I thought I heard her calling my name. My mind devoid of all reason and common sense, I hurled myself bodily against the main door, which finally burst open. I tumbled out of the Behemoth, arms cart wheeling, and slammed down on the sand. I heard my right wrist pop as a needle of pain stabbed my arm. My head hit the ground and my world became fuzzy.

The night was quiet except for the stiff breeze coming in off the Gulf. I was spread-eagle on my stomach on the sand. The back of my hand stung like hell where slivers of glass remained embedded in the flesh. Using my elbows for support, I looked over my shoulder at the Behemoth. The door stood open, light blazing within. I struggled to my knees and walked on them back to that door and looked inside.

It was serene and quiet. I crawled into the beast, leaving the door open behind me. I turned the knob on the bathroom door and it opened easily. The interior of the bathroom was pattered in deep red and bright silver slivers. I went back and experimented with the main door and got the same result. I continued to leave it open anyway.

Ghosts 67

Mary Worth was gone, history. In the safety of the Behemoth, I closed and locked the main door, got a bowl, a towel, and some rubbing alcohol and tweezers, and spent the remainder of the night picking glass bits out of my flesh.

Bishop was going to be pissed when he saw the broken mirror. He wouldn't believe me about Mary Worth.

Truth was, I couldn't explain it. Some things you just can't explain. Bloody Mary Worth is one of them.

About Joseph L. Lanza

Joseph Lanza practices business and commercial law with the Vethan Law firm in Houston. He previously worked for legendary Texas attorney Richard "Racehorse" Haynes for sixteen years and as a briefing attorney for the Fourteenth Court of Appeals for two years. His contribution to this anthology won first place in the Houston Writers Guild organization spring 2008 short story contest, and his novel, *Life Swap,* based on the adventures of Bishop and Ceré, won first place in the 2012 spring novel contest. Mr. Lanza has authored and co-authored several articles on topics related to his legal practice specialties.

The Man in the Fedora
by
Ann Conti

My company cut back everyone's hours, because business had declined since Hurricane Katrina. When I returned home at the end of my shortened workday, I went upstairs to my bedroom to change clothes. When I entered my bathroom, I noticed that the toilet seat was up. I distinctly remembered putting the seat and lid down after I had cleaned the toilet with Pine Sol that morning. Not only was the toilet seat up, but the Pine-Sol had been flushed away.

Irritation raged through my body. The toilet seat being up brought back memories of my ex-husband. He always left the seat up. Several times, I didn't notice the seat was up and I fell right in. My fault for not looking before I sat down. If a Saints or LSU game was on television, he leaned out the bathroom door to see the television in the next room. His aim wasn't so great. All the beer he had been drinking took its toll. You'd have thought that he was watering a garden instead of using the bathroom.

But my ex had never been to the house I bought after our divorce. In fact, he didn't even know where it was. So he certainly couldn't be the culprit.

"Did you use my bathroom today?" I asked my sister who lived with me now because her house was destroyed by Katrina's wind and flood waters.

"No. Why would I do that? There's another bathroom upstairs for me and a half-bath downstairs."

She seemed a bit pissed as though I were accusing her of something.

"I was just wondering because the toilet seat was up, and I thought you might have used it for some reason."

Shock and fear flooded her face. She stared away then whispered, "The toilet seat was up in the downstairs half bath, too."

"What!" I hesitated a moment. "Has a man been in the house?"

My sister had several guy friends who visited her and sometimes spent the night. I hoped she wasn't going to start bringing them to my house. She and I had different taste in men.

"No. Why would a man come into the house? No repairs need to be done inside, and I haven't had any visitors," she said.

"That is very eerie," I said.

"Yes, it is."

We were silent for a while, pondering this mystery.

When Hurricane Katrina coldcocked New Orleans, I was in Houston at my son's house. I watched in horror on TV as my hometown was disemboweled. I was safe, but so many others were not—not even the ghosts.

We were allowed to go back home for a "look and see" on September 5th. By the time Hurricane Rita headed for Galveston a few weeks after Katrina, we were allowed to return home for good.

Blowflies had descended on the city. They laid their eggs in carcasses. Animal carcasses, human carcasses that had not yet been found, and human carcasses that had long been buried but exhumed by the flood. The devastation–the smell of death–was overwhelming. I felt an incredible sense of loss, but I hadn't actually lost anything. What had it been like for those who stayed behind? What did people feel who watched as their property, their loved ones, their city washed away?

I stood in front of my house and watched my neighbor drag water-soaked carpet outside putting it beside the discarded sheetrock that had sucked up the rising flood waters and was mildewed. Joe was a first responder and had to stay behind during the storm.

"Hi, Joe. Can I help you with that?"

"Ya back? Looks like your house is the only one on the block that didn't get water."

"I guess I'm lucky. But just a little lucky. There's a debris line around the cement foundation an inch below my front door. If the water had come up a bit more, I'd have been flooded too.

"The biggest change in my life is that my sister is living with me because her house was destroyed. Joe, I'm so depressed because of all of this. I know I don't really have the right to feel that way. I mean, I haven't lost anything, and I was able to leave so I didn't have to witness anything. What was it like Joe? What was it like? You must be so glad that it's over now."

"I haven't had time to think about all that really. During the storm, we just had to deal with whatever came up. And deal with it fast. To save whatever lives we could. And now, we're looking for missing people."

"You're still looking for bodies?"

No one knew at the time that in addition to Katrina's tempestuous winds and storm surge, the levees would explode hurling enough water into the city to bury almost every home, business, and, yes, above-ground crypts in the cemeteries, exhuming bodies and killing over 1,000 living people.

"Oh yeah. We find one every now and then. Usually it's an old person who drowned when the waters filled their house. But sometimes it's a body that floated out from its grave when the cemeteries flooded. Lots of graves were disturbed. Just like live people, a lot of spirits have been uprooted too."

"What do you mean, spirits?" I didn't know if I believed in spirits of dead people wandering around.

"I've seen all kinds of weird things happen."

"Like what, Joe?"

"During search and rescue I've been in a couple of buildings that didn't have electricity, but they were lit up as bright as a Christmas tree. You'da thought a party was goin' on. And one time when I was searching a building in Gentilly, I heard footsteps and doors slamming, but the building was completely empty."

"That must have been weird."

"Freaked me out man, but I gotta stay tough for my job, ya' know."

Joe went back inside his house to drag out more debris for trash collection.

Several nights later, I was sleeping when something woke me up. I opened my eyes and watched as the silhouette of a man wearing a fedora entered my room. Mind you, he didn't open the door—he passed right through it while it was closed.

My heart was pounding so loudly I was afraid he would hear it. I tried to do controlled breathing to slow it down. Why hadn't I paid more attention in my yoga class? I didn't want him to realize I was there. I lay as still as I could and watched the shadow of the man in the fedora glide through the room and vanish before he reached the other side. It was as though he had never existed. And who knows? Maybe he hadn't. I thought I must have been dreaming. Was this man real? How did he get inside? I set the burglar alarm before I went to sleep. Yet, there had been no warning beeps.

What did he want? Was he going to attack me? Was he going to steal something? Could he be a looter?

The man in the fedora said nothing to me. Nor touched me, nor anything in the room. In fact, although I was terrified, he didn't seem to know I was

Ghosts 71

there. I figure he wasn't visible during the day, only at night. Otherwise, my sister would have seen him. And if he was going to come during the day and use my bathrooms to relieve himself, the least he could do was put the seat down afterwards.

Over the next few months, the man in the fedora passed through my bedroom door numerous times. Each time, I shook with fear. Each time I struggled to keep my beating heart quiet. Each time, he glided away.

He didn't seem to use my bathrooms anymore, or at least I didn't find any evidence of it. He just seemed to be wandering through, looking for something or someone. Could he be lost—lost like so many people were after Katrina?

The smell of death smothered New Orleans. The ordeal of Katrina resulted in many suicides and an acceleration of health problems. Many died at a younger age than they otherwise would have. But what about those who were dead before Katrina? Could the man in the fedora be from an earlier era in New Orleans history?

I told Joe about the toilet seats and seeing the man in the fedora hat pass through my bedroom at night.

He laughed about the toilet seats, but then said, "You really could have a ghost, you know."

"This man was wearing a fedora. Men haven't worn hats like that since the 1960s," I said. "Where do you think he could have come from, Joe?"

"Good question."

After a time, the ghost stopped appearing. I suppose he found what he was looking for or moved on to look elsewhere. Whenever I mentioned to people that I had a ghost in my house, they smiled condescendingly to humor me or flatly said that ghosts don't exist. I began to doubt what I had seen. Surely, it was a dream after all.

Six-year-old Robby who lived down the street used to come to my house to play with my Shih Tzu. One day, he was sitting with me on my back patio playing fetch with Polo and telling me all about his school and an illness that he had struggled with since he was a toddler. He talked quickly as though he just had to reveal this information. And the last thing he blurted out was that he had a ghost in his house, that he, his mom, and his grandpa had all seen it. He said the ghost looked like a man wearing a hat like the ones men wore in the old time movies. So there—I wasn't the only one to see this ghost after all.

I only hope his life is now settled, as so many others' lives are now settled these seven years after Katrina.

About Ann Conti

Ann Conti (aka Ann Morcos) grew up in New Orleans. Her current 'day job' is as the Medical Writing Manager in the Biostatistics and Medical Writing Department at US Oncology Research, McKesson Specialty Health. In 1999, she opened her own medical writing and editing company, MorcosMedia™ (http://www.morcosmedia.com). She has published over 90 newspaper and magazine articles, a children's book, *The Tale of Nada Nutria*, and 3 short stories, 2 for children. Her articles have appeared in *CBS HealthWatch*, *Annals of Internal Medicine*, *KidsHealth.org*, *ADVANCE for Directors in Rehabilitation*, *ADVANCE for Nurse Practitioners*, *HemAware*, *Boys Life*, *Sports Life*, *Laparoscopy Today*, *Creative Classroom*, and others. In addition, she has written a screenplay. She is the former editor of the *BELS Letter*, the official publication of the Board of Editors in the Life Sciences, and the former annual meeting editor of *Science Editor*, the official publication of the Council of Science Editors. Ann is a member of the American Medical Writers Association, the Board of Editors in the Life Sciences, the Council of Science Editors, and the European Association of Science Editors, the Woodlands Writers Guild, the Houston Writers Guild, and Mystery Writers of America. In 2002, Ann graduated from the Gretna Police Academy and became Peace Officer Standards and Training (P.O.S.T) certified in basic law enforcement. She has completed her first crime novel in a series featuring Private Eye Coco P. Cappaccio. She enjoys reading, exercising, listening to live music, and family activities.

The Name
by
Sandra Morton DiGiovanni

Waking up nose to nose with a ghost will disconcert the bravest person. I am not that person. I lay between the states of sleeping and waking, aware of my new home, looking forward to tackling all the boxes and furniture. I debated whether to try to squeeze a few more minutes of snooze time, but a full bladder and a need of caffeine decided for me. I threw out both arms and arched my back, rolled to my right side and opened my eyes. Just inches away, a pair of blue-green eyes twinkled at me. I did what any normal woman would do when face to face with a stranger in her bedroom. I squeaked. No screams were available.

I dug my heels into my bed to push backwards. The strange girl stood up and backed away a few feet. Something was definitely off. No danger vibes. Weird, old clothing. "How did you get into my house? Why are you in my bedroom? Who are you?" The questions fell over each other. Her mouth moved, but no sound came out. *Oh, great,* I thought to myself, *a mute home invader.* "Can you understand me?"

A nod.

"Stay right there. Don't move. I'm about to explode." I headed to my ensuite bathroom.

As I peed, I tried to wrap my head around the silent intruder. I looked up, and she stood in the bathroom doorway. "What on earth? Don't you have a concept of privacy? Do you have an audience when you pee?" She backed away, her brow furrowed, mouthing something that looked like an apology. "Geez," I muttered as I flushed. I was surprised by my lack of alarm after the initial shock.

She stood with her back to me, staring out my window. I decided to steer her toward the living area of the house. No matter why she was here, I needed coffee to get the old gray cells working. I put my hand out to steer her, and my hand passed through her shoulder, leaving my fingers tingling. Shock numbed my psyche. I do not believe in ghosts—well, not exactly. I tried touching her again, and again my hand passed through her. She turned to face me, one eyebrow arched, a smirk on her pretty lips.

"Good grief, this is just a dream! A ghost, for crying out loud. Girl, you are not real, just a crazy dream. After all that moving and Mexican food, what should I expect? Stop shaking your head and grinning at me. And you're dressed funny. And nobody wears a grungy apron these days. I said, stop shaking your head!"

She stood, facing me, shoulders shaking in laughter. Her head ducked down, a sly smile rimming her lips. She wore a brown, floor-length, long-sleeved dress topped with a dingy gray apron. Her copper mane was tied into a bun on top of her head. Pale freckles covered a small, elfin face. All this detail in a dream? I don't think so.

"Come on. Whether you're real or not, I gotta have coffee." I pushed toward the kitchen to get my fix. If she was a dream, I'd turn around and she'd be gone. If not a dream, well, I'd deal with that after my first hit of some smooth Kona blend. Knowing my penchant for morning fumbling, I'd put my coffee bean grinder, fake sugar, dairy creamer, and cups on my counter last night. I took my beans from the cupboard, emptied some into the grinder, and let the grinder rip. I looked up in time to see the girl jump. "It's only a coffee grinder." Her head came into mine to look into the process. Uh, her head *into* mine? My brain momentarily shut down. I measured the coffee into the pot, turned it on, and sat at the breakfast bar.

I wondered at my easy acceptance of a resident ghost. Had I gone around the bend? Was this an involved and complicated dream? No, the brewing aroma convinced me this was real. My mind couldn't form anything but the most basic questions, so I started asking.

"What is your name?"

Shaking head, shrugging shoulders.

"Can you hear me"?

Nod.

"Can you talk?"

Head shake no.

"You don't know your name?"

She shook her head no.

I turned my back and fixed my coffee. When I turned back around, she had seated herself on the other side of the bar, chin in hand. "Want some coffee?" Sometimes I can be a real smartass.

No.

"My name is Lee Johnson. This is my first house. I know the house is twenty six years old. Were you always here?"

Head nod and gesture over her shoulder.

"Were you here before the house was built?"

She nodded and repeated the gesture.

"How long?"

Shrug.

"Let me get this straight. This is your spot. You were here before this house was built. You don't know how long. You don't know your name. Do you know anything that can help?" Ghosts don't cry, at least this one didn't. She shook her head, bit her lower lip, then her eyes met mine. Such sadness.

"Give me time to let this soak in. You wear clothes from long ago, but how long ago? I gotta think. I expect friends here pretty soon to help me unpack. Are you gonna stick around?"

My ghost widened her eyes and shrugged. Did she have snark on her face?

"Did you just tell me 'maybe'?"

Nod.

"Smarty britches. Suit yourself. I need a shower, and I don't need an audience." I flip-flopped my way down the hall without a backward glance.

I could get used to this fancy-schmancy shower with all its heads and water speeds. Oil of Olay Body Wash sluiced down my body as I rinsed, and I cursed myself for not unpacking my razor. I'd just have prickly legs and pits when Kay and Hank came over to help. I chuckled when I envisioned their reaction to my ghost.

I doubted they'd be afraid. The three of us are patrons of The Magick Cauldron, sporadically read each other's Tarot, try spells of attraction. But a real, live, live-in ghost? I looked forward to their reaction. Then it hit me. What if they couldn't see her? Would they believe me? I hurried through the rest of my bathroom routine and dressed for a day of unpacking. If Kay did her job, I'd soon be sharing kolaches, coffee, and ghost stories with the other two members of the KHOU researching triad.

I sipped the tepid coffee from my cup as I looked for my ghost. Nowhere in sight. Had I experienced a hallucination? I knew I hadn't, but where was my new roomie?

Beep, beep. *Ah, beware of VWs bearing gifts.* I opened the utility room door to welcome my pals, kolaches, and *look*, a ficus tree.

"Ooooh, Kona or Sumatra?" questioned Hank as he dropped the warm Czech sweets on the bar. "All I had this morning was some Tasters' Choice. Yuk. Gimme coffee and no one gets hurt."

Kay tossed her sable colored pony tail. "You are so pedestrian. That is fresh ground Kona. Hit me with it, Sister. I carried the tree. Serve me first."

My mouth busied itself with warm cream cheese and dough as I pointed at them and the coffeemaker. I am a kolache slut. They can get their own coffee.

Kay and Hank faced me across the bar. We sat and groaned in ecstasy. None of us is a morning person, and the caffeine jolt kept us from growing fangs. The sugar rush is a bonus.

Hank picked up my hand and licked gooey cream cheese from my pinky finger then sucked on it. Anyone else, and the heat would be rising, but Hank was just, well, Hank. Besides, his boyfriend would gut me like a fish if I went there. He topped off his half cup of coffee and sighed lustily as he grazed on a pineapple treat. "So, how was your first night in your new dom-i-cile?"

"The new bed is so comfortable. I didn't want to get up, but I had to pee, and a ghost was eyeballing me. You can thank her for me being up with the smell of a Hawaiian Starbucks wafting around the room," I said. My snark was showing.

Kay grinned like a possum in a garbage can. "A ghost? Kewl beans. Gonna keep her?"

"Thinking about it. Want to meet her? Oh, ghostie," I called. And there she was.

"Holy fried frogs!" Hank snorted coffee out his nose and started coughing. "How'd you do that? She, like, just, uh," as he snapped his fingers, searching for the word.

"Materialized?" offered Kay. Nothing rattles her, not even ghosts, it seemed. She rose from her ebony barstool and started circling my ghost. Her eyes narrowed, and she swept a hand through the ghost's middle. She continued to circle.

Not to be outdone, my ghost started circling Kay and passed a hand through Kay. They looked like two boys circling each other in the school yard. I expected them to start chicken-chesting.

"OK, she can stay," Kay said in judgment.

My ghost rolled her eyes and used her index finger to circle her ear. I had to agree with her that Kay is nutso.

"That's it? Where's the disbelief, the shock? You two are a disappointment," I fumed.

"Hey, I choked," Hank offered. He looked at the ghost and spoke slowly to her. "I—am—Hank. Who are you?"

She started her shrugging, using hand motions. Kay got nose to nose with her. "Spit it out, Sister. We want deets." Kay can be a little impatient.

I felt like I should referee, so I tried to stand between them. Didn't work. I ended up standing IN the ghost. For once Kay was nonplussed.

"She can't speak. Stop. She can hear. Stop. She doesn't know her name. Stop." My you-know-what was creeping in.

"Shut UP!" shrilled Kay. "Or should I say 'Stop'?" Her freckles stood out against her pinked face in bas relief.

I continued. "She was here before the house, but I don't know how long. I think we should do some research to help her find out who she is. She doesn't know. And she watched me pee."

Now it was Hank's turn to circle her, but she didn't take offense while he did it. She stayed still. "Research. It's what we do. But we need to find a way for her to communicate with us so we can ask questions. Look here, Honey, can you write?"

She nodded.

Hank pulled out his ever-present notepad from his shirt pocket and scrounged a pen from one of my boxes. He handed it to her as she reached out to take it. It hit the bar. "Oops," he giggled with a sheepish look that matched hers. "Can you pick it up?" It wasn't gonna happen.

A sudden inspiration hit me. "Sign language!" I bellowed.

She looked perplexed.

"You don't know what sign language is?" I asked.

Head shake.

"She can write, so that means she can read," mused Kay. "Just get a book on signing, and we'll all learn together."

Ghosts 79

"Should I hit Barnes & Noble Booksellers now or after we do some settling in?" Hank wondered. "I volunteer to get the book." He headed toward the utility room, intent on putting distance between himself and physical labor.

"Not so fast, boyo," I objected, grabbing him by the collar. "We can do that later. I didn't just want you here today for your pretty face. I need your manly arms for heavy lifting."

Hank snickered and flexed a pathetic bicep.

"Just sit back down, and let's have another cup. And gimme another kolache—that cherry one," I said.

Kay and Hank took their places opposite me, and Ms. Ghost slid into the stool beside me. She bent her head toward the box of kolaches.

"Can you smell these?" asked Kay.

Head shake, shrug, confused look.

"I've got this one!" I exulted. "You can smell some things?"

Nod.

"But you can't smell these," I prodded.

Enthusiastic nod.

"OK," mused Hank, "you can smell some things but not others. Can you only smell bad things?"

Head shake.

"Oh, I know, I know," wiggled Kay. "You can smell only strong smells, good or bad."

Ghostly enthusiasm. Obviously Kay wins the brass ring.

Hank bent over, took off a shoe and sock and raised his foot toward Ms. Ghost's nose. "Can you smell this?"

Silent gagging and a sneeze. Step backward, tears streaming down ghostly cheeks.

"Dog! Take your stinky feet outside! Kay and I been telling you about your odiferous peds. You made a ghost cry! That ought to tell you something."

Kay punched Hank in the arm while I beat him with my new red dish towel. We drove him out the back door and re-entered. MG was still waving her hand in front of her nose. Rank odor.

"Where's your Febreze? We can make him spray his shoes," Kay suggested.

"I have no idea where I put the Febreze. Besides, that wouldn't help. His feet smell like a garbage barge on a hot day—with sewage on top." I laughed at my own ingenuity.

"True that," Kay snorted.

A disgruntled Hank marched back into the kitchen. MG backed up a few feet, holding her nose. I stood beside MG, and with Kay made up a barricade trio. All of us simultaneously crossed our arms and cocked our hips.

"Very funny," fumed Hank. "About as funny as a fart in an elevator."

Three women cracked up in laughter and encircled him to hug and mollify him. He sniffed and tossed his head. He twisted the shark's tooth he wore on a leather strip and hissed at us.

"You are such a diva," I tittered.

"Yeah, well, you try being dissed by a ghost," poor Hank wailed.

"Come on, y'all, let's get started with this job," said Kay. "Where do you want to start?"

"I have a list," I started.

"Of course you do, Miss Anal Retentive," insulted Hank, intent on some payback.

"Don't make me hurt you, Nunu," I warned.

"If you two don't stop acting like elementary kids, I will give you a timeout," griped Kay.

MG leaned against the bar, ever the interested observer. She gave a thumbs up to Kay, and Kay tried to high-five her. Kay ended up slapping the bar.

"Ahem," I started. "Most of the furniture is in place, but I need to move the china hutch around to the opposite wall. Then I want to move the couch in the living area and my dresser in the bedroom." I took a breath. "I need to get the heavy things first while I have the Hulk to help."

We began the work at hand. Hank and I did the heavy work while Kay monitored to make sure everything was balanced. It had to be "balanced." Kay is as anal as I am. During this work, MG was absent. We moved the final item, my dresser. It came in two pieces. With Kay's eagle eye, Hank and I centered the base of the dresser between the two windows. The top of the dresser with the mirror and shelves was top-heavy, so its movement took more care. Hank and I had just got it situated to move it when MG appeared again, standing right in front of the base.

We stopped and waited for her to move. The top of the mirror started swaying. Kay rushed to help support it. Kay was the only one with presence of mind to remember ghostly physics. "Just go through her, you peabrains!" she gritched as she helped support the top.

My team finished all but my office area. I may be anal, but Kay is the queen. If she got into my office, I'd never find anything again. She'd arrange the books in some obscure order to fit her chakra, and my copies of <u>Wind in the Willows</u> and <u>Lolita</u> would be lost forever. This was a solo effort.

"Hey, I'm gonna order a couple of pizzas with the works. I got drinks, but y'all got any special requests?" I asked as I glanced at my pizza ad magnet on my fridge.

"Order some hot wings and dipping sauce," Hank begged.

"Okay. Anything you want special, Kay?"

"Uh, is this the place that has the cinnamon thingies? If so, I want some of those," answered Kay.

"Okay. I think we ought to go sit outside. It's so nice out there today." I was ready for a break after working about five hours. I emailed our order and followed them outside. I turned back to get my sunshades and saw MG trying to punch the keyboard on my laptop. Laughing, I headed out the back door.

Kay and Hank lazed in the aqua Adirondack chairs. Not me. My tired butt wanted comforting canvas. I plopped down and lifted my feet across Kay's shins.

"Aaaagh! Your bony heels are gouging my legs. Off! Off!" she hollered. She lifted her feet from the patio table and rubbed as my sore dogs hit concrete.

"Cry baby," teased Hank. "Here, prop your bony feet on my lap. I can take it." He and Kay made faces at each other while I settled more comfortably.

Kay looked over her shoulder at the back door. "Where's the ghost? I bet she can't come outside. We are so rude."

I scooched farther down in my seat, giving Hank the back of my calves instead of my heels. "Well, shoot. I didn't buy the house for her. If she can't come outside, tough noogies. That may sound a little harsh, but dadgummit, I can't ignore all this nice outdoor space just because she can't come outside."

"Durn, Girl, do you ever shave? Your legs feel like fine grit sandpaper," Hank complained.

I am no Mary Lou Retton, but I adjusted my position and enclosed his face with my feet and rubbed. Kay convulsed, snorting in laughter, as I stretched his face wide then made him pucker. He looked like a punk Jim Varney, the comedian.

"Vewwy funny," he sputtered, taking my feet into his hands. "Hey, cool toes. What shade is this, Babe? And look at the widdle bitty flowers."

"That shade is Mincing Maroon with Eggshell petals. They ARE pretty, aren't they?" I mused as I took back my feet.

"You want us to come over tomorrow after church?" asked Kay. "And could I bring my laundry over here?"

"Yeah, come on over about noon," I answered. "I'll be working in my office, so we can just hang out. Make some of your Hungarian goulash and bring it. I'll make a hot fudge pudding cake. Hank, you gonna come to help us unravel our ghost mystery?"

Hank stopped working his jaws and thought for a minute. "Nah, I need to work on the homeless project. If I come over here, I could work on it, but we know I wouldn't get anything done."

"That's true," I agreed. "Look, here comes the pizza. Y'all go inside and get the plates and drinks."

Five minutes later we were scarfing down pizza and hot wings. MG popped in to sit with us, pausing to sniff in appreciation.

"Weird," I said, "that you can smell pizza and Hank's feet but not coffee. Do you get hungry?"

She shook her head no, nodded yes, then took another sniff.

"Well, which is it?" I demanded.

Poor MG just bumped her head through my terra cotta bar top in frustration. She patted her tummy and shook her head. Then she pointed two fingers at her eyes then her nose and nodded yes.

"I got this one!" said Hank. He looked at MG and said, "You *smell* some things that have strong odor, you *see* them, but you ain't got no body to hold food, so you don't get hungry?" He grinned.

Kay waved her hand in the air. "Ooooh, pick me, pick me!" With MG's nod Kay added, "You remember how they tasted and wish you could eat."

MG raised her hand to high five Kay. Kay tried to meet her hand and ended up slapping the bar again. "Rule number one, don't high five a ghost. Don't do that again, Sister," Kay warned MG. MG's shoulders shook in a snicker.

Hank stood up and stretched. "I'm gonna shove off. I'll stop at the bookstore and get the sign language books. I need to get my beauty sleep so I can finish my research tomorrow. If I get finished early enough, I'll be over here to help you eat the goulash and dessert."

Kay and I got up and accompanied him to the door, hugging him.

I lay in bed the next morning and stretched, enjoying the order to my bedroom. I smoothed my deep teal paisley duvet and admired my new furniture. I sat up and looked at my bed head in my dresser's mirror. *Ugh, so sad.*

MG hadn't materialized. *Maybe she's sleeping,* I thought to myself. *Do ghosts even sleep?* I performed my morning routine of potty then coffee, still wondering where MG was. After a cup of Kona and the last kolache, I headed to the bathroom to shower and get ready for church.

I backed out of my driveway on the way to The Bridge, wondering why I hadn't seen MG. At church I found some peace, and I even prayed for MG. I mean, it would not be fun to hang around a bunch of live people who got to eat, drink, and sleep. My Kia knew her way home. Good thing. My thoughts were so jumbled, it's a wonder I didn't run any red lights. At least I don't think I did.

I unlocked my door, tossed my keys onto the breakfast bar, and nuked a cup of still warm coffee. I stirred some fake sugar into the java. MG was sitting at the bar when I turned around. "Where have you been?" She made a twirling motion with her hand. "All around the place?" I asked.

Nod.

"Kay will be here in about an hour. We're gonna make a plan on how to find out some things." I turned around to put the milk back in the fridge. MG made hand signals of talking or yada yada, then pointed at her eyes. "Are you telling me to face you when I talk?"

Nod.

"Can you hear or not? You said you could."

MG made a wavy hand signal meaning 'sort of.' Then she pointed at her ear before making a swimming motion. At my confused look, she repeated everything slowmo. I got it.

"You can hear like you're under water. It's easier to pair talking with lip reading."

Excited nod.

"Would you think I was rude if I read the paper?"

Head shake.

"You want to read something?"

Nod.

"What section?" I asked as I slowly held up different sections. After a few seconds, I laid open the Sunday comics and told her to wave her hand under my nose when she wanted me to turn the page. She went through the comics, the front page, and travel in the next half hour. I looked up and found her gone. Just then, Kay's VW beeped, and MG materialized again.

"Brought some pad Thai from our favorite place. Hey, MG, you like Thai food?" Kay stood, wafting the odor of our lunch. Kay sniffed and shrugged.

"She can't smell that. Too bad. Smells scrumtdeliocious. What happened to the goulash?" I asked.

"I got involved in the newest Jodi Picoult book and read until about four o'clock this morning, so I slept in," Kay answered. "I wasn't in the mood to do goulash. That and the fact I forgot to unthaw the meat."

Kay unpacked the food while MG looked at it, seeming to decide if it looked edible. MG tried to poke her finger in it, but the finger went straight through the plate. My ghost heaved her shoulders in frustration.

"BTW, Hank texted me while I was at the restaurant that he was coming over with the sign language book. Of course he whined like a girl when he found I was getting Thai food. I don't know what his problem is, griping about our food choice. He wasn't even coming over today. He's bringing something from Mickey D."

"Oh good, you got both chicken and shrimp." I poked and divvied up the food.

We sat and inhaled pad Thai. MG kibitzed. About midway through the meal, motorcycle noises filled the kitchen, heralding Hank's arrival.

I must say that mixing the smells of Thai food and Mickey D is just plain wrong, an abomination of scents. Hank opened his meal, set it out, then took out a couple of books and four cheat charts, one for each of us. He set out the cheat chart for MG to look at while we ate.

MG started signing almost immediately. *"Hi. Can you read this?"*

Both Kay and I were forking pad Thai, so Hank put down his quarter pounder to look at his chart. "Yeah, I can read it. Just slow down. I know the alphabet from elementary school, but I gotta brush up. Chillax."

"You have to help me find out who I am. Then I can cross over," she signed.

Hank consulted his chart and faced her. "We do research for a television channel for news stories and stuff. Do you know what television is?"

Ghosts 85

"Yes," she signed. *I've lived with people for a long time. I've seen television. I know something about computers. How are you going to find out who I am? Do you think you can?"*

Kay answered for all of us as we took turns interpreting. "We will have to do the bulk of our research after hours. Hank and I have more time out of the office than Lee does, and we'll search through courthouse records to see who owned the property and when they owned it."

"How old are you?" I asked. "Sign slowly. Hank, you write this down."

"I don't know my age for sure. I think about twenty. I came here to the plantation with my ma when I was just walking. We were slaves for Mr. Don and Missus Ella."

"Slaves. Plantation. Mr. Don and Mrs. Ella," Hank said. "Do you know where you came from?"

"Some of the black slaves told me I was born on the slave ship from Ireland. My ma died early on from swamp fever, it was. I died from it years later."

"You don't know anything about what year it was? Who was President?" I asked.

"I don't know any of this."

"What did your master or mistress call you? What was your job?" Hank was scratching his head. "Lee," he said to me, "are you googling some of this?"

I took some notes from my googling. "I just found that Irish slavery to America ended with the Irish Revolution in 1798." I looked at MG as she busied herself with the chart. She looked up. "Hank, start interpreting again."

"I don't remember ever being called anything but 'You, Girl.' From my early days I fetched for the madam. I repaired her clothes and fixed her hair. I slept in a tiny room across the hall from her. And I emptied her chamberpot."

"Who cared for you when your mama passed?" queried Kay.

"The black upstairs maid named Susu till I was old enough to carry things. They called my ma Tildy."

Hank shuffled some papers. "We need to make a timeline, but I think we need to make it backwards. Lee, who sold you this house?"

"Melanie and Joel Carpenter," I answered. "They lived here for sixteen years. I could call and ask who they bought it from. Melanie said they were just the second owners."

"Then we can do a property title search at the county courthouse in Richmond," Hank added. "I can take care of that on my half-day next week."

We decided on a routine to follow for the speediest results. I turned around to MG. "How many other people have seen you in all these years?"

"Susu could see me sometimes, but not always. I don't know why. I scared her several times, but she got used to seeing me. I was with her when she died. I wanted to go with her so bad, but something stayed me. I saw her angel guide and held out my hand. He held his out to me, but heaven closed before I could reach him." MG looked sad, and tears shimmered in her eyes.

I wish I could have hugged her. I told her this, and she just looked sadder. "Who else could see you?"

"My master's little girl could see me. We even tried to play together. When she told her mother she could see me, her mother took her to a doctor. She began ignoring me. Nobody in my master's house ever saw me again. Many years after he died, a big fire destroyed the big house and most of the outbuildings. I stayed near the foundation bricks. Hunters came by, soldiers, but nobody saw me again for many years"

"How did you learn to read?" asked Hank.

"After my master's house burned, a small cabin was built here as a school. It was here for many years. I sat in a class like a student, but no one ever saw me. Then the school cabin was added to and a small house was built. Two different families lived in it. After the first family moved away, the second family moved in. The mother and older daughter saw me and tried talking to me when no one else was around. They were frightened at first, but ignored me later when we couldn't communicate."

"Slow down a little," begged Hank. "My hand is cramping. Maybe we can figure out something. Did any of the people who lived here have a car?"

"Yes! The last family I mentioned moved in with a horseless carriage. They had two babies while they were here, and they grew up. Does that help?"

"Yea," I cheered. "That helps a lot. What do you remember next?"

MG was gone.

"Where'd she go?" asked Kay. "She just disappears. I know ghosts don't go to the bathroom—do they?"

"Maybe she runs on some sort of ghostly energy, and her battery runs out," I guessed.

Several hours later, and still no Ms. Ghost. I would have to ask her about that. Kay stretched and stood. "I need to get home and get ready for Manic Monday. Thanks for letting me do my laundry. I get off early Wednesday, so I can do some research. Hank, don't you get off early Tuesday? You can do some research, and I can build on yours."

Ghosts 87

"I'll go to the county clerk's office Tuesday to see about tracing ownership of the property. You can research the families at the main library in Richmond. How does that sound?" Hank slung his backpack over his shoulder.

Kay nodded. "That sounds workable. Hold the door for me Hank."

I walked out the door with them and sighed. "I feel kinda guilty. She's my ghost, and y'all are doing the work."

I became the center of a Kay-Hank sandwich as they hugged me. "You can't get away as easily as we can," Kay answered, rubbing my back. "See you tomorrow at 7:30 sharp for the staff meeting. Hank, that doesn't mean 7:31."

"Not even if I bring the lattes?" Hank continued his muttering as he kickstarted his manly motorcycle.

I waved to my two pals and headed to my fridge for a Coke. MG sat at the bar. I faced her. "Why do you disappear like that? Where do you go?"

We both used the cheat sheets. MG had a lengthy answer which took time to interpret.

She signed, *"I don't know why I disappear when I do. It just happens. I may end up in the shower, the dining room—this part of being a ghost drives me crazy. I can't control it."*

I thought of a question that bothered me. "If—*when*—we find out your name, how will you know it's the right name? Will you cross over immediately?"

MG pursed her lips. *"I don't know how I know this, but I will know if the name is right. But as to how long it will take me to cross over, I don't know."*

"Can you go outside?" I asked.

"Yes. I was outside watching you move in. It's like disappearing and reappearing. I don't know when and why it happens."

I finished my Coke and put the can in the crusher. MG pointed at the crusher and asked why I did that. After giving her a brief lesson in reduce, reuse, and recycle, I prepared for Monday.

Monday and Tuesday passed like a flash. All three of us were busy on the homeless project and doing interviews with workers and clients at Second Mile Mission. I was one tired puppy when I tossed my keys on the counter. MG sat at the bar waiting and signed, *"How was your day, Dear?"*

I rolled my eyes and sank on a stool and looked at my roomie. It occurred to me that while she wore the same clothing and hairstyle day in and day out, she never seemed overly mussed or dirty. Before I could ask her about that, the sounds of Hank's cycle and Kay's VW reached my ears, soon followed by Hank's shrieking. When he was excited, his voice raised a couple of octaves. Kay was trying to calm him down as they entered the utility room and into the kitchen.

"I found it! I found them!" It didn't seem possible for Hank to reach an even higher pitch. MG had her hands over her ears. The first owners on record were Donald and Ella Kelly. Their family owned the property from 1790 until 1863 when it burned down. They bought it and handed it down to their son who handed it down to his son. Then it burned down." Hank's face was red and sweaty. "I rock!" His happy dance did NOT rock. He opened his mouth to sing and choked instead.

Kay patted him on the back when he started coughing. We all looked at MG. "Do you remember the name Kelly?" questioned Kay.

MG shook her head and signed. *"Slaves and servants had no reasons to know last names. We just used Master and Missus."*

Hank spread out a sheaf of papers. "These are copies of documents that Ms. Joan Horky got me from the archives. Remember her? She's the one who helped us out last year."

"I remember," I stated. "She saved me about a week's worth of work on that property case we researched about the Ku Klux Klan. So where do we go from here?"

Kay picked up the two pages dealing with the Kelly property. "I'll go to the main library in Richmond tomorrow. I'm supposed to be in court at 1:00, and the boss said to just report over there. If I get to the library at 10:00, I'll have a few hours to work."

MG was signing "Thank you" to both Kay and Hank. Then to Hank, she signed, *"If I weren't a ghost, I'd be wrapping myself all over you. You are so cute."*

Apparently there were some things MG didn't understand. A huge grin covered her face as Hank played thermometer. When he got embarrassed, he turned red from the feet, and the red traveled up, stopping at the top of his ears. I actually saw this happen at the beach when some girls came on to him. His speedo didn't cover much, so the red was easy to follow.

Hank beat a hasty retreat while Kay and I collapsed in laughter. Can ghosts look quizzical? I'm here to say they can. Kay explained Hank's situation to MG. I swear she turned a little red before she collapsed along with us.

Kay opened a jar of spaghetti and meat sauce while I stacked linguini in boiling water and stirred. "Hank said to wait for him before you tell us what you have," I told her. "But tell me, does it look promising?"

"Very promising," she replied. "Where's MG?" she asked.

"She's out and about," I answered, nonchalant as one might be if she had a resident ghost. "And here she is," I added as MG materialized in her usual ebony bar seat. "And here comes our own hottie," I smirked as MG looked chagrined.

"OK, I'm here," Hank said, "and keep Miss Hot Pants away from me!"

We three estrogen carriers snickered. At least, I could almost swear I heard MG's snicker.

"I think I have something for you, MG," said Kay.

MG looked puzzled. She signed, "*What's MG?*"

Ever-tactful Hank looked her and said, "Duh? Ms. Ghost?"

Kay fluttered her fingers at him to dismiss him. "You said your mom's name was Tildy?" At MG's nod, she continued, "In 1802, Master Kelly purchased sixteen Irish slaves in New York. Tildy O'Hare and her daughter Mary were two. This is a copy of the receipt. You must be Mary O'Hare. Does that feel right?"

MG put her head down and shook it.

"Darn! I was so sure this was it! Are you certain?"

"*I'm still here, aren't I?*" MG signed with one hand and wiped ghostly tears with another.

Hank forgot his issues with MG and tried to put his arm around her. Didn't happen. His arm went straight from her shoulders to his own side. "Whoa! Little tingle there."

Kay took off running out the back door. A minute later, she came back in carrying a folder. "I was so sure I was right, I left the rest of the information in the car. Help me look."

MG lifted her tear-stained face as she looked over Kay's shoulders. She motioned for Hank to help. I kept my ears peeled while the three of them looked.

Hank pointed at a name. "Tilda Fitzhugh and, aww. Sorry. It says 'and son.'"

I mixed the pasta and sauce, but none of us was hungry.

"Hey," I said, "Tillie Johnson. Hmmm, maybe one of my ancestors. And it says daughter Bridget. Are you Bridget Johnson?"

Sad face and more tears.

"That's it," said Kay. "I'll go back as soon as I can to see if he bought any more Irish slaves. Maybe he bought more on another trip."

I plated up our portions while Kay poured some merlot. Our appetites seemed to have fallen off as we chewed without tasting. The sheet of paper was facing me as I ate. The bottom names were smudged a little, but I stared anyway, not really seeing. I looked up and MG was gone. My friends and I sat in silence. I looked down again, something bothering me. There was no Tildy, Tilda, Tillie, but….

Hot and cold hit me as it sank in, and I screeched, "Yes! It's here!" Hank and Kay looked at me, the stable one in our triad.

"Tildy is short for?" I urged.

"Matilda," they yelled in unison.

"But there was no Matilda on the list," protested Kay.

I paused triumphantly. "And a nickname for Matilda could be?"

Dawning came to Kay's face. "Mattie."

"Mattie Murray and her daughter Bridey. MG! Come here," I called. "Her mother had two nicknames, Mattie and Tildy, both forms of Matilda."

There MG was. "Are you Bridey Murray?" There MG wasn't.

A soft, musical *goodbye* floated in the air.

About Sandra DiGiovanni

Sandra DiGiovanni is a retired theater teacher living and writing in Sugar Land. During her 31 years of teaching in Needville, she authored countless programs for her theater classes and her thespian troupe, including Veterans' Day programs, programs performed at Barnes & Noble Booksellers and Parents' Night programs. She adapted works and directed one act plays for performance competitions at the Texas Renaissance Festival for three years.

While sponsoring a thespian troupe at Needville Middle School and Needville Junior High, Sandra directed 10 University Interscholastic League One Act Plays plus other one act plays just for fun. She also mentored student directors for three years. Her club members and thespians garnering a host of trophies.

Ms. D, as her students called her, said goodbye to the field of education and hello to a more serious writing endeavor. She recently finished her first novel and is in the revision process with a myriad of short stories tossed in for good measure.

Transparent Bob

by

Joseph L. Lanza

I thought I couldn't get in trouble locked inside my own home.

Wrong. Trouble found me in the form of a ghost.

It was eleven at night, rain and thunder raged just beyond the walls of the restored shotgun house my husband and I call home, power kaput, and I found myself sitting at the round laminate table in my kitchen talking to a ghost by candlelight.

I'm Ceré Rosas, one-half of Texas Gulf Coast Paranormal Investigations, based in Tivoli along the middle Texas coast. The other half is my husband, Bishop Temple, who was in Austin spending quality time with his fifteen-year-old daughter Diana. Not that I begrudge him time with Diana, but I was a little put out with him.

You see, two days ago we'd found a packet of cash in the saddle bag of Bishop's motorcycle. No idea how it got there; wrapped in plastic wrap, a few ounces of coffee grounds mixed in, taped all around. In other words, drug money, and someone had screwed up big time. We turned the money in and made a report, but my anxiety level was still sky high, and Bishop had promised to be back earlier that evening.

Instead, a ghost arrived. His name was Bob.

Bob the Ghost.

A gust of wind whistled past the windows while I appraised him. As ghosts went, he was remarkably solid and well-built, angular face, curly black hair, dark green eyes, and strong capable hands. Not strong enough and not capable enough to fend off the person who killed him.

"My best friend, Juan Flores, killed me," he said sadly.

"Your best friend?"

Bob the Ghost must have heard a note of doubt in my voice because he added hastily, "It's not what you think."

"What do I think?" I countered.

"That he and my wife were, you know…."

" Oh! No!" I protested, waving my hand ineffectually. "That's not what I was thinking."

"Sure you were, but you're wrong. He did it for the treasure. Gold coins cached in a honky-tonk," Bob went on," Juan and I bought the place and refurbished it together. We'd heard stories growing up, about how gangsters hid gold coins there in 1914, but no one ever found them. We mostly thought it was a tall tale."

My interest piqued as lightning flashes briefly illuminated the room, flaring against the kitchen floor, vividly etching every appliance in the kitchen in stark white relief and strong black shadows. Thunder rolled over us. I waited for it to pass.

"Where's the honky-tonk?"

"Orange. Near the Louisiana border." He paused and scratched his head. "You're really short."

I'm four feet eleven inches and weigh maybe a hundred pounds. My hair, black cherry red and falling to the small of my back, probably weighs more than the rest of me.

"And you don't dress very neatly."

I was barefoot, wearing jeans and a tank top.

"Those jeans look like they're ready for the rag pile," he continued, "I mean, it's kind of sexy and all, but … uh … kind of trashy too. I'm digging a hole for myself, aren't I?"

"You've already dug it," I assured him, narrowing my eyes at him, my voice dripping acid. "Let's just get back to your problem."

"You're going to need to resolve it before morning."

"Before morning?" I asked, surprised, "Why?"

He shifted uneasily from foot to foot, uncrossed his arms, shoved his hands in the pockets of his ghost jeans. Rain clattered against the house, flung by another gust of wind, and faded like a mournful horn during the night.

"Um," he said, "I'm on a schedule. Sorry, but I can't tell you anymore."

"Can't help you," I said.

"Why not?"

"I'm afraid of people."

"Strictly speaking, I'm not people. I'm a ghost."

"True," I conceded, "Which is why I'm talking to you."

"We'll need to use the Internet."

Bob must have missed the memo that said, "I can't help you." I glanced around the dark room, and said. "Uh, hate to tell you this, no power, no Internet." My notebook computer sat on the kitchen table. It whirred to life. "Runs on a battery," I told Bob, "The Internet doesn't." Google's homepage appeared on the screen. I was obviously losing this round.

"Logon to my Gmail account." Bob gave me the account name and password.

"Why?" I asked suspiciously.

"I want you to send my killer an email."

"No way!" I protested, "They'll trace it back here."

"So?"

I stared at him. Could he really be that dense? Reading my thoughts in reverse, Bob the Ghost said, "Who cares if they trace it back here? Every record on the face of the planet is going to show you had no electricity and thus, no access to the Internet. Let's get on with this."

"What do you want me to write?" I asked, still suspicious.

"Write, I saw what you did, and I know who you are."

I raised an eyebrow. "That's the title to an old horror movie. Besides, it's not strictly accurate. I didn't see him do anything and I don't know what he did."

"It's my email account," Bob patiently explained, "Flores won't know it's you. Not yet."

"Not yet?" I asked, *sotto voce*, my stomach shrinking to the size of a peach pit.

"Well, you're going to have to call him to pull this off. And then you're going lure him down here."

"Ah ... no thank you," I hurriedly replied, raising my hand. He gave me his ghost stare.

"No," I insisted, emphasizing the point with raised palms facing outward, fingers spread, "Absolutely not!"

"Don't you want to see an injustice righted?"

"Not if it gets me killed!" I retorted.

"Nothing's going to happen," Bob assured me, "I'll be there to protect you."

"How can you possibly protect me?"

"All you need to do is get Flores down here. I'll do the rest."

Ghosts 95

I was uneasy, and Bob's ghostly stare made me nervous. A voice inside me counseled against sending the email. Truth is, I have a lousy track record when it comes to following rational advice. I was also burning with curiosity. This was, after all, a *bona fide* paranormal event. What type of investigator would I be if I didn't see it through?

"Okay," I said, giving in. "That all you want me to do?"

"C. C. yourself," he instructed.

"Excuse me?"

"Carbon copy yourself. That way, when you call him, it won't sound suspicious."

I thought about the request. "I know I'm going to regret it, but okay."

I typed the message and sat back. The enter key depressed of its own accord and the missive flitted into the ether.

"Cool!" I exclaimed, pointing, "I am *not* touching that key again. It's got a ghost's fingerprint on it! How cool is that?"

"You're a strange woman, Ceré Rosas," Bob said as my phantasmal connection to the Internet faded and my notebook computer dropped back into hibernation mode.

"You call him in half an hour," Bob instructed. "Juan checks his email like clockwork."

"Did I tell you I don't like talking to people?" My voice jumped half an octave.

"You're talking to me."

"You're a ghost, remember?"

"I thought you were joking. Are you saying you've got a phobia about talking to people?" Disbelief was written all over his face.

"Bingo," I said.

"But you talk to ghosts?"

"Go figure," I told him.

"Well, get over it," he ordered, "Tell Flores you're a psychic and you got a message from me. Tell him you're going to tell the cops where the coins are. Give him your website address so he can look you up."

"I thought he killed you because you found the coins?"

"I was unclear," Bob explained. "We found the coins, but I hid them again. The dumb fuck killed me before he knew that fact."

"Yeah," I agreed, "that was pretty stupid. So you expect Flores to come tearing down to Tivoli in a thunderstorm after I tell him I know about the coins?"

"I *know* he'll come down to Tivoli," Bob said. "Now call him."

Okay, I stupidly thought, I can do this, I can do phones sometimes. I just move my lips and make words come out. And then I planned to hide. Let Bob take care of it.

We waited in the semi-darkness. The thunder was more distant now, the rain slackening. At eleven forty five Bob gave me the phone number. Gathering my nerve, I dialed it on my cell.

"Mr. Flores?"

"Yes?" The reply was cautious.

"My name is Ceré Rosas. I'm a paranormal investigator in Tivoli, Texas." I spit out the web address, and charged forward, eager to get it over. "I've had a communication from Bob regarding the gold coins you both found, and about his death."

"Yea? My real name is Santa Anna," he scoffed, "and I'm the president of Mexico."

"Take it as you will, Santa," I said, "I'll be calling the police in the morning to tell them what I know. I have the ear of the local sheriff, so I know he'll go looking where I tell him, and when he finds the coins, you're goose is cooked. You don't believe me about the cops, go look at the website. Bye." And I hung up. I'd run my words together so quickly the speech sounded like a machine gun burst.

"That was really good," Bob said, "I'm impressed."

So was I.

"Thank you," I replied, "Now I'm going to go hide in the Behemoth."

"The what?"

"The Behemoth is the nickname for our recreational vehicle," I told him, as I went to Bishop's desk and pulled out his grandfather's Army Colt .45. I hate guns, but I didn't want it where Flores could get his hands on it, so I decided the best course of action would be to take it with me to the Behemoth. There were smarter things I could do. Too bad I didn't think of any. "Want to tell me where the coins are in case I pull this off?"

"There's a secret compartment at the base of the bar, next to the beer taps," Bob said.

Ghosts 97

Why bother asking? Any idiot could have figured that out. Flores must be about as smart as a bag of hammers. I navigated the miscellany of objects cramming our back screen porch and walked into the yard. When I looked back, Bob was gone.

I struggled through the cold rain to the parked RV, about a hundred feet away. After I let myself in, I shucked my wet jeans and tank top and dried myself. Pulling on one of Bishop's University of Texas tee shirts, I got a Nancy Drew novel and read by flashlight, huddled on the floor, back against the bed. Nancy Drew makes me feel cozy, and at the moment, I needed cozy.

Time dragged, and the longer it dragged, the edgier I got. About three in the morning I heard the grinding of an engine and the crunch of tires on gravel. Moments later, a car door opened and closed. I extinguished my small flashlight and hunkered down.

Hollow thuds told me someone had stepped onto the shotgun's porch. I was certain my visitor was Flores. The car door opened and closed again. What did that mean? Was he leaving? I waited, listening, and heard a mummer of voices. Oh God, there were two of them! As the crunch of boots on gravel suddenly grew closer, I held my breath.

"I don't suppose you have any suggestions?" I whispered fiercely, hoping Bob the Ghost would hear, and added, "Constructive ones?"

No reply, but more boot crunches and they stopped outside the Behemoth. Peachy. I heard the screen door to the shotgun's back porch open and bang shut. The second person was at rear of the house. My heart thudded in my ears, and I was trembling. How do I get myself into these situations? I was supposed to have a nice quiet evening at home. Now I was about to get murdered inside the Behemoth instead.

I gripped the .45 tightly in both hands. Tiny hands compared to the giant weapon in them. The barrel wobbled left and right, up and down. Something clinked at the door to the Behemoth. Flores was forcing the lock, and I had no doubt my ghostly acquaintance had steered him towards me. Bob the Ghost had set me up.

The door opened and a hulking shadow filled the doorway. I held my breath hoping he would go away, but he climbed in. Shaking, *really* shaking, I closed my eyes and, not really wanting to hit the intruder, just pointed the .45 in the general direction of the front of the RV, and pulled the trigger. The gun jumped in my hands. Orange light filled the interior of the Behemoth, a sound like a bomb pounded my ears, and I heard the sharp crack of metal on metal following by smashing glass.

"Shit! Ceré?"

I recognized the voice.

"Bishop?" I squeaked. Omigod! I almost shot my husband!

"Who the bloody hell were you expecting, Rosas? Freddie Kruger? And what are you doing in the Behemoth?" Bishop's use of my last name told me he was truly pissed. I rallied. Always best to go on the offensive when husbands ask you awkward questions.

"What the hell are you doing in the Behemoth," I countered, coming to my knees, trembling from anxiety over what I'd almost done. I was closing ground with hysteria rapidly.

"I'm not in the Behemoth," he replied irritably. I heard the rain drizzling down outside. "In answer to your question," Bishop continued, "I thought you were in the house asleep, and didn't want to disturb you. Instead, I find you shacked up out here firing off a small cannon like you're under siege."

"Which," added a new, deeper voice, "she is."

The rumble of distant thunder was the only noise in the wake of that pronouncement. Perfect timing. Flores had arrived, sneaking up behind Bishop, probably while I was industriously shooting at him. I skipped hysteria, did not collect two hundred dollars, and went straight to numb.

"Stay where you are and keep your hands in plain sight," Flores instructed Bishop, "Miss Rosas, or whatever your name is, slide the gun out the door, or I shoot your husband."

Where the hell was Bob the Ghost? I crawled forward and slid the .45 so that it clattered down the steps and fell to the ground.

"Shit lady," Flores exclaimed, "Be more careful, will you?"

"You'll be the death of me yet, Beloved," Bishop said. His voice held a sardonic note, despite our predicament, and I found it oddly comforting. Bishop, steady as a rock. I heard a muted clunk as Flores tossed the .45 aside.

"Now step outside," Flores ordered. Timidly, I stepped out into the drizzle. The tee shirt flapped around my knees, and my bare feet sunk into mud and wet grass. I looked at my husband, a six-foot-two buzzard of a man, bald head, beak for a nose, ice chip blue eyes.

His eyes said, "What have you done now, Beloved?"

"Where's the other person?" Flores demanded.

"What other person?" Bishop asked.

Ghosts 99

"I heard someone go onto the back porch."

"You heard a broken screen door swinging in the wind," Bishop scoffed, nodding his head. Flores took a quick look towards the shotgun. So did I. The screen door to the back porch swung and then slammed shut as a gust caught it.

"Okay," Flores said, mollified. "Give me the money, and I'll be on my way."

My throat constricted the way it does when I'm around people, only tighter from fear. I use sign language when my people phobia robs me of speech. I started to move my hands to sign the answer, and Flores jerked his pistol my way. I stopped and forced myself to speak.

"You won't hurt us?" My words were a harsh whisper.

"No," Flores replied, "I just want the money."

"Oh, yeah, right," Bishop jeered. "Just give me the gun so I can put the bullet through my own head and save you the trouble."

Flores glared at us. "My patience is wearing thin."

I tried to find the courage to speak. Tears of embarrassment welled in my eyes. How was it I had no problem talking to a ghost but couldn't force words out of my mouth when my life depended on it?

"I want the money." Flores pointed the gun at me. "Talk!"

"My wife suffers from—" Bishop started to explain.

"I don't give a fuck what your wife suffers from so long as she gives me the money!"

"What money?" Bishop asked, frustrated.

"The money she's holding on this drug deal!"

"Drug deal!" Surprise forced my voice out of my throat, "I didn't say anything about a drug deal! I said he told me where the coins were!"

"Fine lady, then tell me where—" Flores complained.

But I was on a roll now. Anger gave strength to my voice and nothing was stopping my rant.

"Only problem is, Bob hid the coins before you killed him and you didn't even know it." I laughed hysterically, "You can't kill us because I know where the coins are, and you don't. So if you kill us, you won't find the coins."

Flores turned and fired one shot into Bishop.

"No!" I shrieked, jumping towards my husband.

The pistol butt caught me across the side of the face, and I tasted blood. Flores reversed the trajectory of his hand and pistol-whipped Bishop across the side of the head. He sagged against the Behemoth, semi-conscious, then dropped and didn't move.

Flores grabbed my tee shirt, tearing it half off my shoulders as he slammed me back against the Behemoth, put the gun in my face and forced the barrel into my mouth. He pulled the hammer back and cocked it. I was so terrified, my crossed eyes were glued to the gun barrel. Flores' gaze briefly dropped to my exposed chest, before his eyes found mine. I whimpered, and the intensity of his gaze forced me to look up from the gun barrel.

"Wrong, sweetcakes." Flores growled, his voice low and slow. "You know where the money is, hubby doesn't, which makes him expendable. I only hit him in the shoulder. Next shot's between the eyes. Now, I'm only going to ask you one more time. Where . . . is . . . the . . . money?"

He slid the barrel out of my mouth, bobbing it up and down, punctuating each word. I cowered, crying hysterically. Everything had gone wrong. I thought this whole fiasco was about missing gold coins, but Flores seemed to have some a drug deal gone bad in mind. And where was Bob the Ghost?

"I don't know anything about any money," I sobbed, "All Bob mentioned were gold coins, just gold coins."

The gun shifted towards Bishop. Panicked, I grabbed for Flores' arm. He backhanded me with his left hand. My head struck the doorplate and little lights popped behind my eyes. Flores grabbed my hair and twisted my head back, putting the gun to my temple.

"Please, please, listen to me!" I sobbed. "All Bob told me about was coins, I swear."

Flores rapped my head against the side of the Behemoth, and I fell on my bum. Water soaked my panties and my tee shirt was up around my navel. I tried to pull it down.

"Coins is code for drug money," Flores said, menace saturating his voice and body language. "Bob stashed cash and was supposed to text me to make the pickup. It wasn't there, so he had an *accident*. But then you called, so I'm guessing that you or your husband were somehow tied in with Bob and have the cash. Only you didn't tell me where the cash is, you told me you were going to call the police."

Bob the Ghost had never said anything about drugs. This was about that drug money we'd found! Bob had messed up, and the bastard had tricked me, making me the victim of a particularly cruel and deadly form of revenge.

Flores was insane with rage and I knew my world had ended. I didn't have the money, and he was going kill us. End of story, end of my life.

It couldn't get any worse.

It did.

Flores stepped back and raised the gun. I mustered the courage to make one last plea for clemency, "Please... Bob set me up..."

I went cold. Bishop's daughter Diana was creeping up behind Flores. She *was* the second person I'd heard earlier, the one whose presence Bishop had denied. She must have hidden and come around the side of the house. She had her Apple notebook computer in her hand. She was going to crash it over Flores' head, but I could tell she would never get close enough.

And then Flores' gaze suddenly shifted to my right and his gun swung around. He actually took a step back, fear on his face, but maintained his composure.

"What the fuck's going on?" Flores demanded shakily as I turned my head to the side. Bob the Ghost was standing beside the Behemoth, hands in his pockets, rocking back on his heels, doing nothing but smiling.

The gun swung back, "I'll shoot this bitch if you don't tell me where the money is!"

"Go ahead," Bob replied. "Revenge is sweet, Juan, especially when you're dead. See you soon. You too, Ceré."

"You fucking bastard!" I screamed, "You lousy fucking bastard!"

Bob just laughed, and, in a final act of betrayal, targeted Diana by saying, "Look behind you, Juan."

She had been sneaking closer, and I threw myself at Flores as he began to turn. His gun discharged, a solid thump spun me in place, pain seared the left side of my chest, a white-hot poker into my lung, and as I fell I saw Diana launch her notebook computer like a Frisbee. It sailed towards Flores' head and crashed into his temple. Flores landed on top of me, his gun hitting the ground beside us. He groped for it and Bishop grabbed it at the same moment Flores did, miraculously getting his thumb between the hammer and anvil as Flores pulled the trigger.

Diana picked up the broken computer and slammed it edge-first into Flores' head again and again, her own face terror etched and tear streaked as her eyes darted frantically looking for some sign of Bob. But I knew Bob was no longer there. Out of the corner of my eye, I had seen him fade away, laughing.

Blood splattered Diana's blouse and pretty face, and I felt the warm fluid drench me. When Diana finally lifted her hands, blood covered them and her eyes were glazed. She reached for Bishop calling, "Daddy, Daddy," her voice small and tremulous, like a little girl.

My every breath was agony, a searing pain in my chest, but my eyes sought my husband. He was on hands and knees, dazed, and one arm took his daughter into his embrace. They half-crawled, half-stumbled towards where I lay in the mud, coughing blood. Bishop lifted my head, his face stricken. His left shoulder was drenched in blood and I saw it oozing out of his wound, and more blood caked the right side of his head.

"I love you," I whispered.

I've rarely seen my husband's composure break. Tears ran down his cheeks. Diana hugged him from behind. Before either of them could say anything, inky darkness swallowed me, but I thought I heard the word love in two distinctly different voices.

The first time I regained consciousness, there were tubes in my nose and tubes in my mouth and tubes in my arms and even a tube you know where. I'm not talking about that last one. My second dalliance with consciousness was much better. Most of the tubes were gone, Bishop was holding my hand, and I knew I was going to live.

"What happened," I mouthed. Fortunately, Bishop can read lips. He'd even learned to sign so I'd be more comfortable in public. His face was haunted.

"Diana killed the bastard."

"Oh God. I'm sorry—" I started, but he put a finger to my lips.

"Not your fault. Diana will be fine." He moved stiffly, favoring his left shoulder.

My eyes found his, and my lips moved silently, "How about you?"

"I'll live," he replied, "Now, mind telling me what the bloody hell that was all about? And why on earth did you let that man into our house? I thought you had better sense?"

"I didn't let him into the house," I protested, "He was a ghost!"

" Ceré . . ." Bishop started, but I glared daggers at him. He shut his mouth and I told him everything. As I did, I found my voice again.

"You do realize you're not making any sense?" he asked when I finished.

Ghosts 103

I scowled. At least, I think it was a scowl. Hard to tell through the narcotic haze of the painkillers they'd loaded into my body.

"Ceré," Bishop continued, "I know you believe …"

"Shut up, Bishop," I said, not wanting to hear him try to explain events away. I know what I saw. "Please," I added.

Bishop smiled down at me, "You won't buy into some kind of covert hypnotism theory?"

"Nope."

"How about hallucinations induced by a drug-laced drink?"

"You're reaching, Bishop."

"Holographic image?" He suggested playfully.

"Skeptic," I teased as I closed my eyes and whispered, "Love you." I fell asleep with him caressing the back of my hand. Life was good again.

Ashes
by
Lynne Gregg

"My parents are drunks, my girlfriend is dumping me, I'm flat broke, and I can't remember the last meal my mom cooked." Jim Reagan spoke aloud to himself as he foraged through the fridge. "Things better look up for me soon or I'm checking out of this place."

He was one month from graduating from high school. *Man, I thought my senior year would be the best and the summer before college even better, but instead, every day I get slammed between the shoulder blades with another problem.*

On their usual verge of divorce, his parents both drank too much and fought constantly. Jim was an only child and always ended up a key figure in all their fights. "You were the one who wanted kids; I thought they were just a bunch of trouble and expenses." Jim's dad slurred.

"How can you even think of us not having Jim? He's done nothing but made us proud." His mom defended him, unaware he was standing in the kitchen. Jim knew he made his father feel old and inadequate. His mother always stood up for him against his father's verbal attacks, but this made his father even more furious. Things weren't good, but they were bearable when his parents managed to stay off the booze. That didn't happen much anymore.

And then there was Patti, Jim's beautiful, petite, brunette girlfriend of two years. She said she fell in love with Jim's sun-streaked blonde hair, tanned muscles, and eyes that were intensely blue. He still possessed all these qualities so why had she told Jim last night that maybe they shouldn't remain tied to each other. They had scholarships to separate colleges. She thought they should start seeing other people now. He really needed Patti, but he agreed with her quietly because he had sensed for a while that she might be seeing someone else. *I don't want to think about it or I'll bash some guy's face in.*

"Why delay the inevitable? What do I need her for? What do I need anyone for? I just need to get a decent job, make some money, and get the hell away from this town." He was talking to himself again. He'd been doing that a lot lately.

Ghosts 105

Saturday morning he studied every ad in the job section of the newspaper. The ad that appealed to him most read:

"Unusual job, good pay, no experience necessary, part-time for student ok, start immediately, phone 281-555-3848"

By ten that morning Jim had made a few phone calls and set up one interview. The man on the phone didn't want to give out much information. He gave the address and said, "Come before one o'clock because we get busy after that."

As he drove, Jim rehearsed the good qualities he could say about himself. "I'm a hard worker. I make good grades. I got a scholarship to Tech. I worked after school and summers at a paper company for two years. Now what will I say if he asks me why I'm no longer there?"

Jim didn't want to tell him he had quit to party at the end of his senior year, but that was the truth. Maybe he won't ask.

In a navy Polo style shirt and a pair of Dockers, Jim felt he looked his casual best. He had decided against wearing his suit because he didn't know what kind of job he was applying for. He figured he would have a better chance of landing the job if he weren't dressed better than his future boss.

As he neared the address the man had given him, he realized it had to be the cemetery. Jim decided as he drove under the wrought iron arch of Memorial Park that *no matter how much money they offer me, I will not dig graves.* He considered turning around and going home, but curiosity kept him going.

He stopped his car outside the caretaker's office. He ran his hands over his hair to smooth it down, hitched up his pants, and walked inside. A short man with salt and pepper hair and wire bifocals was seated behind a desk covered with neat stacks of funeral brochures.

He looked up when he heard Jim and pushed his glasses up higher on his nose. "May I help you, young man?"

"Yes, I've come to apply for the job. I called earlier," Jim said.

"Oh, certainly. I'm Mr. Richards. You must have spoken with Mr. Jebens. I'll call him for you." He said this in a gentle monotone he probably had acquired from years of discussing funeral arrangements.

"Thank you." Jim sat down on a blue velvet sofa. Nearly everything in the room was blue and smelled stale. *I'll bet they call it tranquility blue. A good color for discussing the departure of a loved one,* he thought in a tone that mocked the little man.

While he waited, Jim listened in on a phone conversation. Mr. Richards was giving headstone prices to some obviously bereaved person. *I'll bet the person on the other end of that call is a hell of a lot sadder after hearing those prices — for a piece of a rock,* Jim thought.

The next call was better than the first. Mr. Richards was trying to hide the disgust in his voice while he told the caller, "No, ma'am, we do not bury dogs at Memorial Park. I can give you the number of a very respectable pet cemetery that will help you."

There was a pause and then Jim heard, "I'm sorry you promised Fifi she'd be buried next to you. That is not a possibility here."

After another pause, "I'm sure when you bought your burial plot, no one here told you that we would bury your dog next to you. I've been employed here for over thirty years, and that has never been our policy. Call the pet cemetery. I'm sure you'll be pleased when you drive out there. Again let me say I'm sorry for your loss."

Jim wondered if the pet cemetery was the one on the outskirts of town. He remembered driving past it and seeing the little granite poodle markers on many of the graves.

He remembered the story on the news about the funeral of the city police dog killed in the line of duty. The television cameras had zoomed in on the body of the dog at the pet cemetery. It was a German shepherd all stretched out in a satin-lined casket. The satin was a print with little black dog bones on it. Six cop pall bearers carried the casket. The news coverage was like a miniature version of the funeral of a president.

His thoughts stopped when the door blasted opened and a large man stepped into the room.

"Hello, I'm Andrew Jebens. I understand you want a job."

Dressed in a gray uniform with a beer belly that hung over his belt, the man had short curly hair and a red face with fat cheeks. He huffed and puffed when he talked like he'd just run a mile, when in fact; he'd just walked about ten feet from his pick-up to the door.

"Yes, but." Jim had planned to qualify his answer, but the big man didn't give him time.

"We need someone to work in our crematorium. Do you know what that is?" He used a red bandana to wipe the sweat off his forehead as he talked.

"Yes, sir."

Ghosts 107

Before Jim could speak again, the man quickly went on. "We'll train you for a week. The pay is two dollars an hour over minimum wage. Can you start Monday?"

Jim gave up trying to say anything to this rapid-talking man and just nodded his head.

"We'll need you after school and all day on Saturday. You can miss once in a while but not when we have a body scheduled." Mr. Jebens handed Jim some paperwork and started for the door. "Oh, I don't believe I got your name."

Jim offered his hand. "Jim Reagan, sir."

"Okay, Jim, fill out this application. Leave it on the desk with Mr. Richards. I'll see you Monday. I've got an oven to attend to." He hurried out the door and yelled over his shoulder, "Wear work clothes!"

The week of training for the job was all a blur to Jim. He had so much on his mind, and so many things about the crematorium startled his senses. Since he was not dating Patti and his parents remained in their usual alcoholic stupor, he didn't tell anyone about his job. He decided he'd give it a try first to see if it worked out. After four days, Jim was operating the oven, and by the end of the week, Mr. Jebens trusted him enough to let him drive the hearse to pick up bodies.

"You have to be at the hospital by seven o'clock in the morning. They like to remove bodies before visiting hours start. You drive to the loading dock and tell them which body you are there to pick up. Someone will bring the body out to you. You just load it up and drive back here. You know how to do the rest." He walked out before Jim could even think of a question.

On Saturday morning Jim drove more carefully than usual through the early morning traffic with the hearse. He felt uneasy listening to his usual rock station on the radio. He punched the buttons on the hearse radio until he found some elevator music, but that gave him the creeps so he shut the radio off. Until now he had only been alone with the dead in the furnace room where it was perfectly quiet. He found himself sitting up military straight with both hands suctioned to the steering wheel. He tried to think about football or the last movie he'd seen, but as hard as he tried, he couldn't keep his mind off the body riding with him. The hearse seemed to get cold once the body was loaded. Ghost? Jim believed in them.

How did he die? Did he take a long time to die, or was it over in a couple of seconds? Was the man a free spirit now? Was he glad to be rid of his earthly problems? "I can't freaking believe I almost feel envious of this guy."

Jim pulled into the service driveway at the cemetery and jumped out to open the elevator door. He slid the stretcher out of the hearse and double-checked the security straps that held the body on the stretcher. He did that out of habit. He could still feel the thick knot that lunged from his stomach to his throat the time he almost dropped the little old lady off the gurney. *The thought of her body dropping on the oil spotted driveway and having to pick her up would have been the deal breaker on this job.* He had managed to catch her before she slid all the way off the stretcher, but he still felt like he had abused the poor old woman. Thank goodness, Mr. Jebens had not been there to watch that.

Jim felt his stomach rise as the elevator descended to the basement. The door opened, and Jim was instantly swallowed up by the cool draft and the solitude. He wondered *about those cold spots and cool air shifts when he was with the bodies. Ghosts?* A lot of dead people were wheeled through this room. *Were some of them trying to come back?* He pushed the cold metal stretcher into the furnace room, noticing as usual, the faint smell of mildew and ashes.

In a month, he had spent so much time here that he knew every inch of the room. He knew the high and low spots of the Spanish tiled floor. Two straight lines ran from the elevator to the oven, made by the stretchers' wheels over the years. The beige tiles on the wall always looked cold and shiny. One tile next to the oven door was cracked. The crooked lines of the crack had turned dark brown from the oven's heat.

The ceiling was beige like the walls with a large brown water ring near the elevator. It had leaked years ago, and no one thought it needed painting. Very few people came into this room alive, and the dead ones didn't care. A tarnished brass light fixture hung near the center of the room. It looked like it could have swung from an old riverboat. A dusty cobweb floated from one side of the light, but it was too high to reach, and nobody cared about that either. Did the ghosts make the cobweb quiver like that? No air conditioning or heating was ever installed down here.

The oven was simple, but interesting, if you'd never seen a cremation oven before. It had a three-foot-square door with two large hinges on the right side. It was made of rough, speckled iron. The plate on the front said *Dominic*. The door swung open wide exposing an iron slab for the body to rest on.

The oven controls were simple, one round knob and one small red light. When the round knob was turned on and the door was closed, the red light came on. After the burning and cooling period, the red light would go off, and the safety lock allowed the door to be opened. The unburned bones were removed; the ashes were swept into a small cardboard box, and carried out of the room.

Jim never liked to be near the oven during the burning. He now understood where all the eerie stories about cremations came from. He'd heard that the bodies sat up and screamed when they burned. Ghosts wanting to come back?

While he was training, Jim stayed near the furnace to learn all the stages. Every drop of his blood seemed to drain from his head the first time he heard the scream from inside the oven.

Fortunately, Mr. Jebens had been there to explain. "The heat from the oven makes the vocal cords contract, so you hear that screeching noise. Don't worry, boy, we ain't burning no one alive."

Then the thumping started. Jim looked ready to tear out of the place.

"That's just the leg muscles contracting from the heat. They pull on those large leg bones, and you hear them hitting the sides of the oven," said Mr. Jebens. "You'll get used to it."

Jim remembered he took a deep breath, nodded to show he understood, and then asked himself under his breath, "Why in the hell did I ever take this job?"

A faint noise from somewhere in this empty room creeped Jim out. "I guess I better get started," Jim said aloud to break the silence and cover any other noises. "Mr. uh . . . let's see, the toe tag says Wilbur Rothchild. Okay, Mr. Rothchild, it's time to fire up the furnace and put an end to your mortal body. This is what you said you wanted."

Jim rolled the iron slab out of the oven and wheeled the stretcher parallel to the slab. He unstrapped the body. He took a deep breath. He grabbed the cold body by the left arm and left leg and pulled it onto the slab. He felt a cool breeze pass over them both.

"You probably had to defend this cremation decision to your family. I can hear you telling your mother, 'Very sound idea, Mother, no fuss, no fanfare, inexpensive. Who likes to think of themselves just lying around taking up space for centuries?'."

"Or you were poor and couldn't afford a fancy funeral with all the trimmings. Is that it, Mr. Rothchild? It's hard to tell if a man is rich or poor by the time he gets to me. Sometimes the hair is a give-away, but I usually make my decision when I see the hands. If a man has smooth pink hands with manicured nails, it's pretty certain he wasn't poor. If a man comes in with thick yellowed fingernails on rough hands with black fingerprints that could never be scrubbed clean and calluses as big as quarters at the base of each finger, then I know that man wasn't rich, but he was a worker.

"Did you lead a good life, Mr. Rothchild? Did you do everything on your Bucket List? Or did you reach forty five and go into a decline because you never achieved the goals you had set for yourself at twenty-five? Were you faithful to your wife? I know you were married by the white circle on your left ring finger.

"I better get this over with. I wonder if I'm going crazy because I spend so much time talking to dead people down here. I don't think I could be indifferent about them like Mr. Jebens. I'm the last person to see these bodies before they become unrecognizable. No one ever thinks of ashes as he or she, tall or short, good or bad. Ashes are nothing. In this room, at my hand, this body will turn from a remarkable creation into a pile of ashes."

Jim looked closely at the body one last time, trying to draw from it any last contributions to this earth.

"Maybe I'll write some day and remember a strong jaw line I saw here and describe it. Maybe I'll touch someone who is lonely with a warm hand because I'll remember the cold bodies down here.

"Whew! I'm getting macabre. I'd better finish and get out of here."

Then without so much as a goodbye, he adjusted the dial, quickly shoved the body into the furnace, shut the door, and listened to make sure the fire started. He hung Mr. Rothchild's toe tag on the door and headed for his car.

He started driving with no particular destination in mind. He didn't want to go home to his parents' drinking and fighting, so he just drove around thinking about where his life was headed and why. He couldn't face his old friends since Patti broke up with him. So far he had been successful at avoiding all of them. That is, until now.

At a stoplight a carload of Jim's crowd from high school pulled up beside him. As they motioned for him to roll down the window, he felt awkward; out of touch.

"Hey, man, where you been hiding?" hollered Mark, a friend since elementary school.

"Under a rock!" Jim yelled back.

"Let's go to the beach this weekend, or are you tied up? Mark grinned, lifted a beer can to his mouth, tipped his head back, and took a drink.

"Call me!" Jim yelled, but the light turned green, and his old friends sped away without hearing him. He was alone, unhappy, and confused.

He decided to get something to eat at the local drive-in. Before Jim's order was ready, he spotted Patti driving in with a guy he didn't recognize. He pretended not to see her in case she looked his way. As soon as he paid for his food, Jim drove away quickly hoping Patti would not see him here alone. He wanted her to think he was having no problem filling the time in his life that she used to fill.

Jim drove to a nearby park to eat. He unwrapped his hamburger, but suddenly he was not hungry and set it on the seat next to him. He felt a chill rush past him as he sat.

He thought back to football season. The Fighting Bears—they'd had a great year, and he had been a valuable part of it.

He thought about kissing Patti and how her hair smelled like watermelons when he pulled her close to him.

He remembered all the times he and Patti had sat together in dark movie theatres, sharing popcorn and whispering to each other.

He could picture Patti on Prom night in her long black dress. He smiled as he remembered how great he felt in his tux when he arrived to pick her up.

It had all seemed so perfect. What made Patti change? His feelings for her hadn't changed.

After staring out at the park for a long time without really seeing anything, Jim took a pencil from his pocket and smoothed out the white sack his hamburger has come in.

Without a moment's hesitation he wrote on the sack as though the words had been in his mind for years.

"I am nothing.

My life is nothing.

Ashes are nothing.

Scatter mine nowhere."

He stared at the paper in disbelief, crumpled it up, and threw it out the window. He drove back to the crematorium. He needed to put Mr.

Rothchild's ashes in a box. They were to be scattered over Crystal Lake in the morning by Acme Flying Service. The pilot would be by soon to pick them up. Jim had acquired a sizable collection of toe tags. Each time he marked the container with the cremains, he put the toe tag in his pocket.

Two days later Mr. Jebens blasted into the caretaker's office.

"Richards, have you seen Jim?"

"No, sir, I haven't," he said as he answered the phone.

"You can't get good help anymore. He not only doesn't show up for work for two days, he leaves me with an oven full of ashes and about forty toe tags hanging on the door. Not funny! If that damn kid shows up, tell him he's fired!"

At Patti's house, she was spending the evening at home alone in front of the TV. It was warm outside and the windows were open, but she felt chilled and assumed she might be getting sick.

That same evening at Jim's house after the third round of martinis, Mrs. Reagan spoke to her husband. "Do you feel a chill in here? I do."

"I believe I do, too," he answered.

"I wonder where Jimmy is."

"He's probably running around with some dumb bitch," said Mr. Reagan.

"Now don't you say such things about my Jimmy. He's a good boy," she slurred.

"Good boy, my ass. He's a damn know-it-all!" Mr. Reagan yelled garbling his words.

"Well, he's already more of a man than you'll ever be!" returned Mrs. Reagan.

They were off and running, well into round one. But it didn't matter now; Jim wouldn't be there to hear them.

That same evening at Jim's house after the third round of martinis, Mrs. Reagan spoke to her husband. "Do you feel a chill in here? I do."

"I believe I do, too," he answered.

"I wonder where Jimmy is?"

About Lynne Gregg

Lynne Gregg grew up in Blue Grass, Iowa, population 495. She had total creative freedom as a child and began writing sagas by the time she was eight. Her love of language led her to become a secondary English teacher for nearly thirty years.

She attended college all over while her husband was in the Air Force. She finished her Bachelors and Masters Degrees at the University of Houston. When the jet fuel finally ran out she and her husband settled in Houston.

Once she retired from grading compositions, Lynne and co-author Karen Jennings published *Shake on It and Spit in the Dirt*, a multicultural, monster mystery for the middle grades set in East Texas. Lynne and Karen are frequent presenters in schools. A sequel set in Houston's Third Ward is in the works.

Lynne has been a member of Houston Writers Guild for fourteen years, and has won many of their writing contests. She has published short stories and memoirs in several magazines such as *Woman's World* and *Super Twins*. She is currently writing a book about her daughter Angela who lost her battle with juvenile diabetes.

The Jumbie House
by
Pamela Fagan Hutchins

After our estate sale, I cleaned up the remaining items, stacking unwanted paintings and chipped vases in the garage as I listened over and over to the Dixie Chicks' album *Home*. It sounded as mournful as I felt. My husband and I were leaving our island home for Texas the next day, and our house was not happy about it. We lived in—I might as well just say it and get it out there—a jumbie house in the rainforest. Jumbie as in voodoo spirit. Yeah, right. I know. I didn't believe it either at first. I promise I'm not some crazy woman who needs her head shrunk. Living at Annalise just showed me there's more out there than our first five senses can detect. Maybe it comes from living near the water, but when I moved to St. Marcos to dry myself out and get over Nick, I discovered a sort of sixth sense that makes me aware of things. Things that were almost undetectable back when I lived in Dallas, like someone had hit the mute button. But on St. Marcos, by the sea, I can hear them, feel them. I could feel her—the house, Annalise. And right then she felt like a teenage girl with her sulk on.

"I'm going to miss you, Annalise. I'm really, really sorry about this," I said aloud.

I discovered Annalise on a guided rainforest hike when she was an abandoned shell, like myself. I guess you could say we saved each other. But, still, wouldn't Annalise, if she were human—a live woman—do the same as me? Nick wanted me to go back to the states with him so we could raise his orphaned nephew. It was the right thing to do. It was the only thing to do. Wasn't it?

Nick walked in and some of my melancholy lifted.

"Ask me how it went," he said.

I raised my eyebrows. He could never tell a story without making sure he had an eager audience. Nick had visited the airport, which currently was only running local flights since a Category Four hurricane came through the island ten days ago. It hadn't so much as nicked Annalise's fortress, but the airport was damaged, and the major air carriers wouldn't resume operations for weeks.

"How did it go?" I asked.

"Great! If you worked for LIAT Airlines, you'd be $100 richer right now. And all you have to do is let one slightly oversized dog sail past the cargo scales tomorrow. Which you would, of course, because of the $100." He tipped his shoulders back and puffed out his chest.

"Thank God," I said. We had feared Poco Oso, my giant young German shepherd, would be stuck in the islands forever because I'd hand fed him too many jerky treats. Noticing Nick's stance, I added, "And thank *you*, baby," trying to hide my smirk. I walked toward the side door to give the dogs their nightly feed. And share the good news. And adding a Milkbone for Oso.

"Wait." Nick's tone stopped me short. "Don't go outside yet."

"What's outside, Nick?" I asked.

"Trust me. It's nothing, and I'll take care of it."

"Which is it: nothing, or something you'll take care of?"

Nick looked back and forth from me to the door—me, the churning waters of Scylla, it, the rock face of Charybdis.

"The dogs found Sheila."

In addition to Oso, we had five watchdogs at our remote house. Or we had, until Sheila disappeared a few days ago, only to return and drop dead that morning right as we'd parted with a coffee table for $25 that should have brought twice that much. She was swollen with stings from African bees. The rainforest wasn't for the faint of heart.

"What do you mean, *found her?*"

"The dogs think they're in the Fiji Islands instead of the West Indies."

It took a moment, but when understanding dawned, it dawned like a strobe light.

"They're eating Sheila?" My turkey and Swiss sandwich churned against the mango in my stomach.

"Past tense. She's pretty far gone. I'm sorry, Katie."

The prickly feeling in my face meant the pale between my freckles had turned pasty. I sank onto the bed and put my head in my hands. Nick sat beside me. We held onto each other for several quiet moments.

"Are you going to bury her?" I asked into his chest.

"We sold the shovel this morning."

The man who bought it had said, "Five dollah, me son, and not a penny more, or you be stealin' food from the mout' of me chirrun dem."

For some reason, that was the thing that brought on my tears. "We can't just leave her there," I protested, chagrined at the shrill tremor in my voice. Softer, I added, "Or what's left of her."

"I'll cover her up so nothing else can get at her," Nick promised as he stroked my hair.

I wiped my eyes and nodded. Nick went out to deal with Sheila and the cannibals.

Annalise was still and quiet. *Some help you are,* I thought.

I fought against the image of the dogs over Sheila's body. It was too horrifying. Sheila had mothered Oso when I first got him. I flinched as I heard a thud and a crack outside. Nick must have dropped something over Sheila. Rocks or bricks, maybe.

I tried to be rational: these were island dogs, one step removed from feral. Not house pets. It wasn't as if they'd killed her to eat her. She just happened to be available. But no matter how I tried to spin it for myself, at the end of the day, they ate their friend. What a way to finish our last day here.

Later that evening, while we had supper on the back patio, I watched the bats come out from under the eaves. Each island sparrow stopped at the pool for a sip of water before flitting into the night. It sounded from the whir of their beating wings like there were thousands of them. I had always appreciated their appetite for mosquitoes, and found them achingly beautiful tonight. My nerves settled as the macabre vision of Sheila faded. Only twelve hours before our plane departed, ours and Oso's. The other four guard dogs would stay with the house sitters and Annalise until she sold.

We threw away our paper plates and tidied up the kitchen for the last time. My pulse throbbed in my ears as we walked the long hall to our bedroom, another final exercise. I took a soak in our claw-footed tub, then put away everything but what I'd need in the morning. All our bags were packed and ready.

As we climbed into bed, Nick brought up the cash.

"Are you at all concerned about the money from the sale? We did advertise in the paper, and we had a lot of people we didn't know up here." He ran his hand from the front to the back of his dark hair several times, his nervous tell.

We'd made nearly eighteen thousand dollars that day. There were people on this quasi-third-world island who would go to great lengths for that kind of cash, and notice of an estate sale generally meant an untended house. Not only was the cash attractive, but the items left in the house would appeal to a certain class of person as well. And we weren't parting as friends with some of our island neighbors. Faces flashed in my mind of some of the less savory contractors that I had fired, of my ex boyfriend Gene who hadn't liked being dumped when Nick showed up on St. Marcos, of the many friends of Pumpy, a former senatorial aide whom I had helped land in jail for murder. Tonight was the last chance for some of them to bid us farewell in their own special ways.

"I hadn't thought of it at all. And it's dark as pitch out there now." I hesitated a minute. "Well, we've got the dogs, we've got the flare gun, and the gate is shut. We'll be fine, right?"

Nick nodded. "I'll put the money under my pillow. I didn't mean to scare you," he said as he peered at me in the dark.

I probably looked like a ghost again.

Right then, the quietness if the night vanished and the wind gusted through our open windows, whipping the curtains into a froth of sea-foam green gauze. I swallowed and put on my brave smiley face. Nick gripped my hand and returned the expression. Two courageous souls facing the night together.

I wished we had more than the flare gun for protection, but getting a real gun on St. Marcos practically took a federal order, unless you were willing to buy it on the black market. It wasn't like we could call 911 if the bad guys did show up. On St. Marcos, no one called the police if they could help it. Cops and perps were nearly indistinguishable. The front page of the *St. Marcos Daily Source* featured stories every week about bad cops involved in drug trafficking, kidnapping, murder, and running guns.

Local friends had told us never to harm an intruder, even if he was armed, because the police would always side with a local. Some even told us to kill the would-be burglar, rapist, kidnapper or murderer, and throw the body over the Wall—a 6,000-foot drop about a mile off the northern shore. Nick and I didn't think we could go that far, but decided that if we needed help, we would call my friend Rashidi, not the police. Until then, our sole protection consisted of five dogs, an aluminum baseball bat, a jumbie house, and a flare gun.

We tried to sleep, but lay wild-eyed in the dark while the clock's minute hand advanced as if wading through a vat of molasses. The wind grew stronger and built to a howl, but no rain came. Objects inside the house shifted, banged, and fell to the floor. We heard a thud in the living room and something crashed upstairs. I prayed the wind was the culprit. If it was anything else, the storm was blowing too loud for us to hear it.

"If it gets any worse, we're going to need to shut the windows and close the hurricane shutters again," I whispered.

The dogs growled, then barked, and finally howled like crazy. Were they scared of the wind? Or was something out there? The night visits from the Senepol cattle and scrubby island horses that roamed the hills didn't bother them.

The bed felt like it was about to go airborne and the sheets already had; the edges of the cotton floated like poltergeists. I clutched at Nick's hand, as if it would tether me down if I held tightly enough.

"Are you sure you locked up?" I asked for the sixth time.

"You know I am."

"Nick, let's push the furniture against the door."

He sprang up to move the armoire. I fell in beside him and pushed with all my might. My brain ticked through our points of vulnerability. No one could get to us in the master bedroom through the windows, since it was suspended in the middle story of the three-level house. A determined house-breaker could get to us with a tall ladder, but not in this wind. The only entrance to our room was the door, and we had just blockaded it with two chests of drawers and an armoire. That was all we could do. We got back in bed and listened to the wind, the dogs, and the bumps in the night, and waited for morning. I prayed that Annalise would forgive us for moving and hold the line if anyone got past the dogs.

We must have fallen asleep sitting up, because I woke up in the middle of the night with my back against the headboard and my left hand holding Nick's right. Something was different. And wrong. Nick awoke, too.

"The lights," I said to him. "We left them on in the bathroom and now they're out. And if we lost power, the generator should have come on, but it didn't."

Shit, shit, shit.

"Do you want me to go outside and check it?" he asked.

"Absolutely not! Let's leave the furniture in place and stay here together." We huddled close. This might be the longest night of my life. Longer even than the night of the hurricane.

Many uneasy hours later, we woke to a peaceful tropical morning that belied the night before. It was late. Neither of our phone's alarms had gone off. I suspected Annalise the electronics-zapper might have had a hand in. When she was happy she was mischievous, and liked to reset clocks and turn on the stereo. She wasn't happy now, though, so maybe this was her way of making us late? I didn't have time to dwell on it. We had survived the night, we were relieved and exhausted, and if we were going to make our plane, we had to put it in high gear.

We threw on our clothes, grabbed our bags, and ran for the garage where Oso waited for us. He was the only one allowed to sleep inside; being mama's baby has its privileges. We shoved him into the truck's cab and hustled down the driveway as the other dogs lounged half-asleep in the grass, a pile of rocks marking Sheila's final resting place behind them. They barely acknowledged our departure. They had worked hard last night.

Nick backed the truck down the driveway toward our lane, but then slammed on the brakes. All the construction scaffolding that we had left carefully stacked against the side of the house lay across the driveway, blocking our path.

"Annalise?" I asked.

"That's my guess. She really doesn't want us to go."

We jumped out and Nick called me over to his side of the truck. He hefted a corner of the scaffolding platform and pointed at a machete, a patched Rasta cap, and a dried stain on the ground that looked like blood.

"Oh my God," I breathed.

"She may not want us to go, but it looks like she isn't going to let anyone hurt us either."

"It wasn't just anyone—it was Junior. That contractor I fired last spring. That's his cap," I said. "Annalise hated him. She used to dump his paint cans and move his tools. She scared him off the property last time he was here. Looks like she did it again."

Thanks to Annalise, this had only been a near miss. I ran back to the house and put my head against her cool yellow plaster like I had so many times before. And whispered my thanks and farewell.

"I am so sorry, Annalise. I promise to find a good family to come live here with you."

Silence from the jumbie house. I couldn't wait for an answer. Nick and I dragged the scaffolding out of the way and got back in the truck. I felt a sharp pain in my heart as we went through the gate for the last time. It was done. We were leaving. I pressed my body against Nick's side. Oso turned back toward the house and barked madly, jangling my seriously frayed nerves.

"Wait!" I yelled, and Nick slammed on the brakes, making Oso yelp. I jumped out of the car and ran back toward the gate, snapping pictures as fast as my phone's camera would let me: the lane, the gate, the forest, and the house. The beautiful house. Sunlight had broken through the treetops and was warming the backs of a mare and her black colt as they grazed beside Annalise's steps in the front yard. The scent of the fermenting mangoes in the orchard seared my nose. I committed it all to memory, knowing I would probably not get another chance to soak in this house that I had brought back to life over the last two years. And who had brought me back with her.

"Are you going to be all right?" Nick asked when I climbed back into the truck.

"Drive."

He jammed the truck into gear and stomped on the accelerator, and we lurched forward with our tires spinning and gravel spraying behind us. I scrolled through the pictures on my Treo, squinting in the bright morning sunlight. I drank them in, one by one. As I clicked to the last picture, something about the one just before it tugged at me, and I went back to look at the picture of the horses. The mare and foal were standing in front of Annalise, looking as I'd seen them moments before. But there was something else. I held the phone further from me, trying to bring it into focus.

And then I saw her.

My hand opened and the Treo clattered to the floor. Oso whined and shoved his nose under my elbow. My hand flew to my mouth. I turned and looked back at my house, to see what my eyes told me was true but my mind could not believe. Already, the forest was impenetrable and I saw nothing but a wall of green.

Nick kept his eyes on the road as he whipped through the narrow opening in the trees. "What's the matter?"

I picked up my phone again. Annalise. Annalise? On the front steps of my house stood a tall black woman in a white blouse and loose, calf-length plaid

Ghosts 121

skirt. A matching scarf was knotted over her hair. She looked straight into the camera with somber eyes and no expression as one of our dogs stood beside her, nuzzling her leg. In her right hand, she held Junior's cap and machete. In her left, she held his severed, bloody head by his dreadlocked hair.

I bit my lip and shook my head. My heart ached for the terrifying warrior goddess I had left behind.

"Goodbye, Annalise," I whispered.

Then I rolled down the passenger window and threw up.

About Pamela Fagan Hutchins

Pamela Fagan Hutchins lives, loves, laughs, works, and writes in Houston and Nowheresville, Texas with her husband Eric and their blended family of three dogs, one cat, and the youngest few of their five offspring. Pamela has received numerous awards for her writing, including top Manuscript awards in mainstream fiction, narrative nonfiction, ghost story, and contemporary fiction from the Houston Writers Guild, and in romance from the Writers League of Texas. She is the author of *Saving Grace, The Clark Kent Chronicles, How To Screw Up Your Kids, Love Gone Viral, Hot Flashes And Half Ironmans,* and *Puppalicious And Beyond* and a contributing author to *Prevent Workplace Harassment* and *Easy To Love But Hard To Raise*. *The Jumbie House* is an adapted excerpt from the Katie and Annalise series. Watch for the next book in the series, *Leaving Annalise*, in 2013.

Pamela is an employment attorney and human resources professional, and the co-founder of a human resources consulting company. She spends her free time hiking, running, bicycling, and enjoying the great outdoors. For more information, visit http://pamelahutchins.com.

The Stop
help is where you find it
by
E. L. Russell

Darkness had fallen on the lonely rural highway. Tired and hungry, Alice turned down the scratchy radio and scanned her GPS for a motel. As far as she could tell from the screen, she had spent the past hour driving through an empty gray region with no discernible features except a few thin twisted black lines. Her car was not on any of them. She was off the grid.

A dimly lit gas station came into view. Trying to decide if she should stop, she slowed her car to check it out. Her gas gauge indicated slightly less than a quarter tank.

Need gas. Freaking short cut to the Interstate may be longer than that yahoo claimed. Where is the damn freeway?

Alice drove slowly into the dark station and paused before pulling under a small covered section containing two pumps. The inside lights were off and there were no other cars. One pump's hose had a white plastic bag duct taped to its handle.

Crap, they're closed.

She noticed the other pump had a credit card reader and pulled next to it.

I hope that still works.

Before she unlocked her doors, Alice checked her mirrors and turned to look out both rear windows for any signs of danger. Not seeing any movement, she removed her credit card, put her purse under the armrest, and unlocked the door.

A sudden noise in the tall weeds behind the station caused her to stand close to the car door. Her eyes searched the shadows for several seconds before she swiped her credit card and waited for approval. After she inserted the nozzle into her car, she continued scanning the darkness surrounding the small station.

Another muffled noise in the weeds made her stop fueling to look around.

Something like a small dark animal scurried between the weeds and the bushes next to the ice machine.

Ghosts   123

Okay, that's enough gas to get to the Interstate.

She clumsily returned the nozzle, jumped into the car, and locked the doors. As she pulled away from the pump a slight thump under her car startled her sending a chill through her body.

Crap! I ran over the critter.

Alice drove down the dark highway without looking back. She locked her hands on the steering wheel and couldn't shake off the cold chill.

Relax. Play some music. Slow down. Take it easy.

She quickly found a soothing tune on the radio. The road enclosed her car in blackness offering only a faint clue about her surroundings.

Nothing's after you.

She stole a furtive glance at her rearview mirror.

Nothing.

Her apprehension diminished in relation to the distant, fading light of the gas station behind her. The headlights revealed little in the darkness ahead. She tried to concentrate on the gentle, late night country music.

Without warning, flashing lights illuminated her rear view mirror and a double blast of short siren woops of a filled the car. Shocked and frightened, Alice glanced at her speedometer.

I'm not speeding!

Keeping one eye on the mirror, she turned the radio down. She didn't know what else she should do.

The siren had scared the wits out of her and she frantically searched the darkness for a safe place to pull over. A slight rise in the road revealed the distant lights of the Interstate.

Crap, so close.

An approaching billboard caught her attention. Its dim lights extended over an old and torn ad.

At least there's some light.

Alice engaged her turn signal, slowed, and pulled onto the shoulder. Her tires crunched through gravel until she stopped under the billboard's dirty yellow glow. With hands still tightly locked on the steering wheel, she furtively glanced in the rearview mirror to catch a glimpse of the cop.

The outline of a large man appeared in her side mirror. He slowly approached her door. The brim of his trooper's hat covered the top of his face. His belly covered his belt buckle. A gold badge hung at an angle on his starched brown long-sleeved shirt. Everything about him made her feel uncomfortable.

Reaching for her purse from the armrest, she felt angry and scared.

Why did he stop me? Crap, what's he want?

He tapped on the window and said, "License and registration, ma'am." Alice glanced at the miniature handcuffs on his tiepin and opened her window. She clutched her purse on her lap and straightened. "Officer, I'm glad to see—"

"License and registration, ma'am," he repeated. His hand held the door, his face, accompanied by his unwashed body odor, edged too close.

"Yes, officer, it's right here." She dove into her bag while cautiously eyeing him.

Handing him her driver's license she leaned away from the window. He bent closer and flashed the light on her face. He carefully checked the interior of her car. He repeated flatly, "Registration, ma'am."

Alice rummaged through her purse and searched frantically for more documentation. Then she remembered. "Just a second, the rental agreement's in there." She pointed to the glove compartment. "Okay if I get it?"

He aimed his flashlight on the glove compartment door. "Make it fast, ma'am."

She stretched against her seatbelt to open it and reached in. She searched blindly with her hand. "I know it's here somewhere."

"Hurry up, ma'am." His voice sounded impatient. "Or I'll need to take you downtown."

His demandingly gruff response startled Alice. "I know it's here. I'll find it." *What's his damn rush? Okay, let me check again. It might be stuck in the back.*

She felt terror for the first time and thought, "This isn't right." Then, still restrained by her seatbelt, she stretched and reached in the compartment as far as she could.

Alice felt a growing terror. The cop's hand brushed her bottom when he reached in to release her seat belt.

God, this isn't right I have to get out of here.

Free of the seat belt, she made a final effort to stretch to the back of the glove compartment.

Something ice cold touched her fingers. Before she could react, a hand grabbed her. She bit her lip and fought an impulse to scream. The frigid hand held her firmly, locked in its grasp.

"Ma'am, I need you to step out of the car."

Considering the cold hand, Alice thought that getting out of the car was a good idea. She started to slide her arm out of the glove compartment when the hand roughly yanked her back.

"Oh dear, God." She screamed.

The man opened the door. "Ma'am, do not panic. Back away from the glove compartment and step out of the car."

Alice could not respond. She pulled with all her strength but her wrist remained painfully locked within the icy grip of the hand.

"Did you catch your sleeve on something?" He grabbed her free arm tried to pull her out of the car.

The hand yanked Alice closer until her head hit the dashboard. Fearing the loss of an arm she cried, "Stop! Please don't—"

The man released her arm and held her tightly around her waist while he began to stroke her thighs. He undid her belt and tugged at her jeans. "Don't worry, honey, this won't hurt."

His repulsive touch eclipsed the terror she had of the hand. Alice frantically kicked at him as she painfully twisted her arm to free herself from whatever coldly clutched her hand.

He moaned then sneered, "Oh, you like it rough?"

The hand in the glove compartment twisted her wrist and forced her palm upwards. It slid a cold metallic object in her hand and bent her fingers around it.

The man stopped pulling her jeans and slid his arm under her blouse. "Oh, yeah—"

Before he could finish, Alice had freed her hand from the glove compartment, twisted on her back and fired at him until she emptied the gun.

He collapsed on her. She screamed with frustration and anger as she kicked and pushed his bleeding body from the car. After she closed and locked the door, Alice examined her blood-spattered image in the rear view mirror.

The radio still played softly in the background while Alice carefully wiped blood from her face, hands, and the gun on her lap.

She turned and stared apprehensively at the open glove compartment. She did not see the hand but felt it was there. Holding the gun with two trembling fingers, Alice carefully placed it on the shelf of the open glove compartment and quietly said, "Thank you."

She didn't look at the bloody body on the ground beside her car. Instead, Alice stared at the gun and waited. Seconds later, a ghostly woman's hand crawled toward the gun, pulled it inside, and closed the glove compartment door.

A radio announcer interrupted the music. "The police have issued an alert to all women drivers to be careful. Yesterday evening the highway rapist struck again. Several hours ago police discovered the dismembered remains of an unidentified woman in a ditch on FM8606 believed to be his seventh victim. Local authorities warn he's liable to strike again—"

Alice turned the radio off and shook her head.

I don't think so, that bastard's done with killin'.

Alice smiled at the distant lights of the Interstate and took off. Her spinning tires showered stones over his dead body.

About E. L. and Enid Russell

E. L. and Enid Russell grew up in northeast Philadelphia and met in college. After a short courtship on the soccer and lacrosse fields respectively, they married and entered into a fifty year adventure of teaching, coaching, traveling, and more recently, writing together. While most of their manuscripts are in the science fiction genre, *the Ghost in my iPad,* is a story for tweens and was scripted for their grandchildren, who, along with their writing, keep them young.

Novels in the Cohort series include: *Deadly Awakenings, Evolutis Rising,* and *Genecaust*; their novellas: *Onset* and *ReSet, and their* short stories: *The Ghost in my iPad.*

Assorted short-shorts and flash fiction include *The Stop, To find a Thief, Critique Circle, Sniper POV, BottomsUp,* and the *Commitment.*

X Marks the Spot
by
Ann Conti

I hated evacuating for hurricanes!

"Are you going to leave for the storm?" Eli asked nervously as the wind picked up.

He was my six-year-old neighbor and was standing outside watching as I packed my car to evacuate for Hurricane Katrina. He loved to come to my house and play with my two Yorkies. He had known them since they were pups and got a kick out of rubbing their ears and playing fetch with them. His grandpa wouldn't let him come over very often though, because he was afraid Eli would make a pest of himself. Buy Eli was a good kid, so I didn't mind.

"Yes," I said. "But I don't really want to."

I hadn't left for Hurricane Georges and my house wasn't damaged. I had lived through Betsy and Camille and others. The one time I did evacuate, it took me 12 hours just to drive to Baton Rouge, which is only 60 miles up the road.

"Are Plato and Toby leaving too?"

"Oh, yes. I wouldn't leave them here alone," I said. "How about you?"

"No. My grandpa wants to stay here. He said we've never left for a hurricane and we aren't going to start now."

A pine tree branch whipped by. Eli jumped to avoid being slashed. The winds were probably blowing at about 40 miles an hour now, as Katrina moved closer to land.

Plato and Toby were inside. Their shrill barks resounded with fear. The now screeching wind sounded like the howls of the screaming Banshee.

"Can I help you bring Plato and Toby to the car?"

"Sure."

I had already loaded my car with the dog food, my computer, and my suitcase with enough clothes to last for three days. Eli and I went into the house. I let him put Plato and Toby's leashes on and walk them to the car. I secured them in their harnesses in the back seat and walked Eli back to his house.

"Eli thanks for your help. Be sure to listen to your grandpa. He'll keep you safe."

"I will."

"I wanted to make sure one more time that everything was secure in my house. I got Plato and Toby out of the car and went back inside the house for one last look.

My plan was to drive across the Crescent City Connection Bridge to the West Bank of the Mississippi River to catch Highway 90 from New Orleans to Lafayette to avoid the crush of traffic that would jam Interstate 10 West from New Orleans to Baton Rouge. Others would do the same. Like funeral procession except cars would run out of gas and be abandoned along the road. In the darkness, they would look like coffins. I never let me gasoline get below a quarter of a tank, so I would make it all the way to Lake Charles. If I was lucky, I would find a hotel that allowed pets and would still have vacancies. Plato, Toby, and I would stay for three days then return home, which is the way it usually was. Three days away, then return home.

I sat glued to my battery operated television set every night. The stations relocated to Baton Rouge, because the New Orleans studios had been destroyed. All that was covered on the local news was how the levees broke. And three days after Katrina had passed over, the city filled up with water as though it were a teacup. The Corps of Engineers had not maintained the levees dutifully, and flood waters smashed through the weakened levee walls. The 17th Street Canal, the boundary between Orleans and Jefferson Parishes, burst on the Orleans Parish side flooding Lakeview. The rush of the waters caused by Katrina's storm surge was powerful. But the canal didn't burst on the Jefferson Parish side. The water raged to the far end of the canal overtopping it, dumping ten to twelve feet of water into Old Metairie, which is where I lived, and burying every home in its path.

I slept restlessly, worrying about the devastation and the lost lives. As dawn broke, I heard men's voices yelling and pounding at my front door. Then a loud crash. I jumped out of bed and threw on my robe. What was going on? I could hear these men running through my house, turning over furniture opening closets and drawers. What were they looking for? Looters had taken over the city. With so many homes and businesses abandoned since Katrina, looters were having a field day.

I tried to stay quiet, hoping they wouldn't find me.

But to no avail. Four men burst through my bedroom door. They were dressed in military uniforms and carried weapons. They weren't looters, they were National Guardsmen.

"Jack, this room is freezing?"

"Yeah, there's no electricity in this house. How can it be cold in here and warm and humid everywhere else?"

One guardsman walked toward me. Was he going to shoot me, thinking I was a looter? I called out to him, but he didn't seem to see me or even know I was there.

"Man that spot I just walked through is really cold," he said to the other guardsman.

"Hey watch out! Rats! They're eating something."

He fired his weapon at the rats, and they ran away. The guardsman bent down to see what the rats had been eating. He shook his head and took a deep breath.

"We're finished here. Let's go."

They left.

I hadn't noticed rats before. These guardsmen must have let them in when the bashed down my front door.

I went downstairs to see how bad the damage was. My door, torn off the hinges, lay flat on the floor. I went outside to see if there was other damage. Not only had they broken down my door, tracked in mud, let in rats, but they had also spray painted a large orange X on the front of my house.

Painted in the top of the X was *9/1*.

In the left side of the X was *TF-TX-1*.

In the right side of the X was *upstairs bedroom cold, rats*.

And in the bottom part of the X was a *0* and *dogs 2*.

Author's Note: Top quadrant of X: date the rescue team left the structure. Left quadrant of X: name of search & rescue team. Right quadrant of X: personal hazards, such as rats. Bottom quadrant of X: number of live or dead victims found inside the structure. Urban Search & Rescue (US&R) Response System Field Operations Guide, FEMA, September 2003 (US&R-2-FG), IV-11.

Ghosts 131

The Ghost in my iPad
by
Enid Russell

Every night for two months now, he heard the voice... and it scared him. It scared him bad.

I'm cold ... it's dark...I can't find the light...

Over and over.

Jengo begged his mom to leave the light on. He looked as pathetic as possible but his mom laughed. "You're a big boy now. You told me so yourself. You're starting sixth grade tomorrow. Good night, sweetie." And she flipped out the light.

It seemed to Jengo there were too many bad things going on. Earlier that evening a local newscaster had broken into his TV movie with, "... *personal items belonging to Katrina Robins were found by a local hunter at the old Bartlett Apple Orchard. Katrina appears to be the sixth victim...*"

The Yellow Banana, the kids' name for the school bus, passed right by the Bartlett place. Maybe he would see the kidnapper. Maybe it was the same man who had stolen away his sister Maddy. Where was she now? He missed her so much it hurt. Maybe that had been her calling him in the night. She sounded so sad... and lost.

I'm cold ... it's dark...

Even though it meant risking his mom's wrath, Jengo reached for Buzz Lightyear, the lamp Maddy had given him for his birthday four years ago. Mom could not resist teasing him about it. That he wanted it on all night. He switched it on.

The voice stopped.

Thank God. He let his head fall back to the pillow.

The earlier promise of a storm erupted into a gully washer with spectacular flashes of lightning followed by ear-splitting cracks of thunder. Startled awake, Jengo grimly waited for the voice... he heard... nothing... not a peep.

Not moving, he rolled his eyes to the digital clock. *Like always...* 3:15. He rolled his eyes toward his feet. *What the...?* The warm glow of his iPad on his desk cast shadows through the room. And above the pounding rain, he heard the faint sound of music. *Zelda music?* He hadn't played that game in ages. Scooting to the end of his bunk, he peeked down. His iPad floated a foot off the floor and images moved across the screen. His eyes followed the slim white cord of the earbuds up from the iPad to... to nothing. The earbuds hung in the air, suspended. Slowly, two eyes materialized between them. They gazed at him, then faded away.

He squawked in fright and jerked backwards. Fear gave way to curiosity. Jengo stretched his neck over the end of the bed for a better look. The same blue eyes floated from under his bed . . . to stare at him . . . eyeball to eyeball. He yelped and jerked back. His heart thumped so loud he almost missed the muffled noise from under the bed. Two tiny taps... then two louder taps.

Tap! Tap!

Although trembling like a bug in a hot skillet, he slipped out of bed. *The iPad? It wants the iPad back? That's crazy. Why do I even know that?* Nevertheless, he put his thumbs on the edge of the tablet and non-too gently, shoved it under the bed. When it suddenly reappeared, he jumped back. His iPad had been rejected. Shock and irritation replaced his fear.

Three more taps... ... louder... more urgent.

Tap! Tap! Tap!

His eyes fell on the earbuds. *Ah.* He plugged them in and slid the iPad under the bed. Something jerked it from his hands into the darkness. The muffled sound of Zelda music drifted out, his lips quirked in a small grin.

Climbing into the Yellow Banana the next morning, Jengo couldn't wait to tell his buddy about last night. He made it through the gauntlet of hotshot eighth graders eager to trip him and slid in next to Billy.

"Hey, Jengo, did you hear about that kidnapped girl?" Billy asked, his eyebrows furrowed in worry. "You think it was the same man who took your sister?"

Billy was the only one he'd talked to about Maddy. Sometimes he cried and he didn't want anyone else to see his tears and how sad it made him.

"Maybe."

With an explosion of movement, Candy Ball, the girl in the seat in front of them popped up. She announced in her prissy know-it-all voice, "The Holiday Snatcher took her."

Jengo looked at her wild red hair and wondered how she got by her mom in the morning. *Nothing* got by his mom.

134 Ghosts

"Who's the Holiday Snatcher?" he asked before he could bit his lips shut.

"Don't you know?" Candy Ball frowned with a supercilious look. "Takes his victims only on a holiday. You know, just like he took Maddy on the Fourth of July and... uh... oh, Jengo..." Her face scrunched in concern. "Uh... and Katrina, she was taken on Labor Day."

"When's the next holiday?" Billy asked, chewing on his bottom lip.

One more scary night alone until Billy spends the night. Whatever was under the bed only wanted time on his iPad, it seemed. But even so, it was creepy. Was that thing the voice? Was the thing connected to Maddy?

At 3:45, Zelda music, not the voice, woke him. Carefully, he peeked over the side of his bed.

"What...?" He jerked back. "Oh my God," he mumbled. A pair of eyes gazed back at him, set in the face of a girl. He could see all of her. Well, actually, he could see through her. Her transparent skin and white dress made her look like a pale reflection in a dark window. Earbuds hung from her ears. Her long hair was bluish... like the rest of her... like her eyes... which were staring straight at him.

"Hello?" he inquired with the barest whisper of sound. He climbed down from the bed for a better look. "You're practically invisible, you know."

She backed away from him as if scared. Or maybe afraid he'd take the iPad, which she held behind her back. Jengo almost laughed because he could see it straight through her. He rubbed his chin and cleared his throat.

"Are—are you the voice I keep hearing?" Jengo asked quietly so as not to startle her. He desperately wanted an answer. "The one—who's cold—and in the dark?"

After an endless moment, the girl gave the slightest nod.

"You're a ghost, aren't you?"

A whisper of musical sound was the response. The girl was laughing. He smiled in wonder and the guarded gurgle of laughter he had suppressed escaped his own lips.

Talk on the school bus Friday morning was all about the Holiday Snatcher. Now, six girls were officially missing, one from as long ago as last Christmas. Disgust was written all over Jengo's face. "The police should have caught the guy by now. Hey, we're passing the old apple orchard where they found Katrina's backpack."

"That place is huge. I bet Katrina just got lost," Billy speculated.

Know-it-all Candy Ball interrupted with a smug look of importance as she popped around in front of them. "It's over 200 acres."

"Yeah, how do you know, smarty pants?" Jengo shot at her, looking doubtful.

"My mom told me, Jengo Albright, and she knows everything."

"What a surprise." Billy smirked and jabbed Jengo in the ribs.

"There's the entrance! The address is... three... four... what?" Jengo strained his neck trying to see behind the bus as it bounced on its way.

"Five," Know-It-All said. "It was 345 Trooper Road."

Sitting back, Jengo frowned in thought. "Weird. That's the same time the ghost wakes me every night. 3:45. Listen, Billy, tomorrow's Saturday. We need to bike out there. I know a short cut."

"Are you nuts?" Billy said, shaking Jengo's shoulders. "There's a crazy man hangs out there in the apple orchard."

On Saturday morning, after the sleep-over, the boys biked to Billy's. Jengo dutifully called his mom when they arrived but he didn't tell her they were continuing on to the apple orchard.

Pumping hard, Billy panted, "What is so important about this address?"

"Three forty five, Billy. I told you. The address numbers are the same as the time the ghost wakes me. I asked Candy if that meant something and —" He was huffing and puffing too. The ride was farther than he'd figured.

"Yeah, yeah, I know," Billy interrupted, "and she nodded. How do you know she isn't just a bobble-head ghost who nods all the time?"

The connection was obvious in Jengo's mind and he ignored the sarcastic crack. When he'd told his buddy about the ghost the night before, it had freaked Billy out so bad, Jengo couldn't even get him to look over the side of the bed.

By the time the abandoned farmhouse finally came into view, they were both dragging. Dark clouds covered the sun and the address on the old sign was barely visible in the gloom. "Yep, 345 Trooper Road."

"Quit whispering, Jengo. You're freaking me out."

"Yeah, I know, but it's kind of weird around here, don't you think? The old farm house perched on the hill looks spooky as heck." A gust of wind whipped his voice away and the sky turned black. An eerie metallic smell filled the air.

"Jeez! We're gonna get soaked," Billy screamed. They dropped their bikes and took off at a sprint up the hill toward the house. As if on cue, the skies opened. Ear-splitting thunder made them duck and they all but missed the ominous growls of two huge snarling dogs.

"Run for your life, Billy!" Cold rain pelted them like sharp arrows as the dogs charged in hot pursuit. Batting their arms behind them to ward off snapping jaws, they jumped on the porch and skidded across the wet boards to slam into the front door, which miraculously opened. Mere seconds ahead of the snarling fangs, they slammed the door shut and threw the rusty bolt home. Their hearts thumped like jackhammers.

Billy gasped, "I thought we were goners. Did you ever see such huge dogs? They're as big as elephants." He looked toward the boarded windows that allowed only the smallest bit of gloomy light to struggle through. Groaning, he moaned, "I wanna go home."

"Nope." Jengo shook his head. "We have to find clue to where Katrina . . . and Maddy are," he added hopefully. He ran his hand through his hair to sluice out some of the rain.

Resigned, Billy reached into Jengo's backpack searching hopefully for food. He came out with a Snickers Bar and Jengo's iPad. "How come you brought this? Jeez, are you lucky. It's still dry. Hey it's on." He bit into the candy bar while staring at the screen. "What game is this, Jengo? These are some *creepy* blue eyes."

"Gimme that." Jengo squeaked in alarm.

Although Billy held on, Jengo snatched the Pad with determined strength, He placed it on the floor well beyond Billy's reach. "Do *not* touch it," he commanded. "That's her. That's the ghost I tried to show you."

Although Billy claimed he didn't believe in ghosts, he had been so freaked out by Jengo's story that he wouldn't listen to the whole thing. Now, he watched the ghost rise slowly from the screen, ready to bolt. He inched behind Jengo. Seeing Billy, the ghost melted back into the screen until Jengo urgently rapped on the wall three times. The ghost stopped her descent. Hesitated. Then seeing Jengo, rose and stepped out of the tablet.

"Tell her to go back, Billy babbled, peeking around Jengo's shoulder at the transparent spirit hovering in front of them. "I really wanna go home."

Outside, the dogs renewed their attack on the door and both boys jumped. The ghost tilted her head, staring at them. Then, turning, she floated through the front door.

Billy exhaled in relief. "She's gone. Thank God."

The barking outside changed to yelps and yips that faded into the distance.

"*She* did that." Jengo smiled. "My ghost got rid of the dogs." He didn't remember exactly when the ghost had become *his* ghost but he knew she had. "She needs a name. Her white dress reminds me of the lilies in my mom's garden."

Jengo turned to his ghost, who had returned, and asked, "Is Lily okay with you? It's a pretty name. I like it."

Other than a slight tilt of her head, there was no perceptible reaction. Jengo grinned, then turned serious. "Good. We have work to do."

Billy, his eyes fixed on the ghost, whispered, "Are kidding me? We need to get outta here while the dogs are gone."

"No, Billy. You know what we need to do." He smiled shyly at Lily as he picked up his iPad and returned it to his backpack.

Inspecting each room and every closet downstairs, they moved as one. Billy followed so close behind Jengo they looked like a four-legged alien. Finding nothing, they started up the stairs. Their slow progress came to a grinding halt when Billy saw Lily floating on the upper landing.

"How'd she get up there?" he asked in panic as he retreated down the stairs.

Jengo grabbed his buddy's arm, preventing farther withdrawal. "Don't be dumb. She can do things we can't."

He took off up the stairs. When Billy hurried to catch up, he inadvertently ran through Lily's transparent body at the bedroom entry.

"Jengo," he wailed as he shut his eyes to the momentary cold, "get her offa me... I wanna go home."

When he opened his eyes, Lily was frowning at him and shaking her head. Then she floated out the door. Jengo glared at him. "Lily says there's nothing here. Quit whining."

When they entered the last bedroom, they were surprised to find it fully furnished. "You check under the bed, Billy and I'll look in the closet."

"No."

"What? Just bend over and see if anything's there. We can't miss anything."

Billy, knees shaking, knelt and stole a quick peek beneath the four-poster bed. "Holy…" He jerked to his feet and raced for the door. "Eyes! Two of them. Another ghost! Run!"

A familiar chiding voice erupted from under the bed. "I am not a ghost, Billy Butt-Head. You're a jerk. You scared me to death."

Billy stopped. "Know-it-all Candy Ball? That was *you* under the bed? Yeah, well, I wasn't scared. What are *you* doing here?"

"Yeah, like that's true and none of your business." Candy clenched her fists. Billy's scream had scared her witless and she was mad it might show.

"Candy," Jengo stepped between them, "what *are* you doing here?"

"I heard you two talking at school and I wanted to help find Maddy, too. Even though she's two years older than us, she was nice to me. Anyway, I figured you'd need my help if you were only taking Butt-Head with you." She shot a malicious glare at Jengo's sidekick.

"How much help can a *girl* be?" Billy shot back, putting his hands in his pockets, the faked image of nonchalance.

"Well, you're here now," Jengo said, resigned to her company, "so stick close. We need to look in the attic."

Billy panicked. "The attic?" Dark clouds were threatening another downpour and it would have been a travesty to call the slight glow in the upstairs hallway light. He could just imagine how dark the attic would be. "There's nothing in the attic."

"You chicken, everyone knows the attic is where you hide stuff." Candy taunted, looking pale herself but maintaining a brave front.

As the two bickered the merits of an attic search, Jengo mounted the short stairway and rattled the handle of the door that blocked their way. "Damn. It's locked."

Lily came drifting through the door from the attic side. For all that she was only a slip of a girl, not even five feet tall, the way she came and went was spine-chilling. Jengo gasped in fright and needed a minute to recover. "Are the missing girls in there, Lily?"

She was so transparent she was barely visible. She shook her head and beckoned Jengo to follow her down the stairs to the basement.

Billy wailed as they inched down the cellar stairs. "First the attic, now the basement. Why is *this* a good idea?"

"You are like a terror meter Billy," Jengo said with dismay. "Maddy might be down there. You *know* we have to check. "This the only place left to look."

Lily pointed to a light switch, which was obscured by narrow shelves holding cans of food. *Why food in a deserted house?* Jengo turned on the poorest excuse for a light he'd ever seen. *Why electricity?*

"That light bulb isn't strong enough to make a shadow," Billy said. "Who'd go down there on purpose? It's a dark pit."

"I *get* the picture, Billy." Swallowing hard, Jengo added, "After this, we can go home. Candy, are you coming?"

Pale but willing, Candy nodded and said in a shaky whisper, "Yes, I'm coming." Turning to Billy, she ribbed him with, "Come on, scaredy pants, I'll protect you." She flexed her arm to show a small muscle.

"No way. If you're so fearless, *you* go down. I'll stay here as the lookout."

Jengo tuned them out…again… and followed Lily, who was already halfway down the stairs. She turned to check he was following.

The basement was a huge disappointment. It was a smallish room with nothing in it but stale air and a dirt floor. Jengo groaned in frustration. Next to him, Candy cowered down as if the ceiling might bump her head.

"This room feels like a coffin, Jengo and it's way too dark to see a thing."

Maddy, where are you? Devastated, Jengo turned toward the stairs, but through the abysmal light, he saw Lily, not ten feet away, silently stamping her foot and pointing down. She beckoned to him.

"What, Lily?" he whispered.

Noiselessly, she stamped her foot again.

Expecting nothing, but to show he was listening, Jengo stamped his foot, too. "What? Hear that? It's hollow." He looked at her with a grin. "A door?"

He knelt and saw footprints in the dry dirt. His eyebrows lifted in astonishment. He looked up at his ghost. "Lily, you're the best." A tinge of pink colored her transparent cheeks and he laughed.

"Candy, look! This must be a trap door." He dropped to one knee and started brushing the thin layer of dirt away.

Almost immediately, they found a big iron ring, which Jengo reached to pull. They were so focused on their find they didn't hear the clamor of barking and screaming closing in.

Billy exploded into view, having descended the stairs so fast he missed most of the steps. "Dogs!" He yelled! Those devil-dogs are coming." He skidded across the dirt floor to where Jengo knelt. "And there's some old guy nuttier than a fruitcake who keeps screaming at the dogs to *get us.*"

At the top of the stairs, they could see a pair of old boots and baggy pants. Gruff commands of "Find em, boys. Get em," boomed down the stairwell. Menacing snarls and deep-throated rumbles circled the boots, and then the dogs sniffed and snarled their way slowly down the stairs.

"We're goners." Billy whispered. "Those dogs are gonna kill us for sure."

But when they reached the last few steps, Lily materialized and floated in front of them. An explosion of frantic yelping and scraping erupted as the terrified dogs turned and tore up the staircase. In their desperate effort to escape through the trap door, they crashed into their owner and unbalanced him.

"You mangy mutts, I'll—I'll—" and with that, he tumbled down the stairs, landing in a very still and very silent heap.

The sound of yipping hounds faded completely and no one spoke until Candy whispered in wonder, "It's a *woman*," She pointed at the rifle that had also crashed down the stairs. "She has a gun."

"Is... is she dead?" Billy stuttered.

"She could have killed us." Candy said, stepping back. "Is she breathing?"

Jengo was near enough to see a fine cloud of dust leave the floor at regular intervals just under her nose. "No, but she's out cold. We should tie her up."

After securing the old woman with the dog leashes attached to her belt, the three turned their attention to the trap door. Pulling on the iron ring, they heaved the door up and descended to yet another subterranean level. They were amazed at what they found.

"It's a classroom," Candy said in wonder, "with desks and books and even a pull-down wall map."

"She made them go to school?" Billy said, incredulous. "That woman tortured them?"

"The girls must be here. But where?" Jengo muttered as he re-examined the room. "There *must* be another door!" He stepped back and tripped over a waste basket, falling on his butt. Papers flew everywhere and he grabbed one, smoothing it out on the floor. "Holy cow! Look at this. It's a math paper—uh—no name."

Excitement thrummed through the air and when Jengo saw his ghost floating at the closet entrance, he went to her. "Where are they, Lily? You know, don't you?" It was more a statement than question and when the ghost turned and disappeared into the closet, he followed. "We looked here. There's nothing."

Ignoring him, Lily sat on a small stuffed chair that was wedged into the corner. Studying her for clues, Jengo moved the chair. A small rigorous nod encouraged him to pull it out farther. He ran his hand over the rough surface of the wall, like he'd seen Indiana Jones do in a movie, and his fingers caught in a deep indentation. When he pulled, a small door, barely four feet high, swung open.

"*Another* secret door," Candy, who'd tailed him, murmured in wonder. "I wonder if it leads to the bottom of the hill under this house. My mom said they used to store hooch here during the days of prohibition."

"Hooch smooch." Billy said. He wasn't interested in illegal alcohol. "This is a maze." He whined his mantra, "I wanna go home."

Jengo grabbed his arm and bending low, pulled Billy through the small door. Candy trailed and they emerged in a dimly lit hallway with five small doors on each side.

Billy's eyes got so big Candy told him his eyeballs would pop out but he was too freaked to make a comeback. They found one large key on a nail over the first door.

"I bet it opens all the doors," Candy said in a meek voice, not at all like her know-it-all self. They collectively held their breath as Jengo turned the key in the first lock.

An eternity passed before the dim light from the hall crawled into the room to share its meager glow and they strained their eyes to see. The room was so small it could only be called a cell. On a narrow cot, a teenage girl in an old-fashioned flannel nightgown came into focus. She starred at them in abject terror. *Not Maddy.*

Before the others could move, Jengo stepped forward and in a gentle voice, murmured, "It's okay. You're safe now. You're with us and we'll take you out of here." With the slightest nod, the girl crumpled into tears. Jengo hesitated then awkwardly wrapped an arm around her shoulders.

Behind the next three doors, they found more dazed and terrified girls but still no Maddy... and not in the sixth or seventh room either. Jengo was frantic.

Crossing the hall to the second to last cell, he swallowed hard trying not to cry. He turned the key fast and burst inside. "Maddy. It's me..." Nothing.

The last door. He stood for a moment and crossed all his fingers. *Please God,* he bargained, *I'll do anything.*

Candy watched with her hand to her mouth and Billy laid a supportive hand on his friend's shoulder.

In fear of crushing heartbreak, Jengo turned the key and slowly pushed the door open. "Maddy?" he whispered in desperation. "Maddy?" When no one responded, a single tear escaped and rolled down his cheek.

As he hung his head in defeat a whoosh of air broke the silence and he was tackled to his knees. He dropped like a stone. He knew that tackle. She had used it often in their play. "Maddy!" he cried in jubilation. "Maddy!"

"Jengo? It's you? Really?" His sister collapsed on top of him and hugged the breath out of him. "You found me! I knew you would." She held him in a strangle hold and he loved it.

Too drugged to celebrate their escape, the four listless girls huddled close like one lethargic amoeba. "How come you're not dopey, too, Maddy," Jengo asked. That was a great tackle you gave me."

"The old lady gave us pills but you don't think I swallowed them, do you, Jengo? Not after the first time, anyway." She jerked her head toward the group of groggy girls Look how stupid they make you."

In silence, the girls followed Jengo up the stairs with Billy and Candy nudging them from behind. Jengo was feeling home free when a voice boomed down the stairwell.

"Where do you think you're going? Get back to your rooms."

Like automatons, the five girls reversed their progress, forcing Candy and Billy back down the steps with them.

The old woman had regained consciousness and somehow untied herself. With her feet parted, she shouldered the rifle like an extension of her arm... then fired it at the ceiling.

The thundering explosion brought down plaster and wood splinters. In a freighted frenzy, the girls turned as one toward their cells, only to stop abruptly when a small figure floated through the group and hovered before them.

Jengo's jaw dropped as he looked at Lily. She was practically a normal person... hardly transparent at all.

Billy's baffled look went with Candy's whisper. "I don't remember that girl."

Turning, Lily pointed at the shrieking crone with the full length of her arm and then floated upward toward her. When the woman spoke, her words shocked Jengo to the core.

"Where did you come from? You're dead," the crone gasped as if she knew Lily.

Taunting the kidnapper, Lily hung in front of her and the woman's face changed from one of surprise to abject fear. Dropping the rifle, she put up both arms to ward off the apparition. "You *can't* be here. I killed you."

Jengo's jaw dropped and he felt tremendous rage at this lunatic who had killed his ghost.

Lily floated closer to the old hag.

"Stop! Please stop! It was an accident. I didn't mean to kill you." The old woman blubbered and fell to her knees wailing. "You are *not* here. You're dead."

As they watched, Lily became transparent and floated through the kneeling kidnapper only to stop and hover at her back. When the women stood and turned, Lily raised her arms and in a small voice said, "Boo!"

The old woman screamed and collapsed at Lily's feet.

Standing in the yard in front of the house, the FBI agent spoke into his phone. "Yeah, the old woman is completely bonkers. All she did was babble when I got here." He looked at the big house in the encroaching darkness and mumbled, "Scary."

"These girls are cold," Jengo interrupted with impatience. He'd called 911 on the cell phone his mom had insisted he take. *Thank God.* "Is that ambulance coming with the blankets or what?"

The Agent couldn't help but smile at the gutsy kid. Not for the first time, he wondered how he and his friends had managed to find the kidnapped girls when the FBI team had found nothing. They were heroes in his book.

"It'll be here directly," he assured Jengo. With his hand over the phone, he watched the boy return to his rescued flock. The trio had given the girls their jackets and they were all huddled close for warmth.

Yanked back to the telephone by his supervisor, the agent answered, "Yes, sir. She's the Holiday Snatcher all right. All the missing girls are here except the first victim." *If these kids hadn't filled me in, the whole thing would still be a tangle. No sir, there is no sign of the first girl. The kids told me the old* lady said in some kind of garbled confession that she had killed that first one."

The sergeant tried to get off the phone. Hell, he was getting cold himself standing there yakking while the night closed in but he wanted clarification on that last bit. "You say she was a retired school teacher? Oh, that's tragic… she lost her granddaughter about two years ago in a fire?" *Jeez,* he thought, *she kidnapped girls to replace her granddaughter.*

Getting ready for bed, Jengo replayed the day in his mind. *Maddy was home.* He grinned absently. The paramedics had assured him that in spite of shock and dehydration, the girls would be fine, but where Lily had gone? He wondered if closure on the mystery of her death meant she would go to heaven… or wherever ghosts went. His last thought as he drifted toward sleep was he missed her.

Tap! Tap!

Jengo's eyes flew open. He saw a warm glow of light at the foot of his bed. *She's still here.* A tremendous smile lit his face. It was 4:10. *I bet that means she's on to something new!*

Jengo jumped out of bed and ran toward his ghost.

"Lily, what's next?"

The Ghost Rider of the Bar-B-Bar
by
Thomas J. Dowling

"Allow me to introduce myself. My name is Buck Lang; this is my wife Dorothy and daughter Rebecca. Welcome to the Bar-B-Bar. We hope you enjoy your stay."

"Why, thank you. I'm Bessie Rogers, and I'm from Springfield, *Missourah*. Pleasure to make your acquaintance. I do intend to have a pleasant stay, even though I have serious business to attend to first."

Serious business? Rebecca thought. *Nobody takes anything very serious 'round here.*

After a big meal and what seemed like hours of boring adult talk to Rebecca, the Bessie Rogers, the new school teacher, excused herself to her cabin.

Rebecca's excitement kept her awake long into the night. She hadn't been to school in over two years. Ever since the wild boys scared off the last teacher by putting a rattlesnake under her desk. No brave soul had dared replace her. The next morning, Rebecca and Buck accompanied Bessie by horseback to the one-room school house. It was a mile from the ranch down Enon Road, near the small Ozark town of Enon, Arkansas. The rocky road wound through a forest thick with oak and hickory trees. It passed by the top of a large bluff that overlooked Long Creek. The ledges below the bluff contained caves once used by the Osage Indians.

Rebecca wasn't allowed near them. She wondered what treasures they held.

When they arrived, Bessie introduced herself to the waiting parents and children. Rebecca knew Bessie would have her hands full. While most of the local children were respectful, there were three older boys who didn't like school and skipped it as often as they could. Hunting and fishing was a better use of their time than reading, writing and 'rithmetic.

Bessie appeared strict and intolerant of laziness, which suited Rebecca just fine. She was used to rising early to gather eggs and feed chickens. School gave her an excuse to skip chores. After the days grew shorter and the weather turned cool, fall arrived and with it, dance season.

Early in October, Bessie announced that school would end early on Friday to give the students' time to get ready for the dance. When the four o'clock bell rang, signaling the day was over, three older boys sauntered home together, Eb, Emmitt and Roy.

Eb kicked a can down the road and declared, "I'm done with schoolin'. I wanna go huntin'."

"I don't need no book learnin'," Roy gave the can another kick "I'm tired of gittin' up so danged early. They's days I just wanna sleep all day."

"Huh, like your Mom would let you do that," Em said, giving the can another kick.

Emmitt poked Roy in the ribs. "You sleep in Miss Bessie's class, she'll beat you with a switch."

"I don't like them gol-durned switches. Daddy loves to lay it on me. Hurts like hell."

Eb looked amused. "Boys, we need to do something. I gotta plan we can scare this teacher off just like we did the last one with that cute little rattlesnake. Then, they'll just shut the school down. Here's what we're gonna do."

Roy and Emmitt huddled around Eb to hear his plan.

"After the dance, Roy and I are gonna put on bed sheets and jump out in front of her horse as she's leavin'. She'll think we're ghosts and git real scared."

Roy thought for a moment. "What if she thinks were robbers and tries to shoot us?"

Eb answered, "Emmitt will hide behind a tree. He'll rope her from behind so she can't draw her pistol. We'll tie her to a tree and leave her there all night. She'll leave town whenever she gets free."

The night of the dance, the boys met on the road outside town. Eb threw a sack of sheets and rope behind some bushes.

"That oughta hide 'em for now, let's git to the dance. Don't say nuthin' about this to no one."

The boys displayed their best behavior. Everyone was having fun dancing to the music of the local fiddler, Jake Mattox.

Rebecca and her parents escorted Bessie to the dance. Rebecca thought Bessie looked pretty in her red and white gingham dress.

When the hour got late, Rebecca's parents took her home on the family wagon. Bessie stayed behind to dance with Chester Williams, the town's handsome blacksmith.

Back at the dance, Eb tipped his hat and said goodnight to Bessie. That was his signal for them to setup the ambush.

The boys walked down the road and hid their horses. They found the sack holding the sheets and rope. Emmitt tied his rope around the trunk of a tree while Eb and Roy donned their sheets.

Eb slipped behind a large oak.

"Hey Eb, where are you?" Roy whispered.

No answer.

Roy walked by the oak. Eb jumped out from behind the tree waving his hands and yelled, "Boo."

Roy screamed and jumped back. He tripped over a tree limb and fell to the ground.

"Ha, ha, scared you good, you chicken! Hey Emmitt, didja see that? I just scared a ghost."

"Shut up, Eb."

"Ya'll be quiet!"

The clip-clop of hooves was heard up the road.

"That must be her, git ready boys," Eb said "and don't make no more noise." The leaves rustled as the boys slithered behind the trees.

Bessie's horse kept a steady gait. When she passed Emmitt's hiding spot, Eb and Roy jumped in front of the horse, blocking her path.

"*Boooooo*," Eb moaned. "*Wooooooo*," Roy groaned.

Emmitt snuck up behind the unsuspecting rider.

"I ain't afraid of ghosts." Bessie reached for the pistol that she tied to the saddle horn.

While Bessie wasn't afraid of ghosts, her horse was. It reared up as Emmitt threw the rope. The rope landed around Bessie's neck instead of her body.

The rope went taut around Bessie's neck. She gasped for air as she desperately clawed at her throat. The horse bolted, snagging Eb's sheet. The force separated Bessie's head from her body. The bodiless head landed in front of Roy, who fainted when he saw it. Eb looked directly into Bessie's lifeless eyes and ran into the forest, screaming hysterically. The rest of the body stayed on the galloping horse as it faded into the night.

Rebecca scraped her soles on the boards of the wooden dance floor. "Can we go now? I don't feel much like dancing."

Buck nodded.

"I miss Bessie," Rebecca said as they walked down the creaky steps of town hall. "It's been a whole year and nobody knows what happened."

"Fetch the horses, darlin'."

Rebecca led the horses back to Buck as he said goodbye to his friends.

They rode slowly down the trail.

"Can we ride faster? This is where they found her head."

"Stay behind me. The bluff is straight ahead."

Rebecca nudged her mare to quicken its pace.

"Did you hear that?" Buck asked.

"Someone is riding up behind us," Rebecca replied.

"They're riding fast, better get off the trail and let 'em by."

Buck led his horse into a small clearing, Rebecca followed.

The sound of a galloping horse grew louder.

"Only a damn fool rides a horse fast at night. Wonder who it is?"

A rider dressed in red and white flew by.

"Watch out for the bluff," Buck yelled.

The horse and rider vanished at its edge.

"Tha-tha-that was Miss Bessie. I seen that dress before," Rebecca cried. "She's a ghost and still ridin' her horse."

"I don't believe in ghosts. Besides, no ghost horse makes a galloping sound like that."

"Oh, I don't know. I wanna go home. *Now!*"

They rode back to the ranch house where Buck told his wife, "I think somebody rode over the bluff tonight. I'll check at first light."

The next morning, Rebecca watched Buck knot a long rope and tie it to his saddle.

"Papa, I'm coming with you."

Buck didn't argue.

When they reached the bluff, Buck tied one end of the rope to a large oak. He disappeared over the edge. Rebecca heard his boots scrape the rocks as he climbed down.

150   Ghosts

Faded red and white material dangled from a tree branch. *Bessie's dress.* His neck hairs bristled.

At the bottom, he eyed a gruesome sight. The skeletal remains of a horse stared at him from the mouth of a small cave. Its two front legs were stretched forward, as if trying to climb out of the hole. Below were the remains of Bessie, still wearing her red and white dress.

Buck shivered when he recalled the ghostly rider from the night before. He fell to the ground trembling and tried not to panic.

Once Buck regained his senses, he noticed that a dirty old sheet was partially wrapped around the horse's bridle. *Wonder where that came from?*

Buck reached down and freed it with a slash from his knife. Upon further inspection, Buck found the name "Erikson" scrawled faintly on its edge.

Erikson? This belongs to Ebenezer Erikson. Wherever Eb is, Roy and Emmitt are usually close by. Those rotten scoundrels!

Buck threw the sheet to the ground. He would've bet his ranch that Eb and his friends were behind the death of Bessie Rogers.

About Tom Dowling

Tom grew up in the west Texas town of Kermit. He attended Texas State University where he acquired a bachelor's degree in business administration. He moved to Houston in 1981 and has lived there ever since working in a variety of IT positions – project manager, business analyst, developer, technical writer and trainer.

Tom has been married to his lovely wife, Helen, for 24 years. They have two boys in college and a girl in high school. One of his sons is active in the Marine Reserves.

As an avid baseball fan, Tom coached youth baseball for 12+ years and has a wealth of experience to draw upon for his stories about youth baseball. His first novel about baseball is *DaddyBall: One Crazy Season*, about Little League baseball from a ten-year-old player's point of view. He is currently working on the follow-up novel titled *DaddyBall: The Select Team*, about a player's experience on a tournament team of eleven-year-olds. His plans are to write a trilogy of novels about Little League and youth baseball teams.

My Francine
by
Shawn Caldwell

In 1967, "The Great Midwestern Blizzard" slammed my hometown of Gary, Indiana, dumping twenty four inches of snow and creating drifts as high as fifteen feet, but my true terror arrived during the devious calm after the storm. My memories of these incidents are both strange and vivid.

I slouched on our over-stuffed couch, alongside my dad and watched the weather report. The meteorologists harped on about the storms approach as it elbowed its way across the Northeast coast, its hard gut blowing snow and ice, leaving toppled businesses and glassless windows in its wake.

The day after the storm, my mother stood at the kitchen sink and hummed *Blessed Assurance*. I'm sure she was glad the storm hadn't blown our small wooden home off the frame and into our neighbor's yard. She glared at me and Francine, dubiously, mulling our request to get out of the house. At age five, Francine used those big, sad puppy dog eyes. I danced back and forth impatiently, filled with all the pre-teen angst one might expect.

"Come on, mom . . . just one hour!" I pleaded.

She wiped off one of the plastic plates we'd eaten on for dinner, carefully slid it into the wired frame dish rack and dried her hands on her apron. The reflection of the sun bounced off the white carpet of snow and beamed brightly against her soft auburn skin.

Mom loved to toy with us when we wanted something badly, often going long periods without giving an answer. Her "stubborn" gene, as daddy would say, coming out.

"Go on," she said, reluctantly, glancing at us and wrinkling her nose as if she didn't want to say it. She faced toward the sink and I thought I saw a hint of a smile grow over her face.

We cheered and showered her with kisses, hugs and thanks. It's funny how irony works. We were bursting to get out of the house—feeling cooped-up and in some cases (for me anyway) claustrophobic—sure the four walls of our small home were closing in on us.

Excited! I pulled on my red puff jacket and black corduroy pants. Francine threw on her blue-green parka, a red and blue balaclava and a pair of cotton knit gloves. I had a stupid balaclava, too. But as soon as I stepped outside, I took the damn thing off and stuffed it in my jacket pocket.

"Ooooh! Um, gonna tell momma!" Francine yelled, gaping at me through the eye-circles of her hat, white smoke danced from her pie-hole.

"I'm not wearing that stupid hat. Tell if you want." Francine did a one eighty in the snow, better to throw her voice with.

"Momma—!" She bayed at the top of her lungs and stopped when I placed one finger over my mouth.

"It's been plenty of times I could've told on you and didn't," I said, eyebrows arched in a gesture that felt like they could've froze like that. The breeze off Lake Michigan sliced hard—some days, downright hateful.

She looked at me, crossed both arms and rocked her narrow hip to one side. I tried to think of a way out of this.

"Last week, when you snuck down stairs in the middle of the night and ate the oatmeal cookies," I said.

"That was you!" she countered.

She was right. I guessed that happens when you collect as much dirt as we had, you can't remember who did what.

I sighed.

"I'll let you have the last orange cupcake," I piped. "It's in the cupboard. Keep your mouth shut, and it's yours."

She glanced at me for a moment eyes narrowed and then cupped her gloved hands over her mouth preparing to be a pain.

"Momma!"

I leered at her and thought about popping her with a snowball to shut her up, but I decided against it. I knew how that would play in the Oscar Haynes Sr., family court.

"Let's play kickball!" Her favorite game, particularly in the snow "I'll get the soccer ball off the porch. And then we'll build the biggest snowman on East 43rd street, okay? Just don't tell momma about the hat."

Francine's eyes grew wide and she shook her head adamantly. I'll never forget the little footsteps she made in the snow—those steps were so light, one small dusting would have covered them completely. I grabbed the old checkered soccer ball from the porch and we marched deep into the hard-packed snow that dressed our yard, totally unaware our lives were about to change.

A quarter into the game, I accidentally kicked the ball over the fence and into the street. Earlier, snowplows had rumbled through and cleared the ribbon of white snow from the streets, but large mounds of slushed ice still sloped on both sides.

"I got it Oscar!" Francine yelled and the first hint of nausea churned in my stomach.

"Francine . . . wait!"

She sauntered through the gate and high-stepped over the embankment—the strings on her parka swinging, her little steps barely making indentations in the thick snow, her young innocent eyes focused on the ball, the ball . . .

I watched helplessly, as the snot-green Chevy Impala's brakes squealed and the rubber tires broke, grasping for traction as it swerved. The car's inertia carried its hulking frame directly toward her. She raised one arm, one last futile defensive pose.

In the split second that felt like hours, but was mere seconds, I saw my sister hit and tossed several feet in the air, landing in a thick patch of snow. I felt paralyzed and my mind shut down, only allowing a sort of surreal perspective.

Just past the spot where Francine landed, I saw another Francine, except this one looked sketched or oddly transparent. She wore the same clothes: the blue-green parka, the balaclava, and the knit gloves. Her body glimmered and faded in and out. She gaped at her arms, appearing as shocked as I was. She tried to scream and her mouth creaked open, unhinged, but no sound came out. She reached for me and oily-black tears leaked from her eyes.

My body quaked from the sight. Death stared directly at me and I couldn't move.

I glanced down and saw the real Francine lying twisted, awkwardly in the snow bank—no faded images, no sketchy transparencies, no black tears.

Trickles of red branched down her forehead and dripped from the corner of her mouth, staining the snow with a crimson hue. My throat went dry and my heart thumped in my chest.

I shook my head to clear my thoughts and peered up. Transparent Francine was gone and my baby sister, my only sister, lay on the ground motionless.

The feeling returned in my legs and I stumbled toward her, tears welling in my eyes, a prisoner to that window of my mind. A truly bizarre experience, but it wasn't until the funeral that I realized, bizarre was only the beginning.

My grandmother, Madea, straightened my tie and gave me the once over before we walked into the funeral service. She kissed me on the cheek and whispered, "You got to be strong, hear?" She tilted her head in that shy way custom with most of the women in our family. Her warm brown eyes sparkled in the dim lights in the church foyer.

"You've grown to be so handsome, Oscar Jr." Madea told me and smiled, wanly. "Come on, we'll do this together." We joined my parents who waited by the doors to the sanctuary.

Inside, the choir a mixture of members from Greater New Salem, Hope Mission and Calvary Baptist church sang, "I will trust in the Lord."

Our older cousin, Henry, a senior and star basketball player at Marquette delivered the eulogy. Before the service he told me it was his first eulogy, and then he told me I'd better not laugh if he got too nervous and tripped at the pulpit. I forced a smiled and appreciated his attempt to make me feel better, even if it was brief.

Revered Minor stepped forward and gave the sermon. The congregation, which spilled into the walkways, nodded and said "amen" in all the right places. Cries for mercy and rants for deliverance echoed the hall.

While Reverend Minor spoke, I got flashbacks of that awful day. I went into these blurry dreams which began with me standing in our yard after the snow storm. Francine stood in front of me, but she never looked at me, she only gazed at the black and white soccer ball rolling along in the snow — the damn ball seemed more and more like the soccer ball from hell, calling her toward the dangerous street. "Come on, little Francine, follow me..." It said in a voice reminiscent of Penny-Wise the clown, baiting her with a fist full of colorful balloons. I relived the whole situation each time more helpless than before.

"I got it Oscar," Francine yelled and trudged through the wrought iron gate and into the mud and ice slushed street.

"Francine, wait . . ." I tried to caution but was relegated to watching the disaster unfold, helpless.

A small nudge in my side broke me from my trance. I was completely unaware that I was still in the church. My dad looked at me incredulously. He leaned over and whispered, "Were you going to sleep?"

I shook my head.

Reverend Minor's truculent voice thundered through the walls of the church as he quoted another bible verse, "No weapons formed against us shall prosper!" His moisturized S curl was brushed back behind his ears and down his neck. The sanctuary lights gleamed on his forehead. "You see, to some of us God took our baby girl Francine home a little too early. But who are we to judge?"

The time came to view the body. Immediate family, of course, sat on the first pew and were first to go. I held hands with momma and daddy—Aunt Evelyn and Uncle Joe came up to the casket, too. Aunt Evelyn wore her signature black hat with jutting peacock feathers and Uncle Joe adorned his black suit and red tie, his narrow face and small eyes looked pale under the low lights. Undoubtedly, Uncle Joe had delighted in a few spirits of his own.

I saw Francine's body. I think it's important I repeat this: My baby sister's dead body did lie in the casket. Her face was colorless, and she wore a faded shade of pink lipstick (probably my mom's last minute idea, my daddy would've never allowed it) and even in death, perhaps, now more pronounced, high cheekbones accentuated her face.

We gaped into the open casket and I was startled by mom's horrified shrieks—realization kicked in and she understood Francine was gone, a cold shell in this frail wooden coffin. Never again would she bark about me hogging all the Chips or laugh when I stuck two straws up my nose and made ridiculous faces while I chased her around the house.

Tears streamed down my face. The screaming and shrieks gave me a sickened feeling in the pit of my stomach, that same feeling when you're on a roller coaster and it takes a sudden, hard dip.

I took a deep breath and when I breathed out a white mist issued from my mouth. I glanced around to see if anyone saw it—they hadn't. But the atmospheric change wasn't the biggest thing. I heard a low, familiar giggling sound emanate from the casket.

If it had only been the white mist floating from my mouth or only the giggling sound from the casket, I would've dismissed the whole thing—my wildly and admittedly warped imagination consuming me.

I stepped away from Francine's casket, shaken. Uncle Joe was the first to notice my knee-jerk reaction and he placed his hand gently on my back.

"You okay, kiddo?" He asked, in an outside voice that drew a few glances. And I was suddenly assaulted by a mixture of Uncle Joe's cheap cologne and a hint of Wild Irish Rose. I envisioned Uncle Joe leaning over the counter and telling the cashier "Gimmie a pint of Rosie with a skirt."

I didn't answer him, not at first, anyway. There were other factors needing to be considered. Like what the heck was happening? My lips were dry and cracked. I breathed out again and this time I saw no white air.

I turned and nodded to Uncle Joe, informing him everything was all right. Of course, this was a lie because something definitely was not all right. My parents took notice and gaped at me with a sort of concerned curiosity. Both their faces looked hard and worn, as if, they had aged ten years over the last week.

In the background, the choir hummed a low version of my mom's favorite song, "Blessed Assurance". Several sobs and prayers were murmured among the mourners.

My dad stepped closer and put his arm around me.

"You okay?" He asked me, almost echoing Uncle Joe. I felt a small flash of anger come over me, or maybe it was angst. I wasn't sure. But why is it people always ask you if you're okay at funerals? It's the most stupid thing you could ask family members at a funeral.

"Are you Okay?" I don't know dad—Francine's dead, let me think on it—no, I'm not okay! Now just what in the hell are you going to do about it? She's dead, for Crissake! I thought this, but didn't say.

I pulled away from him, stepped back toward the casket and bent over to kiss Francine on the forehead.

My lips touched skin as warm as Madea's homemade rolls. And, again, there was the soft giggle in my ear and as I stood within inches of her face, I saw Francine's high cheekbones move, her eyes opened and she winked.

I sprang away from the casket.

"Did you see that?" I yelled, unable to control myself. I turned to my dad, who regarded me with a slightly embarrassed gaze. His eyes were low and against the backdrop of the dim church light his lids resembled shiny pennies.

"She's alive. Did you see it daddy? Francine winked at me."

My mom's sobs slowed and she glanced at me with vein pulsing red eyes. Both their faces, mom's and dad's, were moving from sadness, to questioning and then to traced mixtures of anger and resentment.

"What?" Dad croaked. He regarded me with a look which suggested that *this better be good—damn good.*

"Francine, she winked," I said, sincerely and then turned toward the casket. Francine's face was motionless and grey. I bent over and touched my lips to her forehead, again. This time it felt like a thick plastic strip strewn over a block of ice. I frowned, confused.

The music had stopped and the organist craned his neck and peered into Francine's casket, trying to see what was going on. The choir was no longer humming and they were gaping at me curiously. Most of the congregation stared blankly, some sat up in their seats and tried to see what was going on while others, who heard me clearly shout "She's Alive!" covered their mouths and whispered to their neighbors.

"Oscar, Lets go," dad insisted. His tone wasn't happiness. He grabbed me firmly around the shoulders and he and my mother ushered me outside.

Dad closed the church doors behind us. Arms crossed, they both glared at me with that stern expression parents give after a bad report card, or a broken vase, or after you've been caught rifling through your dad's adult movie stash. No words were spoken, but I knew I'd better start talking.

"Francine . . . her forehead was warm the first time I kissed it. She felt alive," I added, miserably.

"Oscar," my mom said and stepped toward me. Dismay and concern branded on her face. "She's gone, hon." She placed the back of her hand against my forehead to check my temperature. Relieved that there was no fever, she tilted her head and under the veil of her black hat, I saw remnants of desperation and melancholy in her eyes.

"Oscar, we all loved Francine, but you can't say stuff like that during a funeral. You'll freak everybody out," dad said, his voice rose.

"But I—"

My mother whirled on him, with a look of deep resentment etched in her face. "He wasn't trying to freak everybody out, Oscar! He's going through this just like we are." The dark grey clouds in the sky drew closer, and a soft dust of snow blew against the montaged church windows.

"I know that Evelyn? But to yell 'She's Alive' in the sanctuary." There were only two times my mother and father called each other by first names: when they were angry, or on the other side of the bedroom door, during sex.

"She's his sister just like she's your daughter. Maybe this whole situation has been a bit much," My mother hissed. Irritation had crawled into her voice.

"Evelyn, I don't need you to remind me she's my daughter. I know she's my daughter! And don't try to make this *my* fault."

"Oh, so it's mine?" my mom waged and pointed to herself. She shook her head and gazed at the parking lot. The lot was full with cars. Most wheels were nestled in fresh snow that had fallen while we were inside. A soft breeze brushed several windshields with powdery snow.

She offered a sour chuckle, but there was no humor in it. My father glared at her with a mixture of contempt and hurt. He licked his lips as the December wind flapped his pants against his leg.

"You think this is my fault?" She asked him softly and tears gleamed in her eyes.

"I didn't say that."

"You didn't have to. It's all over your face," she told him. She tightened her coat around her waist and went inside.

"Evelyn—", he called to her, but it was too late.

The next week dad went back to work at Indiana Steel, deciding happily to cut his two week bereavement short. Which I thought was good; he and my mother seemed they would soon kill each other if he moped around the house one more day. She was doing enough moping for both of them.

Most days mom sat in the dining room, spiking her coffee with Jack Daniels, ogling the window which gave a terrific 3-D view into our yard. How often had she run through her mind the awful day when we lost Francine, thinking perhaps, if she could just wind back the clock and change the events? I was sure she was beating herself up and wondering if she had kept a closer eye on us would the results have been different? Could she have done something?

Over the next several weeks, mom and dad fought regularly, each time seeming more aggressive than the last. And then on that day, the realization that someone could get hurt washed over me like a cold shower. They slammed doors and screamed and shouted at the top of their lungs. The last fight was the worst.

"I really don't care what you do, just stay out of my face," mom screeched.

"Don't worry!" My dad assured her. His speech was slurred. "Drink yourself to death . . . go on, you'll be right there with her." He was a fine one to talk about drinking yourself to death. He staggered a bit as he waved the bottle of Irish whiskey in the air. "Then, what you gonna do about the boy?"

"What am I gonna do?" My mother roared from the other room, from which she had barricaded herself in. "It's always all on my shoulders, isn't it Oscar? What am I gonna do? Not we . . . but me! Her voice was shrieking and dismal. My knees went numb.

"Open this door, Evelyn."

"I don't want to see you right now," Mom said.

"I didn't ask you what you wanted to see. I said open the goddamn door," my dad insisted in that low controlled voice—a little too controlled.

After a few moments, he took a step back and kicked the door with one rubber-soled boot. It sent the door crashing open, ripping the lock from its hold and sending splinters of coarse wood and shrapnel flying through the air.

The door slammed against the opposite wall of the room. My mom screamed. I crouched down behind the sofa, heart thudding, wanting the fighting to stop—hoping it would all just go away.

I heard glass breaking and pictured my parent's bedside lamp, a porcelain structure decorated with a big pink flamingo, toppling over and shattering into a thousand pieces. Then I heard arguing and skirmishing.

They appeared at the bedrooms doorway—panting, sweating and glaring at each other with a disgust I'd never seen. My dad still held the bottle of Irish whiskey in one clutched hand, my mom's arm in the other.

"Let me go, Oscar," she said, breathless, and with one last burst of energy, she yanked her arm free and knocked the bottle of whiskey from his hand. The bottle sailed across the room and smashed against the wall, spilling its contents.

My dad stared at the shattered bottle, as if he'd lost a best friend and then glowered at mom. His chest heaved, and sweat glazed over his twisted face. His eyes danced with fire. He raised one hand and slapped my mom across the face.

The sound carried across the room like thunderclap and for a moment I felt life flash over me. I saw the whole family standing in the middle of the living room on Christmas morning, laughing and talking, engaged in a game of twister.

"Left foot on green . . . left foot on green, Francie," my dad called to her. And then I flashed to our trip to the Grand Canyon—me and Francine smiling widely and gaping over the rail at the enormous phenomenon in the earth's crust. Dad laughed and pointed to the different landscapes, marveling at the canyon's depth. My mom refusing to look down, scared she'd get dizzy and fall in—and finally dad placing Francine on his shoulders so she could get a better view.

I flashed back to our living room and saw my mom place her hand over the spot where dad had slapped her. She regarded him behind horrified, disbelieving eyes. Never in their marriage had he raised his hand to her, inebriated or sober. Daddy looked back at her blinking stupidly like a man who wasn't sure where he was.

He reached for her. "Evelyn, I'm sor—"

Mom shook her head and pulled away.

She stormed across the room, grabbed me by the arm and led me toward the door. She stopped abruptly and turned toward daddy. He stood there hunched over, eyes red, floating in a sea of dismay.

She glared at him. And though neither said anything, neither of them acknowledged it, I think we all knew that this was it. The line in the sand that had been engraved so deep, particularly in the last several weeks, had been crossed. This was the end of the Haynes family as I knew it.

My mom was about to leave, with me in tow—but then, something strange happened. Something I think none of us would have ever guessed. In fact, if it were told to anybody else, they would've called us crazy and dismissed it. Or they would've said it was some sort of technical glitch in the things voice box.

The volume on the television grew.

On the screen, a man wearing a wide brim hat and a trench coat was talking to a lady. She was preparing to board a plane. Behind them, several planes took off into the distant blue sky. The wind blew and their clothes flapped against their lean bodies. As the volume continued to increase, the image on the screen began to shimmer and fry.

The man said "Please, please don't go!" And then like a mystifying, echoing, recording, the television repeated. "Please, please don't go!"

The volume rose louder and the scene played itself over and over again "Please, please don't go!" The trench coat hero begged.

I had turned the volume up on this television many days, many of them to drown out my babbling baby sister. So, I knew its limits. And the sound box on our old model Zenith TV was far more than exceeding it.

The sound elevated until it was almost unbearable. We held our ears, wondering what was happening.

"Please, please don't go!" The image on the screen shimmered and faded but repeated the phrase. Only now the voice was turning deeper, slower and more guttural.

"Puh-leeze, d o n ' t g o!"

And suddenly a gust of cold air blew through the house, whisking across the walls, knocking the old calendar from its warped, rusted nail and tossing the magazines on the coffee table across the floor. I looked around and noticed none of the doors or windows to the outside were open.

The trench coat man reached for the woman. "Please don't—"

Mom and dad both gaped around with shocked and bewildered eyes. Mom grabbed me with both hands and stared toward my dad, not sure what to make of it all.

"Oscar!" she screamed, her voice barely audible over the harsh wind gusts and the blaring television.

Dad broke from his trance and stumbled over to us, watching the magazines pages rifle in the cold air. Pictures, some of me in my checker board shirt and Francine in large floppy pigtails, smiling with a toothless grin, were knocked from their perch, leaving only ghostly impressions of faded squares and circles. We could've been standing in the middle of a small hurricane. Everything was loud.

"Let's get out of here," I heard my dad say, his voice faint and fading. We turned toward the front door and that's when the couch, which I crouched behind during the fight, began to rock.

The couch started to shake, tossing my mom's custom made pillows left and right. The four wooden legs of the couch rose from the floor, hovered there for a moment and then shot across the room like a rocket, slamming itself against the front door.

Ghosts 163

The chair on the other end of the room began to rock and then levitated and soared through the air, crashing against the kitchen entryway, blocking all chance of exit.

In my heart I knew what it was. Somewhere, perhaps, deeper inside, I think we all knew *who* it was. I can't say how we knew, because, perhaps, it's beyond any human understanding—it's all I got. The television, the wind gusts with no ventilation from the outside, the constant rants of the man on the television. "Please, please don't go!"

The wind calmed and I heard the soft click of the television dial turn, slow at first, but then fast. A rhythmic click, click, click…

My mom and dad's arms were around me. Something I hadn't felt in quite some time. In that embrace I felt love. I felt care. Inwardly I felt myself smile and I knew why. The idea, the cool mint of inspiration consumed me.

The television clicked back to the same program and the man held the lady by the arms and stared into her watery, blue eyes.

"Please, baby. Nothing's that bad. We live some, we lose some, but forever's in the heart." He reached up with one gloved hand and touched his chest. The scene was a bit overly dramatic and the thought made me grin. It was because that phrase had Francine Haynes written all over it.

The presence I hadn't felt since Francine's funeral suddenly covered me. She was here with us, and I was sure. I looked at my mom and dad and they both were horrified; speechless.

The television clicked again and the image on the screen turned to white snow. The sound went away. There was giggling. It was loud and clear. A familiar, unmistakable—giggle.

My dad called out, "Francine . . . Francine? Where are you baby?"

Mom and dad stared at each other, a little bewildered, not quite in horror. I felt my dad's grip tighten. And we stood there in a sort of ephemeral silence.

It was the giggle. The one I associated with Francine since she was a baby. The giggle—the one that five years ago had been the bane in my existence, the ringing in my ear, the nails, screeching horridly across the chalk board of my life—now I associated with joy.

"Francine." Her name escaped, my lips, softly.

I leaped from the seat, my heart pounding in my throat.

"You guy's heard it? It's like I told you at the funeral, she's here!"

Mom and dad peered at each other. They embraced—at first, hesitantly—then, fully.

Francine chuckled, but it wasn't spooky and ominous like you might expect from someone dead (though it is still difficult to think of her as dead)—because in that chuckle I felt delight and happiness. The sound, both cosmic and real, trailed farther and farther away, until we didn't hear it anymore.

"We love you, baby. All ways," Dad said, and he kissed my mom on the forehead. He looked at me and nodded and we sat there unable to articulate anything into words; and not really wanting to. We held each other and enjoyed the indelible memory of my babbling little tattletale, my sassy little co-conspirator, my loving baby sister—my Francine.

About Shawn Caldwell

Shawn Caldwell was born in Gary, Indiana, where he lived the first half of his childhood. When he turned ten, Shawn and his family moved to Morehouse Parish in northeast Louisiana. It was in the bayou state that he found much of the inspiration for his writing.

He received a Bachelor of Science degree in Criminal Justice from Grambling State University and was a retail investigator for nine years, traveling along the Gulf States from the Mississippi delta to Charlotte, North Carolina. He is working on a young adult/fantasy novel titled *Sheila—Quest for the Golden Sapphire*, which is the first book in a series. He also has a suspense/thriller titled *Grand Rouge* and a litany of short stories, whose settings shift between Indiana and Louisiana.

Shawn is married with three sons: Shawn Jr., Tyler and Lawrence and balances time between worship, working in the retail industry, family, and writing stories. He and his wife, Nishera, reside in a small town just outside Houston which they share with a blue-eyed pup named Shep. Shawn blogs several times a month at www.scauthor.wordpress.com.

A Silent Graveyard
by
Frank Carden

West and his grandparents drove from their farm to the Winters' Cemetery just before sundown. In it was buried their next-to-youngest boy WT. While playing cowboys and Indians, he had been killed accidentally by his twin brother AB with a shotgun, believed to be unloaded when he pulled it from a closet. It had been a terrible tragedy his mother had told him, one that still hurt, that no one talked about, especially no one talked about who might have left the gun loaded.

West's grandmother worked around the grave, pulling blooming yellow snakeweed from the sparse brown Bermuda grass covering the grave. On the headstone was WT Taber 1910-1922. WT was killed the year West's mother left home, the year before West was born. With the grave cleaned, his grandmother stood and fastened her eyes on him.

"You look just like WT," she said, stepping closer, her head down, and started crying, soundlessly, her shoulders trembling, but not bending.

West wanted to say something, could think of nothing, and doubted that it would do any good. She looked up, tears slid down across the deep dark lines that crossed her face, too much flat prairie sun, too much sorrow, too much life, and yet she stood straight and slim. She pressed her straight, unyielding lips, cool and wet with tears, across his. It was an unsettling terrible kiss physically, more so emotionally. He fought the urge to brush the back of his arm across his lips to wipe away the kiss, its meaning. It was about a boy who would never grow older than twelve, who would forever play and laugh as only a boy that age can. Yet at four in the morning when his grandmother woke in the darkness, it was about a boy buried in a casket. The kiss felt as though it came from there. Somewhere in that graveyard dug in that hot flat land there was a primordial evil, one that created that kiss, a ghost that lived in all the graves.

In the clinging semidarkness, it seemed that he and his grandmother were the only people alive on the earth. His granddad stood, unmoving, still as one of the grave markers, his hat in his hand, pain across his face, dark against the sky, unable to go to his wife, to offer her comfort. West placed his arm around her, not tightly either, just across her shoulders, lightly. It was the best he could do. At that moment though, he knew he loved her, both for being his grandmother, and for being a woman with a love inside for a son, but with a hurt there too, that she kept hidden, except for that moment when it tore loose, and maybe it was anger too. But she carried it all alone. With her head held straight and even, he had seen her sit and talk, but never smile, with those friends who came into Winters on Saturday. For all the emotions she hid on the inside, he loved her. He pressed her shoulder firmly against his until finally she turned to walk toward the car.

A slender solitary figure in a gray dress with blue flowers, she walked quietly as though not to disturb the silence. His grandmother blended in with the darkening evening of that raw flat treeless land, broken only by the headstones. His granddad took slow steps, watching her. Suddenly, West walked rapidly toward the car, with the feeling that the three had become intruders. That the evil being would envelop them too. In the car, he slid down in the back seat, closed his eyes and waited for the engine to start, for some sound he was familiar with. Some sound that would break the smoldering silence.

About Frank Carden

Frank Carden has published over thirty short stories in literary magazines such as *Serape,* an anthology of New Mexico Authors, *Writers Without Borders, Storyteller, Good Old Days, Sulphur River Literary Review* and in the *Rambler.* His stories were winners in the 2004 and 2008 South West Writer's contest and the 2011 North East Texas Writers' Organization National Short Story contest. His novel, *Love Affairs, WWII,* garnered first place in the Bay Area Writers League (Houston) National Novel contest with the first twenty pages being published in an anthology.

His debut novel, *The Prostitutes of Post Office Street,* published by Solbooks, won the Eric Hoffer Award in 2010. His second published novel is *Billy Bonney aka The Kid.*

As a youth, Carden spent time on a three-windmill ranch in West Texas and in the oil fields. He picked cotton, peas, and housed tobacco. He worked on a shrimper and a tug out of Galveston and spent three years in the submarine service. Carden received a PhD from Oklahoma State and is a professor at New Mexico State University.

A New Caretaker
by
Ginger Fisher

The ad stated simply "caretaker needed" with no explanations as to who or what needed the care to be proffered. It was sufficiently vague, sufficiently intriguing and her pocketbook sufficiently empty to pique Sicily's interest. When she called the contact number a woman's voice answered, sweet and politely dignified, the reedy tremors of old age only apparent when she laughed evasively at Sicily's barrage of questions, telling her kindly but firmly "when you arrive" before giving her quite succinctly the address and cutting the call.

The slight irritation raised by this was drowned completely though in the overwhelming tide of curiosity it aroused. The street name was nothing to her, and when she looked it up on the Internet, she was slightly confused. If she remembered correctly the main drag of that neighborhood was comprised of Mexican bakeries, taqueria, grocery, meat market and dilapidated maintenance garages with good quality work but the dubious reputation of selling inspection stickers at an inflated price for cars otherwise unable to pass before petering out into the small but neatly kept homes of their owners and customers. It was incongruous to the faded grandeur that lingered in the voice on the phone.

On the drive over Sicily found she wasn't mistaken in her assessment, but as she completed the final turn, she seemed to be entering an almost dreamlike pocket of nostalgia like the final vestiges of a previous civilization its remnants poking through the newer culture that has grown up around it. They were large houses, grand testimonials to southern architecture with balustrades and columns, but has become unkempt and crumbling once neatly tended gardens had been allowed to overgrow and oil based paint had cracked and was peeling in thin curling strips from outside walls. Part of the second story porch had collapsed next door to what looked suspiciously like a pre depression era build it yourself home kits like Sicily had seen in an antique Sears-Roebuck catalogue.

As she approached the end of the cul de sac, she still hadn't come across the number mentioned on the phone. It was the final house, it's porch swing dangling useless from its chains on the large gnarled branches of an ancient oak tree marking the boundary of a field large enough to put the back of the closest houses in a hazy confusion of perspective. A black cat, sleek but well fed, was resting on the arm, still suspended, glaring pointedly and imperviously at her as she pulled up.

The house appeared to be in better condition than its neighbor's. She noticed, as she appraised it, but still far from the mint condition of its glory days. It was two-story, painted yellow with red and white accents: a covered porch wrapped around two sides of the house, it's sloping roof supported by delicate columns and fenced in with a waist high slated railing. She walked gingerly up the wooden steps onto the porch, its' boards, slightly springy with age and its whitewashed wicker furniture weathered to grey. She opened a wood framed screen door and knocked after a decent interval it was opened by a painted and coiffured lady of advanced age.

Unlike some older woman who appeared garish with makeup, hers was understated the snow white and dove gray hair worn with assumedly antique combs in the style favored by WWII types. She smiled revealingly small teeth too white and too even to be anything but dentures. "I'm Mrs. Rothschild," she told Sicily as the ushered the younger woman inside.

Although obviously old, remarkably her face was sparsely lined and her voice and movements seemed to belong to a much younger woman. She invited Sicily for tea while they were to discuss the proposed job. Mrs. Rothschild, she never offered Sicily her first name, explained as she deftly heated the kettle and filled a diffuser with a chai tea leaves spooning two teaspoons of honey into bone china cups so delicate you could see light through the sides. She was long widowed; her children were grown with families of their own to worry about mostly in other states. All she really needed was someone to come in for a few hours a day to help her with the cooking and cleaning and maybe some light yard work as she really let the gardens become a mess. She really couldn't pay Sicily that much, a pittance really, although when the "paltry sum" amount was mentioned it was much more than Sicily expected.

Sicily warmed to Mrs. Rothschild immediately and agreed to start that afternoon. A large longhaired ginger cat settled on the old woman's lap purring like a lawnmower as Sicily cleaned the dishes from their tea and prepared a meal for them.

Sicily enjoyed cooking and was pleasantly surprised when she discovered that the appliances although they looked like they'd been new at the time the house was built, functioned quite modernly. She went home feeling quite pleased with her new employment. She didn't realize the full extent of what she was getting herself into until the next day. It wasn't her employer that was the problem. Mrs. Rothschild wasn't particularly choosy about the manner in which Sicily conducted the tasks she set. In fact she continued to be extremely courteous and thoughtful towards Sicily, helping out where she could, although after the first day it was apparent how the house had fallen into such disrepair for despite her apparent youthfulness.

There were a growing number of chores Mrs. Rothschild was unable to complete. No, it was something about the house itself, some intrinsic wrongness she couldn't exactly pinpoint. For starters, due to some trick of the hand blown glass windows which like all glass had begun to warp and drip in that barely perceptible manner over the years, the light in the house was always the thick, syrupy yellow of early afternoon in the summertime whether it was high noon on a sunny day or pouring down rain. The exterior and interior of the house were impossible to reconcile for from outside it appeared to be a very normal two story, but once inside you found a spiral staircase in a central wall that spanned four stories that didn't even include the short steep flight of stairs straight down to the sub caller.

Each room led to every other room by at least two connecting doors. Even the bathrooms had two exits. On her second day of work, Sicily lost her way for more than an hour in the labyrinth of rooms of the second floor. When one of the doors flew shut, try as she might, she couldn't retrace her footsteps, actually emerging on the opposite side of the stairwell hanging than she'd originally started. Another of the house's numerous mysteries was the matter of the cats. There seemed to be in every one of the numerous rooms one, and only feline attendant.

No two cats were alike. There were longhaired and shorthaired cats, Siamese, Himalayan, Persian and missed breeds from no obvious country. Some were haughty, some affectionate as dogs, wrapping themselves around Sicily's ankles making it difficult to tidy up, and some just gazed at her, watching with that piercingly intense quintessentially feline stare that implied knowledge of the inner secret workings of the universe that no price could be enticing enough to share. They seemed chained to their chosen territories. She no much as once ever saw a cat leave its room or two cats in the same room.

Over time Sicily learned to navigate the corridor less passages of the rooms based on the progression of cats. It was more reliable than position of

Ghosts 173

the sun, which through the trick of the glass could appear to pour through an eastern facing window at four in the afternoon or the furniture, which while arranged differently in every room, had an almost standardized antique and proper appearance which blurred it in the mind. She stopped counting rooms because sometimes there seemed as few as twenty, sometimes as many as forty five.

The eeriest thing about the cats was despite their proliferation, they seemed to exist outside the natural scheme, like they'd transcended material needs for although Sicily bought groceries for Mrs. Rothschild, she not so much purchased a single kibble. And despite the fact she'd never come across, or much less emptied a litter box, the pervasive ammonia smell normally associated with such a multitude of cats was absent. Instead the rooms were inundated with the mushily sweet smell of bouquets long wilted to potpourri and, of course the slightly chemical but organic smell, almost like a bruised new leaf, of the cats themselves.

Despite its oddness, Sicily grew to enjoy her new job. The small domestic chores weren't' taxing. The pay was good and her employer was a genuinely good person. In a short time she grew to care about the older woman in her floral print dresses with pearlescent buttons and neatly starched white linen or lace collars even on her bad days discreetly made up with her hair carefully fixed like a grandmother or great aunt. On good days, Mrs. Rothschild would regale her with gossip and tales of debutant balls from fifty years prior and Sicily would listen indulgently fascinated. On her bad days, when all the youthfulness was gone from her step, her skin almost translucent in its whiteness, it was obvious why she'd placed the ad that had made their acquaintance. Sicily would tuck her in her second story bed. There were two floors up and one down from the ground floor so in fact it was the second level and Sicily would find tasks in the vicinity so she wouldn't be out of earshot. When Sicily asked her what the matter was, Mrs. Rothschild told her nonchalantly "I'm old if you can believe it. Most days I try to deny it, but sometimes these fugues of old age won't let you ignore them.

After a few months Sicily realized that although she had been in the garden and dusted and organized every room in that deceptive and rambling house, Mrs. Rothschild had never asked her to go down to the cellar and clean it out. Surely a cellar like her own grandmother's attic would be a repository for the detritus that collects over the passage of time. When she asked her employer about it, Mrs. Rothschild told her it would be unnecessary because she couldn't go down there. The shock and disbelief on Sicily's face, she'd never been forbidden to go anywhere in the house or grounds before, were so evident Mrs. Rothschild laughed and hastily amended. "It's not just you who can't go down there, no one can because it's physically impossible. Although five years ago, you remember that horrible flood we had, don't you, when it didn't stop raining for a week straight? Well during the storm and subsequent flood part of the ceiling collapse down they're blocking the descent of the stairs. The foundation of the house shifted from it and while the contractor said it appeared to be stabilized now, that might not be the case if we went around messing about and clearing the cellar out of debris. So I decided to let it be.

On the surface the story seemed plausible. Why would an old woman spend extra money to clear out a room she didn't need which may or may not cause more damage to her house. But there was something amiss down there. Sicily could feel it.

Over the course of her employment, Sicily felt fairly confident. She'd gotten to know Mrs. Rothschild well, and there was some nuance, even deception, in her manner that belied the nonchalance and superficial plausibility of her story. Now a locked door that one cannot pass through is much more psychologically stimulating and irksome than a locked door that one has the key to. So Sicily inflamed by curiosity, spent the next few months searching for a way through the sealed off cellar door. At first she tried every key on the rings she could find, but that seemed too simple and likewise, unfortunately, nothing came to fruition from it.

She searched through drawers, scrubbed behind every portrait hoping to uncover secret hiding places and though she went through their contents but did not find the object of her search. She cleaned and scoured rooms she'd never even seen before, but all to no avail. The mystery of the cellar door remained stubbornly locked. At last her fervent ardor for the search faded to an almost petulant scrabbling around when she discovered some new niche that seemed a prospective hiding place. Finally when even the tops of every door and every inch of the decorative crown molding in the house was spotless from her efforts, she decided to abandon the search. Although she doubted the veracity of her employer's story still, she had a grudging respect for her ability to keep its secret. Things started to go back to, if not normal, than business as usual in the yellow house as the cellar faded from the forefront of Sicily's mind.

Ghosts 175

One morning right as day was breaking Sicily woke up filled with an unnatural anxiety, almost a sense of foreboding. Although she normally didn't go into work until 10 am and it couldn't have been much past five, she had an overwhelming desire to go and check on the big house. She tossed and turned restlessly in her bed, as unable to find sleep again as she had the cellar key. Finally she couldn't deny her instincts any longer. She rose and made ready to go to work.

The sun was barely over the horizon when she turned on Mrs. Rothschild's street. The fiery display or muted oranges pinks purples and blues that comprised the sunrise bleached the colors out of the street making it appear more dilapidated and run down than ever although still filled with a majestic mysterious beauty. A slight fog that drifted over the field beyond Mrs. Rothschild's oak tree with it's now mended swing made them seem isolated, cut off from the rest of the world. It seemed that the cul de sac, as insubstantial as it appeared in the dawn, was truly the only thing in existence that moment.

Sicily knew something was wrong the moment she crunched her car into the driveway, but it took her a second glance to pinpoint it. The black cat that acted as a sentry for the front of the house, with its ruffed fur and smoky gray eyes was nowhere in sight. For the entire year's span she'd worked for Mrs. Rothschild, the black cat had never gone farther from the porch than the tree swing. Its absence was an ominous combination with her mounting anxiety. She fumbled with the front door key, but when she bent down to retrieve it, the door swung open at her touch. She entered and was meet with the most confusing and blood chilling sight so far. As if led by the tune of the pied piper, a line of cats streamed out of every room, descending the spiral stair.

Sicily fell in step behind them. Once she'd reached the first floor, she was now unsurprised to see where the destination of the line of cats led. The door leading to the cellar was wide open and the lithe little bodies of the cats descended into the abyss gracefully. Sicily mincingly followed the last of the stragglers into the unknown depths. The steps were poorly lit, poorly maintained, and she had to clutch the wall to avoid tripping over the cats. A soft glow radiated from the bottom as if the room below were lit by lamplight or torchlight, something for softer and stranger than the harsh illumination of electricity.

When she reached the bottom, it seemed an eternity even though it was actually quite a short flight of stairs. She couldn't see what provided the lighting but it danced and flickered in the warm sensuously alive manner that only flame can manage. Of course, that only occupied her mind briefly for the specter had far stranger features. Cats filled the room, on the floor, and on the tables that lined three of the walls.

From her vantage point at the foot of the stairs she could see that they all faced the central decoration of a vast space, an elaborate sepulture on with rested the remains of a woman's corpse, judging by the tattered gown adorning the bones and long hair clinging resolutely to the skull. Suddenly every hair on her body stood on end. It became very hard to breathe in that damp tomb under the ground. Something more or less than a sound throbbed in her very bones. It seemed to be emitting from the intense focus of the cats on that center platform of the dead. A globule of light congealed on top of the sepulture. It flattened out, assuming human proportions when it rose up through the pile of decaying bones sitting superimposed on them until it daintily dismounted. It was the figure of Mrs. Rothschild. A little paler, a little more haggard, almost translucent in places, but surely this was the Mrs. Rothschild she'd always known. Terror and a morbid curiosity rooted Sicily to the spot. She didn't even notice that the throbbing almost electrical vibration from the cats had stopped. The specter of Mrs. Rothschild spoke, "We were hoping you'd find your way down here soon, you know. Don't think for a moment we didn't notice your search for the key. Unfortunately the cats are only able to open it at certain times of the day."

"The cats?" Sicily managed to croak through a throat rusted shut with fear and surprise. "

"Yes, the cats. I told you one was very old. I was old when I died and I've been dead a very long time. You see this house, this street and of course myself, don't exist anymore, but the cats like it, so they keep it intact. And sometimes because of that it gets very hard for the cats to summon my company. It gets harder all the time. Despite their aloof façade, they really crave companionship, which is why we placed that ad."

Sicily was too shocked, too numb by the impassivity, the absurdity this had brought into her once sane world to do more than stutter, "The ad?"

"Yes, my dear." said the phantasm that was once very long ago called Mrs. Rothschild. "The newspaper ad you answered. You see we had to try out the prospects. And I must admit it was a rather good idea. The first two didn't work out at all. The cats didn't particularly like them, and to be honest, neither did I. They had to be…dismissed"

Ghosts 177

The way she said it, as if more than a pink slip was involved, brought chills to Sicily's spine.

"But try again they say. And now the ad brought you to us. I do admit that I'm going to miss all this, but I'm sure I'm leaving it in more than capable hands"

Sicily could barely form a coherent though. "But I mean what…what if I don't want to stay and care for the house and the cats forever?"

"You don't love us?" Mrs. Rothschild asked. "You don't feel the bond with the house, the cats? All that searching, and now that you've found what you're asking for —don't balk at it."

"Apparently, I do," Sicily admitted inexplicably, unable to lie to the audience of staring silted eyes.

"Well, that's good because you did answer the ad after all."

The apparition said it so sweetly and compassionately that Sicily almost couldn't believe how underlying ominous the implied threat inherent in these words sounded. She hesitated a heartbeat while the cats converged at the feet of the phantasm Mrs. Rothschild, but her flight reaction kicked in over whatever spell they were spinning around her, and Sicily bolted up the stairs the way she'd come. However, when she reached the top landing, no amount of sobbing or pounding would make the cellar door unlock.

The first cat to reach her had been a particular favorite of hers, a small fluffy tortoiseshell Tabby. The little creature let out a liquid burbling mew and started turning itself around Sicily's ankle. What had been so warm and comforting the day before was suddenly as loathsome as the touch of a viper, but she didn't have the heart to kick it away despite everything. More cats reached her the padding of their silent paws on the stairs suddenly murderously loud. She sunk to her knees amongst them; fear and desperation overwhelming her as her heart tried to both speed up and slow down simultaneously. The last thing she heard before it all went black was the decayed grandeur of Mrs. Rothschild's voice, still delicate and as sweet as lead paint."Welcome home, child."

Secret Playroom
by
Karen Alterisio Nelson

Janie walked in the kitchen carrying a cardboard box full of plastic storage bowls and set it on the table. Putting her hands on her hips, she looked around at the cluttered room, overwhelmed with the arduous task ahead of her.

"Janie?" her husband Rob called out from the front hall.

"In here"

He appeared in the doorway holding the barbells to the home gym. "Where do you want this set up?"

"In the bedroom at the end of the hallway." She pushed her brown bangs back off her forehead.

"I thought that was my office."

"No you wanted to use this room, remember?" She pointed to the ceiling.

"Yes dear." he winked one blue eye and turned toward the stairs. "No running!" he called out to his daughter as she darted past, racing up the stairs.

"Kaitlyn" Janie called, ", make your bed, I left the sheets on your dresser."

"Okay" she called from the top of the stairs.

With that Janie turned back to setting up housekeeping in their new home.

Sitting around the television in the living room, the little family ate fried chicken from a bucket.

"Do you like your room?" Rob asked.

Licking her fingers one by one, Kaitlyn nodded. "It's way bigger than my old room. When can I have a sleep over?"

Janie chuckled, "Let's get settled in first."

Kaitlyn's cell phone buzzed. She wiped grease from her hands with a napkin and tapped on the screen.

"Everyone is going to the bowling alley, can I go?"

"What tonight?" Janie frowned.

"Please" clasping her hands and holding them under her chin she pled her case.

Rob sighed, "Who is everyone?"

"Lucy, Molly, Bernadette and Jeff."

"How are they getting there?" Janie asked.

"Jeff's driving."

"No" They said together.

"Why not?" she whined, her brown eyes squinted with outrage.

"Because Jeff just got his license, he doesn't have enough experience behind the wheel." Janie informed her.

Kaitlyn stormed from the room and stomped up the stairs.

Rob sighed. "Creep-agers"

A door slammed and they turned their eyes to the ceiling then looked at one another. Fisting their hands and pumping them in the air, Rob counted to three. Janie straightened two fingers as Rob kept his curled in a fist.

"Rock beats scissors."

Sighing, Janie pushed herself up. "Will you make me a rum and diet soda?"

"You got it Babe." He planted a small kiss on her lips. "Good luck."

Climbing the stairs, she knocked once before entering her daughter's room.

Kaitlyn sat cross legged on her bed beside the window, the lace curtains fluttered with the warm night breeze coming in.

"You can't throw a temper tantrum every time you don't get your way."

Keeping her head bent, Kaitlyn pulled at the fringe around the holes in the knees of her blue jeans.

"You don't want to talk?"

"Why can't I go?"

"I told you why. I don't want you in a car full of teenagers with an inexperienced driver. It's a recipe for disaster."

"Jeff's a good driver. You just don't want me to have any fun."

"If you really want to go I'll drop you off and pick you up."

"Forget it." she spat.

"Fine, then you can sit here alone." Pulling the door closed, she returned to the living room.

"Is everything alright?" He asked as he came in the room with her drink.

"She thinks we don't want her to have any fun."

"Darn, she finally figured it out." He chuckled and swigged from his bottled beer.

A bang sounded from the room above and Janie clenched her jaw.

Rob set his bottle down. "I'll take care of this." He took long strides across the room to the hall and went up the stairs.

Stepping in the room, he put his hand on his hips. "Enough with the attitude little girl."

"That wasn't me, Dad. I swear."

"Then who was it?"

"I don't know. It sounded like it came from my closet."

Going to the closet door, he pulled it open and moved the clothes around. "I don't see anything."

"Dad, I swear, it wasn't me." she shook her head emphatically.

"There's no one else here, Kaitlyn."

"I swear Dad I don't know what that was."

He sighed, "Just take it easy on your mother, deal?"

"She's just being mean."

"No, she's not. She loves you and she doesn't want you to get hurt."

"Whatever" she moped and turned to look out the window at the darkness.

Shaking his head in exasperation, he left the room.

Kaitlyn bounced down the stairs with her backpack over her shoulders.

"Bye hon" Janie kissed her forehead and took her coffee to the table.

"Bye Mom. I'm sorry for last night."

"Thank you. Have a good day."

"Bye Dad." She bent and kissed his cheek.

"Bye Katie. Have fun."

Screwing up her face she asked, "At school?"

"I liked school." He shrugged and sipped his coffee.

She rolled her eyes and went out to the hall.

The door shut and they watched through the window as she walked down the walk to the street and turned right, heading to the bus stop four houses down.

"She really does a rough life." Rob joked.

"She's only fourteen it's going to get worse before it gets better."

"God give me strength." He sighed.

Ghosts 181

At three o'clock, the front door shut and Kaitlyn came in the kitchen.

"Hi" setting her backpack down behind the table she went to the fridge.

"How was your day?"

Tossing her brown hair over one shoulder she complained, "I hate my new bus. There are no cool kids on it. Why can't I walk to the old bus stop?"

"Because it's ten blocks."

"So?" she cut her brown eyes to her mother.

"You're not walking ten blocks to a bus stop."

"Why do you have to ruin everything?" Kaitlyn slammed the fridge. The appliance shook with the blow as she stormed from the room and stomped up the stairs.

After putting the groceries away, she went up the stairs. Pushing the bedroom door open she put her hands on her hips. "What happened to my sweet little girl?"

"Her parents moved her away from all her friends."

"We're not in another city. We're ten blocks away. Look around you." Janie raised her arms, "This place is twice the size of the old house."

"I was happy there!"

"You were miserable!" she shouted, "All you ever did was complain about your room, because it was too small, the house was too small, the yard was too small."

Kaitlyn dropped her head and sniffled, "I could walk to all my friend's houses. Here you won't let me off the leash to go anywhere."

"Why don't you call your friends and see if they can come spend the night? Huh? It's Friday."

Kaitlyn nodded. "I'm sorry Mom I don't know what's wrong with me."

"You're fourteen. I've been there, done that. I know how you feel."

She wiped her face with her hands.

Janie rubbed her back. "Are you hungry?"

Nodding again, Kaitlyn slid off the bed and followed her mother to the kitchen.

Janie stood at the sink, looking out the window at the old metal swing set in the glare of the flood lights in the back yard. The swing moved slightly on the rusty chain then it shook as if someone had jumped off the weathered wooden seat. A shiver ran through her as she leaned on the counter, inspecting the yard for a cat, or raccoon, whatever may have caused the swing to move.

"Weird" she murmured.

"What's weird?"

Crying out, she turned to see Rob standing behind her. "Will you take that swing set down?"

He raised a blonde eyebrow to her, "Can it wait till morning?"

She chuckled, "Sure"

They went to sit in the living room to enjoy a movie and a few adult beverages. Above them, the sounds of muffled loud music, bumps and bangs accompanied the giggles of four teenage girls.

"Maybe she'll get out of her funk now." Rob said hopefully running his hand through his blonde hair.

"It's an adjustment for her."

"It's ten blocks, Janie. We didn't move her across the country."

"She's emotional."

"She's nuts." He sucked on his beer.

The banging and giggling quieted.

"Finally" he groaned and pointed the remote at the television, lowering the volume.

When the doorbell rang, Janie held out her hand. Rob took his wallet from a back pocket and pulled out two twenty dollar bills and handed them over.

A teenage boy in a football jersey and red Pizza Time ball cap on his head stood on the stoop.

"Markey?"

"That's us" she handed him the cash as he handed her the pizzas. "Keep the change."

"Thanks" he jogged back to a little car parked in the driveway.

With the warm boxes in her arms, she went up the stairs and entered the empty room. Frowning, she set the pizzas on the dresser and turned down the volume on the portable player.

The closet door opened and the girls filed in the room

"What are you doing in the closet?"

Molly answered, "There's a little playroom back there."

Kaitlyn flipped open the lid on a pizza box. "Sausage? I said pepperoni."

"Check the others, you spoiled brat." Janie snapped.

Kaitlyn shuffled the boxes and lifted another lid.

"Help yourselves girls." Janie said.

Uttering quiet mingled thanks, they went to join their friend around the tower of pizza boxes.

Janie opened the closet door. The clothes were spread on the rod exposing the back wall. "How did you find this?"

"We heard a noise and we went investigating." Bernadette informed her.

Janie stepped in the closet.

"What are you doing?" Kaitlyn frowned.

"I'm going to see what's in there. Is that alright with you?"

Rolling her eyes, Kaitlyn bit off the end of the pizza slice.

Running her hands over the cedar wood, she felt for the edges of a door.

"You have to press on the dark spot, Mrs. Mackey." Lucy said.

"Thank you Lucy." She put her palms to the wall and pressed. The little square door popped open an inch and she pulled it back then sank to her knees and crawled through to the small room.

A bare light bulb hung in the middle of the room. Three baby dolls sat in little white wooden chairs around a little white wooden table set with pink plastic tea cups and a matching tea pot. Building blocks and a stroller sat against one wall. Thick dust covered everything except where the girls had disturbed it.

Getting to her feet, she went to the table.

"How sweet," she said, picking up a baby doll, one side of her mouth turned up as she righted the doll's faded blue bonnet and set it back in the chair. The plastic blue eyes shifted to look at her. She cried out and turned then dove head first through the little door like she was body surfing. Scrambling to her knees, she pressed the door shut and stumbled from the closet. Wiping dust from her blouse, trying not to quiver, she said, "I don't want you going back in there."

"Why not?" Kaitlyn asked through a mouthful of pizza.

"Because those dolls are creepy."

She swallowed, "They're just dolls Mom. Do we have any soda?"

Janie pushed her brown hair behind her ears with shaky hands. "Yeah, in the fridge." Sliding out the bottom pizza box, she took it down to the living room with her.

"Alright, pizza." Rob rubbed his hands together as she set the box on the coffee table.

Picking up her glass, she gulped the rum and diet soda then let out a long burp.

He laughed as he lifted the greasy lid.

"There's a secret room in Kaitlyn's closet."

He stopped with his hand hovering over the crusty edge of a slice of sausage pizza. "Come again?" he frowned.

"In the back of the closet, there's a door to a child's playroom. The table is set with tea cups. The dolls are having a tea party." She gulped again.

"Hun, guess that's who the swing set was for."

"One of them looked at me."

He stopped with the pizza halfway to his mouth. "One of who?"

"The dolls, one turned its eyes to me."

"Doll's eyes move like that, Janie. Remember that creepy doll my mother gave Kaitlyn? The one with the long plastic eye lashes?" he did a body shake. "I hated that thing."

"I swear it looked right at me." She shook her head.

Setting the pizza slice back in the box, he stood and took her glass. "I'll make you another drink."

"Thanks" Sinking down on the leather sofa she ran through the scene in her mind again, uncertain now if the doll had actually looked at her or if she had imagined the whole thing.

The girls came down the stairs and tromped to the kitchen. Through the archway, Janie watched them standing by the fridge.

"Mom says you have a playroom in your closet?" Kaitlyn nodded.

"It's so cool, Mr. Markey." Lucy gushed. "There's a little table and chairs and the dolls are having a tea party."

"Show me this secret playroom."

Janie went to the kitchen to make another drink while they tromped up the stairs. A few moments later they were coming back down.

Shrugging one shoulder he said, "It looks like a little playroom. None of the dolls gave *me* a dirty look."

"Go ahead and laugh but I'm telling you, something isn't right."

Janie opened her eyes to the dark room. The digital clock on the nightstand told her it was three in the morning. Someone was still awake, muffled giggles came from Kaitlyn's room.

Donning her robe, she went to Kaitlyn's door and pushed it open. The giggling stopped. Taking a head count, she took note of the still lumps under the covers. Two lumps lay in the bed and two on the air mattress on the floor. Frowning, she pulled the door shut and went back to her bedroom.

When she opened her eyes again, the sun was shining in the window. She rolled over. Rob was gone. She rose and looked out the window at the back yard where he was taking apart the swing set. Wrapping up in her robe she went to the bathroom and brushed her teeth then pulled a trash bag from the box under the sink.

Entering the hallway, she heard the girls giggling in the living room and she dashed in Kaitlyn's room, going to the closet before she lost her nerve.

Pressing the little door open, she crawled in on her hands and knees, clutching the white plastic bag. Quickly she went to the table and shoved the dolls in then knotted the end of the bag and duck walked back through the door and pushed it closed.

Jogging down the stairs, holding the bag at arm's length, she went out to the garage, stuffed the bag in a trash can and shut the lid fast. Breathing a sigh of relief, she went back in the house.

A young girl of about six years old with long brown hair stood at the top of the staircase looking down at her with dark eyes. A long white dress hung to her ankles, showing her bare feet.

Janie froze, gazing up at her as goose bumps covered her arms. Swallowing past the lump in her throat she croaked, "Are those your dolls?"

"It's my swing too." She glared.

Janie swallowed again, her head swam and her pulse quickened.

"Put them back." The little girl's mouth became a thin white line as she crossed her arms over her chest.

"Those dolls" Janie began.

"Put them back!" she stormed, stomping a foot, making the entire house shake.

The girls screamed in fright from the living room and Janie nodded. "I'm sorry."

"The swing set too." She pouted and Janie nodded again.

With that, the girl turned around and disappeared through the Kaitlyn's door.

Finding her legs, she ran down the hall, past the girls huddled in the living room doorway and out to the back yard.

Rob was setting the rusty metal pipes in a pile. "You have to put it back together." She breathed.

Putting his hands on his hips he growled, "What?"

"She wants it put back. She's mad."

"Kaitlyn's never going to use this."

"Not Kaitlyn, there's a little girl, they're her dolls and it's her swing set, and she wants them all put back."

Shaking his head in disbelief, he walked past her. "Get it together, Babe."

Grabbing his arm to stop him she pleaded, "Rob, please. I threw the dolls away and when I came back in the house she was on the balcony."

"Mom! What was that? Was there an earthquake?"

"Earthquake?" A confused Rob asked. "Has everyone gone insane?"

"Girls, everything is fine, it was probably a gas main exploding."

The girls exchanged matching looks of surprise.

"We're okay here, promise." Janie soothed.

Reluctantly, the girls returned to the house.

Rob crossed his arms over his chest. "I spent almost an hour turning rusty screws and now you tell me to put it back together? It's not happening." He walked past and went inside.

She followed him, peeking in the living room at the girls sitting on the floor with their heads bent as they tapped frantically on their cell phones, no doubt searching the social network for anyone else who experienced the earthquake. Rob went up the stairs and she went back to the garage.

Plucking the bag from the trash can, she gingerly carried it back to Kaitlyn's room. Squatting in the closet, she pressed the little door open, removed the knot and opened the bag. Plastic faces stared up at her and a shiver ran through her. Taking the bag by the bottom, she shook the dolls out on the floor of the little room.

A small pale hand appeared and Janie scrambled away, watching in terror as the little girl sang quietly to herself and took the dolls, one by one to the table, setting them lovingly back in their rightful places.

Keeping her eyes on the little specter, she crawled backward on hands and knees, out. Pressing the door closed, she got to her feet and came from the closet.

Ghosts 187

Her entire body shook, a dull ache was forming at the front of her skull and she was certain she was going to heave. Walking in her bedroom, she looked out the window at the swing set in the back yard. "Uh, Rob?"

"Yeah?" he asked from the open bathroom, clutching a towel in his hand.

"She took care of the swing set for you."

He leveled his blue eyes at her. "Who did?"

"The little girl."

"Janie" he began patiently.

She pointed to the window. "See for yourself."

Coming to stand beside her, he looked out. His brows came together as he stared in astonishment. "My god" he breathed, "we have a houseguest."

"I think we're the houseguests." She murmured.

About Karen Alterisio Nelson

Karen Alterisio Nelson, author of *Millions of Reasons to Lie* is a New England native. She's been a wife and mother for nineteen years, and a lover of the written word her entire life. Nelson and her husband have two teenage boys and live in a small town northwest of Houston, Texas.

Swirlship
by
Joseph L. Lanza

Legend. Mystery. Temptation.

Dale Martine deftly guided his incorporeal body over the reddish-blue water of the Astral Sea, a spiritual out-of-body realm, gliding toward the shadowy outlines of a ship suspended, turning sluggishly, at the center of an immense churning cyclone.

The Swirlship.

Everything about it was unknown. Name, origin, the events that led to its fate. No legend or historical event in the physical world accounted for its presence. It appeared only at very rare intervals, and all that was known was what was visible; shadowy, indistinct outlines at the center of an astral tempest.

Surprisingly, passage through the wall of the cyclone was remarkably smooth, but as soon as Martine touched down on deck, he knew he was trapped. His contact with the Astral Sea was severed abruptly, the shadowy outlines of the Swirlship clarified, and the cyclone was replaced by a gray, misty sky; primary indications of a dimensional shift. He waited for the area beyond the misty sky to stabilize and clear. When it failed to do so, Martine realized there was no beyond. Was there a way back to the Astral Sea?

The ship was 82 meters long and 15 across with three masts and a single boiler stack. The upper deck of the vessel was in shambles. The mainmast was shattered twelve feet above the base and lay in a tangled wreck, burying the deck and superstructure under splintered wood, tangled rigging, and torn sailcloth. On the remaining masts, tattered remnants of sail flapped madly in the wind, a wind noticeably absent at deck level. The doors and hatches were battened down and secured from the inside. A life preserver gave a minimal clue: Vladmir Petrovsky.

Martine took routine precautions, psychic in nature, to ensure his wellbeing, carefully placing into motion various thought processes within his psyche to protect against foreign intrusion or psychic attack. He also stretched out his awareness, using his psychic talents to explore the ship and its isolated world. He immediately encountered low-grade mental emissions that, although vaguely familiar, he was at a loss to identify. They were random, of varying strengths, and non-intelligent in nature. And although Martine was able to catalog two hundred sixty three individual sources of emissions, he had extreme difficulty sensing the ship's interior. At times his awareness of a particular spot was particularly sharp, and at others, totally blank. The 'blankness,' he discovered, moved around.

He needed to get inside. All doors and hatches were rusted shut. He fought his way through the debris to a ladder that ran up the outside of the boiler stack and climbed. A second ladder ran down the inside of the stack for maintenance purposes, and Martine began to climb down again. Halfway down he was under attack; it came without warning.

Martine felt his mind being crushed. Waves of energy flowed out of him, and then back in. His mental shields snapped shut against the second wave, blocking out the assault. Simultaneously, he probed outward, trying to sense the origin of the onslaught. His attacker changed tactics and tried to feedback psychic energy across Martine's thoughts, seeking to bypass the mental shield. Martine momentarily cut his thought probes, but the damage from the initial shock was done; nausea washed over him as he fought to hold on. He started down the ladder again. Still the attack persisted.

One of the rusted rungs broke under Martine's weight. His body tumbled downward. His left leg caught on the rung two down and his whole body pivoted on that point. Agonizing pain exploded as his leg snapped. Martine turned the pain around and slammed it out through his defenses, down along the probing thoughts that sought him, stabbing his assailant's mind.

That counter-attack was devastating. The assault reeled back upon itself and ceased, but for one brief instant, through the mysterious, moving blankness that was indefinable, Martine got a glimpse of his adversary.

Powerful. Ruthless. Evil. He couldn't identify it.

Martine reached the bottom of the ladder. The attack drained his resources considerably. He employed the splintered remains of a spar to make a splint and, unable to stand, a crutch. He willed his mind to block out the pain, reflecting that he had never before imagined it possible to damage his astral body. Evidently he could, and he wondered if his physical body had suffered any effects.

Martine looked across at the service hatch. It too was rusted shut. He tried to budge it, but had neither the strength nor the leverage. His nemesis was once again testing his defenses, but it too was weakened by the conflict. His unknown enemy's advantage lay in the fact it could regenerate its power over time while Martine's resources were tied up quelling the pain in his leg. He tried to climb the ladder, but couldn't, and he lay at the bottom, looking up, pondering his circumstances.

How to get out of here, Martine mused, there has to be a better way to do this? Then it hit him.

Float fool! After all, you floated onto this crate, didn't you?

Propping his left leg up on top of his right, Martine tentatively floated and hovered, chastising himself. At first he felt like a fool for climbing up and down the ladder. In retrospect, that action proved fortuitous. Floating high off the deck, the consequences could have been worse.

The entity did not renew its assault while Martine glided gently up and out of the stack, keeping one hand on the ladder. He still had to get inside the ship. He floated around the superstructure, intent on examining each door or hatch in turn and trying to open it, but found a door already open, beckoning him to enter; a door which had not been open before.

Something stood just inside the door. It wore the frayed and ragged remains of seaman's clothes, and much of its flesh had long since decayed away. What skin was present was festered and putrid, giving off an overwhelming stench. Hair hung in scraggly tufts from its head, and it reached for Martine with long, black fingernails.

Although Martine backed away, if he was to get inside the ship, he would have to devise a method of circumnavigating the decrepit crewman. There was one approach worth trying. Martine extended his hand toward the man and pushed mentally. The human shell flew backwards and fell. Surprised, Martine sped past it, hugging the ceiling. He quickly raced through the maze of passages, repelling the fetid corpses of the crew and passengers he encountered, until he found the captain's cabin. Entering, he bolted the door.

On the captain's desk he found what he was seeking. A letter, and, stunned, Martine read it.

> August 3, 1917.
>
> To any who may find this.
>
> I, last Grand Master of the Order, am recording this information should we be swallowed up by the storm which threatens to destroy us.

In the years before Charles V of France condemned Jacques de Molay, our Grand Master, and other members of our Order, six trusted Knights secretly traveled to Constantinople in the East, taking the secret knowledge and treasures of the Order. They prospered for many years until 1453 when Mohemet II, prince of the Ottoman Turks, besieged the city. Again six trusted Knights departed and journeyed to Moscow, the last bastion of Christianity open to the Order.

The Order continued to prosper. Over time we came to be among the most trusted advisors to the Czars of Imperial Russia.

Like the Grand Masters who proceed me, I have seen the last hours of the empire which has sheltered us for so many centuries. Once again, six Knights travel to a new haven, the United States of America, with the secrets of the Order.

We have been at sea a week now. Our ship has been battered for the past two days by a terrible storm in the North Atlantic, and I greatly fear all hands will be lost. The captain is dead, swept overboard the first night. I cannot allow the knowledge of our Order to perish. I must take desperate measures. Our hope lies in the oldest treasure of the Order, acquired by our Knights in the Holy Land during the First Crusade, and kept by us since those times. May God, our Father in Heaven, protect us.

Konstantine Petrovich III,

Grand Master, Order of the Knights of the Temple.

Martine sat back, comprehension dawning. Knights Templar. In their desperation, they called upon some force to aid them. But how? More importantly, what force? A key question. Where did they conduct the ritual needed to call upon such a force? Another key question. Obviously something went wrong and led them to this fate.

There was scratching at the door. Several crewmen were trying to enter. Martine realized now they were the sources of the marginal physic emissions. His assailant had drained them, all two hundred sixty three passengers and crew, rendering their conscious minds non-existent. It was draining him, also. How long before the end?

Martine looked about for a means of escape. There was an iron door, sealed tight, leading to the deck. He forced it and floated to the original entrance, back into the interior of the ship, searching for the room where the Templars conducted their ill-fated ritual of conjuration.

In the passenger dining room old pentagrams and symbols marred the floor, and all had been disturbed, rendered useless. Martine's gaze was drawn to one pentagram in particular, and he froze. A spherical vessel of tarnished brass reposed there, more symbols marked its equator, and a hole gaped in the top where a seal once rested. The broken seal lay on the floor next to the vessel, a sigil plainly visible in the wreckage.

Examining the sigil engraved on the broken seal, Martine learned his assailant's identity; he knew its origin, and why it was.

A flash of light reflected among the rubble. Gently, Martine brushed the remains of the seal aside revealing a dagger. Elegant, untarnished silver, flaming edges, and engraved upon the blade, the Holy Tetragram. God's name. A holy relic.

Martine wrapped the dagger's wrist cord around his hand, made his way topside, and went to the stern to wait. His assailant was moving now; advancing, seeking Martine. Marshalling his reserves, Martine called upon his innermost strength.

He felt its thoughts; it made no attempt to hide them, and Martine knew the reason behind the Templars' fate. They released their doom from the brass vessel and compelled it to save them from the violent storm. Obeying twisted logic, it did what they asked, placing them in this dimension, trapping them forever. And itself.

It burst through the deck, an infernal angel with a Stygian Raven's head smelling of brimstone, smashing the decayed planks; darkness surrounded it.

Nephilim. A demon. One of the ten percent that survived the flood; sealed up in ancient times by King Solomon. Martine thought those tales to be myths.

Apparently I was wrong, he mused wryly as in an instant he formed a brilliant ball of light in the bowl formed by his cupped hands. He hurled the light at the demon where it shattered against its breast. The fiend discharged a lance of dark energy. A brilliant white energy sphere, spinning, blossomed protectively, deflected the bolt, and part of the deck vaporized.

The demon assaulted Martine's mental defenses, relentlessly lashed them, picking them apart, seeking his every weakness. Another defensive sphere, inside the first, formed, and Martine released more spheres of white that charged the fiend, only to die against its torso. He shot a bolt of pure psychic energy at its infernal mind and got slammed in return. Several checks on the pain in his leg slipped. Agony swelled up through Martine, blinding him. He tumbled to the deck, then, miraculously, rose to his feet. The Nephilim closed.

"Christ, hear me," Martine sang, forsaking the ceremonial rituals that failed the Templars, and instead placing his faith in the Roman Catholic lay exorcism ritual. He could think of no other tactic. His psychic ability was no match for something born from union of fallen angel and human female.

"God, the Father in Heaven, Redeemer of the world, have mercy on me, Holy Spirit, Holy Trinity, one God, have mercy on me!"

The Nephilim threw Martine back against the rail, and the energy that flowed between them formed a standing wave, part white light, part darkness, growing in amplitude that, when no longer containable, would burst. Martine's spirit and consciousness would be sucked away in the resulting psychic vacuum, leaving the Nephilim victorious.

Martine continued the exorcism ritual. His main defensive sphere, polluted by the dark energy, collapsed and the secondary sphere flared intensely as waves broke against it in swells; more brilliant white light mixing with darkness. He was on his knees, struggling to maintain his last sphere, fighting to continue the exorcism ritual, but he had nothing left. Martine stood on the brink of annihilation, and the gloating demon sensed victory.

One last desperate attempt to finish the exorcism. Holding the dagger so that it formed a cross with blade, grip and guard, hoping that it had not been polluted by the Templar's ungodly ritual, Martine chanted, "See the cross of the Lord, begone, you hostile power; the stem of David, the lion of Judah's tribe has conquered!"

The fiend hissed, then laughed, then charged. Deftly flipping the dagger into his hand, knowing that if the blade were despoiled his own soul would be displaced into oblivion, Martine prayed. The blade flashed brightly!

"I cast you out, unclean spirit, along with every Satanic power of the enemy, every specter from hell, and all your fell companions; in the name of our Lord Jesus Christ."

The Holy Tetragram illumed the burnished blade, and Martine drove it to the hilt into the Nephilim's heart. His own body seared from the pain of physical contact, and the Raven's beak ripped at his cheek.

The miniature world imploded, the concussion crushing Martine, then flew apart, releasing him from its grip. The Swirlship disintegrated into a million fragments and relinquished to eternity what remained of the crew's and passenger's souls.

Martine was back in his physical body, in his own room, and his body hurt and burned. He was drained, cheek torn, and his leg was red and swollen, oddly disjointed. His clothes were soaked with salt brine, smelled of sulfur, and wrapped around his wrist was a cord of fine, white silk, at the end of which danced the silver dagger with flaming blade, unstained, the Holy Tetragram slowly fading.

You're D-dead, Bob
by
J. Dennis Papp

The last time I saw Bob was six months ago. He was flat on his back. In a coffin. But that was *before* what happened at eight o'clock this morning.

I was sleeping peacefully enough, when it felt like a caterpillar was dancing on my right forearm. Lifting my right eyelid a hair, I saw something more round than rectangular. Its hourglass body was larger than a silver dollar and covered with multicolored, spiky hairs. Eight vampire-like eyes held me in a trance, while its thick legs reared for an attack. I swallowed. Hard. Then again.

The instant the monstrous spider sprung at me, dead Bob swatted it aside. At least my hero *looked* like Bob. Most of his flesh was gone, revealing bones and teeth I had never envisioned. His head *did* have a familiar divot of red hair on the top; but his eye sockets were barren. And, most of all, he was transparent.

When I said an automatic "thanks," Bob answered, "You're welcome."

Bam! My eyelid slammed shut.

"What's the matter, Johnny?"

I didn't answer.

"Hmm?" he prompted.

"You're *d-dead*, Bob."

"Yeah, so?"

"How can I see you and talk to you if you're dead?" I demanded.

"Must be pretty easy, since you're doing it."

I covered my head with a pillow to drown out his voice and hide him from my sight. I realized my reaction wasn't the smartest thing to do when confronted with a ghost, even though it had the added benefit of lessening the pungent aroma emanating from his remains. Slowly, I removed the pillow.

"Y-you died six months ago, Bob." It was a snowy night. I had dropped Veronica my wife at home, before taking Bob to his apartment. The SUV hit a patch of black ice and slammed into a tree. Both of us were thrown at the windshield. My seatbelt saved my life. Bob wasn't wearing his.

"Yes, but I have some unfinished business," he replied.

Goose pimples erupted on my arm. The spider had returned. I flicked it away. Bob snickered.

"What b-business?" I asked.

"Something has to be done to rectify this," he answered, handing me a scrapbook. Two maggots fell from his fingers onto the cover. He brushed them away. *Food for the spider?*

Taking a deep breath for courage—but instead receiving a lungful of his overpowering "body" stench—I flipped through the first few pages, seeing newspaper articles that detailed the tragic accident on New Year's Eve and his subsequent funeral. Slamming it shut as though it were contaminated, I flipped the book aside. I squeezed shut my eyes to erase all memory of those events. Regardless, my mind held onto the images, playing them back like a slide show.

"Look at the book, Johnny."

I open my eyes and held up a trembling hand. It stopped in midair—five hesitant fingertips unwilling to go closer. Miraculously, the book jumped at me. I caught it—rather than letting it hit my face—and squeezed it to keep the contents hidden. The book resisted and opened to the first page. I braved another look at one of the clippings. The photo showed a tree trunk bisecting my truck's front end. The left headlight hung from my vehicle like an eyeball dangling out of its socket. Again, I slammed shut the book and flung it to the foot of the bed.

"Johnny, Johnny, Johnny. *Look* at the damned book," Bob demanded.

I sucked up my fear and reached for the scrapbook. Unaided, it found its way to my hands and opened to the same place I had last viewed. I tried turning the page, wanting not to see my demolished SUV. Nothing happened: the pages seemed stuck together. I licked a dry index finger with my sandpaper tongue and tried again. No luck. I was stuck on this page. Something was forcing me to see the picture and read the article.

The blurry words focused slowly. Scanning the article I came to the part where it said the tragic death of the thirty-year-old passenger could have been averted if he had been wearing his seatbelt. My tears fell on the page, making pockmarks on the paper.

"B-ob," my voice crackled, "it says you could have lived if you had been wearing your seatbelt."

He shook his head. "No, Johnny, it never would have happened if you weren't driving so recklessly."

"I wasn't driving recklessly. I was going under the speed limit."

"You weren't paying attention to the road conditions. Your mind was on the damned music and getting home to your wife."

Granted, the radio was playing "Runaround Sue," my favorite song; regardless, my attention *was* on the road ahead—not on getting home after the dinner the three of us had shared.

"That's wrong, Bob. I *was* paying attention," I insisted. "I *know* I was paying attention."

"Who are you talking to, John?" came a female voice.

I turned around and gazed upon the angelic vision of my wife. Her smile became a frown when she saw my weird expression.

"What's the matter?" Veronica asked. "You look like you've just seen a ghost."

Hah!

I glanced over her shoulder and saw Bob sulking on a corner of the bed. A maggot peeked out of his right nostril. He grabbed it and popped the slimy bug into his hollow mouth.

"N-nothing's wrong, Ronnie," I replied, swallowing. "You... you just startled me and put brown tire tracks in my underwear."

Bob smirked.

Veronica scrunched up her nose and said, "Then get your butt out of bed and take a shower." She took a closer look at my face, then added, "And shave."

"Shave?" I complained. "What the hell for?"

"Idiot! Are you going senile at thirty three? You promised to take me to the carnival today. Remember?"

Bob looked me in the eyes and mouthed: "Oh, boy, carnival."

My mind replied: *Dark tunnels. Scary rides.*

His evil smirk told me that he must have read my thoughts.

I forced myself to look away from Bob and smile at my wife. "Oh, I forgot." Then I made a beeline for the bathroom, closing the door quickly so Bob couldn't follow me inside. When I turned around, *after* locking the door, Bob was sitting on the edge of the bathtub.

"You didn't think a door—*locked or not*—could stop me, did you, Johnny?"

Ghosts 199

I shook my head and unlocked the door—anticipating the need to make a speedy exit. I was grateful, at least, that he had left the invisible scrapbook on the bed, and said nothing about what needed to be "rectified" about the accident that had killed him.

After patting my face with warm water, I lathered up and began shaving. Fearful of cutting myself because of a shaky left hand, or of having Bob coax my hand in the wrong direction, I guided the razor with due care. Finishing the job without a nick, I stepped into the tub, closed the curtain, and turned on the water. When I saw movement on the other side of the curtain, I feared a replay of *Psycho*.

"What do you want for breakfast, John?"

I sighed. It was only my wife.

"Not really hungry," I shouted. "Just coffee." I saw her—or *something*—turn and leave.

After finishing my shower, I eased open the end of the curtain and scanned the bathroom. Empty. With added confidence I stepped out of the tub, grabbed a towel—covering my privates —*what for?*—and finished my morning ablutions in record time. Then I dashed into the bedroom, got dressed—not seeing Bob anywhere—and sped down to the kitchen.

Veronica was at the table, eating a bowl of Rice Krispies, oblivious to Bob sitting next to her, spoon in hand, watching her every move. I shuddered when he tilted the utensil over Veronica's bowl and *the* spider started repelling on a single strand of silk right into her breakfast.

Convincing myself the apparition was all in my mind, I turned my back to them, took two quick steps to the counter, grabbed a travel mug, and filled it with hot coffee. When I did an about-face to use the cream and sugar-free sweetener on the kitchen table, I saw that Bob had exchanged the spoon for a ten-inch butcher knife. He looked at me, holding my attention, and nodded toward Veronica. Then he grabbed his shock of red hair, separated his head from his neck, and swept the knife through the vacated space, making it clear what he threatened to do to my innocent wife.

"Don't," I yelled. "Please don't."

"Don't *what*?" Veronica asked.

"N-nothing. Nothing," I replied, all the time watching Bob and wondering what he'd really do with the butcher knife. "You ready to go, or not, Veronica?"

"What's your hurry?" she replied. "I haven't finished my breakfast."

I rushed over, picked up her half-full bowl—keeping it at arm's length—and dropped it in the sink. "You don't want to fill up on breakfast, do you? Especially with all that delicious junk food at the carnival."

Her smile told me she had immediate visions of corn dogs, candy apples, kettle corn, peanuts, and cotton candy.

"No, I guess you're right," she replied, jumping out of her chair as though it were on fire.

As I backed out of the driveway, I checked the rearview mirror and saw the backseat was empty. Hoping that Bob wasn't like a vampire, in that he gave off no reflection in a mirror, I began our trek to the carnival. After a few blocks, I grabbed my coffee mug, took a sip, and rechecked the rearview mirror. Looking back at me was a sneering Bob. I spit out the coffee and roared a string of Hungarian cusswords that would have made my dead mother proud.

"What the hell's wrong with you?" my wife asked.

"Coffee was hotter than I had expected," came my lame response.

Her mouth said *duh*, but her eyes meant *idiot*.

Yeah, well, I thought, *you'd spit out coffee if a dead high-school friend were haunting you.*

Being more stupid than brave, I drove the remaining two miles without glancing at the rearview mirror. When I pulled into the carnival's parking lot, Veronica let out a "Here we are! Here we are! Can't you just smell the popcorn and roasted peanuts?"

"Peanuts, yum," Bob shouted. I gave him a look that said *how the hell can you eat anything? You're dead.* In return, Bob stuck out his rotting tongue.

Forking over $20 for parking and *free* admission, I eased the SUV in the first empty spot I saw and prepared myself for overpriced food, death-defying rides and untold surprises from my transparent dead friend.

No sooner had we entered the Carnival of Surprises, Veronica let out a "*whoopee!*" and pointed out the nearby attractions: Frankenstein's Ghost Ride, Dracula's House of Mirrors, King Tut's Pyramid of Wonders, and King Richard's Concentric Castles. Then she made a beeline to the *Fresh, Hot Peanuts* stand—with Bob right behind—yelling for me to keep up.

I put a ten-dollar bill on the counter and asked for a small bag of peanuts. Bob swung the butcher knife over his shoulder, buried it in Hamilton's head, and shouted, "Small bag!" I jumped backward a foot, then changed my order

Ghosts 201

to a *big* bag. The woman took the bill—as though there were no knife in it—and handed me a *big* bag of hot, roasted peanuts and two singles.

Looking at Bob, I said, "Here's your peanuts."

Veronica took them before my nemesis had the chance. While she broke shells and ate nuts to her heart's content, I steered us toward Dracula's House of Mirrors.

"That's stupid," Veronica said, spitting out some peanut skins. "Vampires don't give off a reflection in a mirror."

"So?"

"Well, then, why would Dracula have a house of mirrors?"

"It's just an *attraction*, Veronica. Not an oxymoron."

"Huh?"

"Never mind," I said, coaxing her in another direction.

"Step right up, folks," the six-foot sideshow worker barked, "and take a dark ride on Frankenstein's Ghost Ride." He pointed his cane at the couple about fifteen feet in front of him and added, "for a mere five dollars each you'll enjoy the time of your life."

"What's a dark ride?" the woman asked.

"Well, miss, this ghost train will travel through dark tunnels and spooky scenery." He winked at the woman's companion, giving him a knowing look. "And take you on a journey you'll never forget. That's what makes it a *dark* ride." He banged his cane on the lectern, then added, "But that's not all. This is also a *shooting* dark ride."

"A what?" the woman asked.

"You see, hon, this is an *interactive* dark ride where you shoot at targets—or ghosts—throughout the ride."

I looked at Bob at the mention of *ghosts*. Holding his midsection with two boney hands, he howled at me. His open mouth gave me a sideways view of his rotting tongue.

"Hit three of 'em," the carny continued, "and you'll win a prize."

What happens if you don't *hit three ghosts?* I wondered. Bob answered my thoughts: *"That's a surprise, Johnny. "That's a* big *surprise."*

"Let's go on the ride, John," said Veronica.

I shook my head. "Don't really want to."

"I want to go on the ride, John," she demanded.

"Yeah, *John*," Bob taunted, "go on the ride."

"All right. All right."

We worked our way toward the line, being jostled by a group of rowdy teenagers. Bob walked through Veronica and smacked one of the raucous teens on the back of his head. The kid turned, looked me in the eyes and growled, "What's your problem, old man?"

Before I could respond, Ronnie got in his face and said, "You're the one with the problem, sweet cheeks."

The kid mumbled something incoherent and laughed. "Okay, granny," he said. With a sweep of his arm while bowing, he let us get ahead of his group.

Bob smacked him again—for good measure.

When it came time for Veronica and me to get in the next car, I felt a tug on my shirt. As I turned to look, the loudmouthed kid shoved me aside, and one of his friends took my place next to my wife.

"Hey," I yelled, to no avail.

After four more cars filled up with pushy teenagers, Bob nudged me into the next empty car, got into the seat next to me, and pulled down the safety bar. Off we went.

"Grab your six-shooter," Bob commanded when we entered the dark tunnel. I did as ordered, using my free hand to wave away his hot breath.

Bang! went my first shot, nailing the ghost right in the head. I looked at Bob and said, "Hah! This is easy." Bob smiled, exposing a mouthful of half-eaten worms.

Shots two and three went wide—each miss punctuated by a "hah-hah" from Bob that was accompanied by a sour-smelling aroma. *Those yummy worms?*

"Three more shots left, Johnny. You need to hit two—or else."

Before I could respond, a weak "Johnny, where are you?" came from around the next bend.

"I'm here, Ronnie," I shouted, doubtful she could hear me.

When I took aim on the next ghost, I heard a female scream, and I missed the shot.

More twists and turns in sheer darkness with no ghosts appearing. Then one popped up, backlit by a red light. I took careful aim and "obliterated" it.

"Good, Johnny, good," Bob encouraged. "One shot left to get one ghost."

"You're preaching to the choir, Bob."

"I don't go to church, Johnny," he snorted.

I let the next two ghosts go by without a shot.

"What's the matter, Johnny, scared?" I dropped the f-bomb. "Only one shot left," he reminded me. Another f-bomb.

As I took aim with my final shot and pulled the trigger, another female scream erupted, causing me to miss.

"You missed. You missed. You missed," Bob shouted.

"Big deal," I answered. "So what's going to happen? Am I gonna turn into a ghost?" I mocked.

Bob just leered at me, his eye sockets lighting up a bright red.

About twenty feet ahead of our car I saw the light at the end of the tunnel.

"Thank God this is over," I sighed.

"Yes, Johnny, it is for you," said Bob. "And *God* had nothing to do with it."

The light intensified, and I saw Veronica staring at each car, expecting to see me.

"Here I am, Ronnie," I shouted.

Her expression became bleak, like fall turning to winter. She continued to gape at each pair of occupants. I shouted her name over and over while waving my arms. The same vacant face never changed.

When our car stopped, I jumped out, never noticing the safety arm had remained in the locked position.

"Johnny, where are you?" continued Veronica's pleading cry.

I rushed toward her, yelling her name. I threw out my arms, then realized I had walked *through* her and come up empty-handed.

"Bob?" she said to the car I had vacated. "How could you be—but you're dead," she gasped, "aren't you?"

He shook his head and smiled.

"Where's John?" she yelled. "What happened to John?"

At that precise moment I knew the consequences of my not hitting *three* ghosts: I had changed places with Bob and become *transparent* Johnny—lost to her forever.

About J. Dennis Papp

J. Dennis Papp, a Vietnam veteran, spent 25 years in advertising, marketing and public relations for various multinational corporations, before retiring from The Newark Public Library, where he was the External Affairs

Officer for 16 years. He graduated from Marquette University in 1966. He and his wife reside in Hamilton, New Jersey.

Havelock Cemetery

by

Joseph L. Lanza

Bishop Temple scared the beejeebers out of me one night in November, but it wasn't his fault. Not entirely. I was standing outside Havelock Cemetery at three in the morning, and I was good and mad at Bishop because he was part of the reason I was there.

With a ghost!

I weigh about 100 pounds. I'm not even five feet tall. I have long braided hair that makes a great leash for a crazed serial murderer to grab. And I have a vivid imagination that made me want to turn tail and run.

But I was determined to prove Bishop wrong. Bishop is my ugly buzzard of a husband who writes about the paranormal and supernatural. Some might suggest stubbornness equated to stupidity under the circumstances. I'd be hard pressed to argue with them, but that fact didn't change my decision.

I clicked on the mini-Maglite at the end of my keychain and flashed the beam around. Old gravestones reached up, broken fingers, and oaks hoary with age loomed, bare branches denuded of leaves.

And the silence of the dead. Happy thought.

Local lore said the ghost, an escaped convict who drowned three-quarters of a century ago, claimed his victims if they didn't reach hallowed ground by dawn. A teen, on a dare, had spent the night in Havelock. He was found dead the following morning, *in his bed, his lungs full of water*. Bishop's job was to crush the rampant home-brewed fable before it went viral. But even Bishop was going to have trouble debunking the Havelock legend.

I liked my lips. I *could leave*, the wise thing to do, or be stubborn and take the chance Bishop was right. It was a no-brainer. Hop on my ten-year-old Ducati motorcycle and get the heck out of Dodge. So why wasn't I going? It was a question for which I don't have a good answer. That happens sometimes.

I slipped an elastic band around my head and inspected myself. One pair scuffed, dusty Red Wing boots. Check. Jean jacket. Check. One tee shirt with a big chocolate stain on it. Check. One pair of ratty jeans. Check. I sighed and wound my long hair around and around and shoved it down the back of my tee shirt. Now I looked hunchbacked. I'd scare the ghost away if it didn't laugh itself to death first. Another comforting thought.

Für Elise began playing. Ring tones, cell phone. I subtracted ten years from my life and dredged up the phone. Bishop. It was a fairly safe bet he was furious since I hadn't told him where I was going, or answered any of his previous calls. I flipped it open. I heard Bishop take a deep breath. He was exasperated with me, but controlling himself. I have that effect on him. There was a lot of background traffic noise.

"Are you okay?"

"I'm fine Bishop."

"When can I expect you home?"

"Probably early afternoon sometime."

A pause.

"Where are you?"

"Promise you won't get mad?"

Another pause, longer. I could hear gears turning. "Okay, I won't get mad."

"I'm back at Havelock Cemetery."

"Sheriff with you?"

"No."

"Deputy Willis?"

"I'm alone."

"Please get out of there."

"I'm going to prove you wrong."

"How!"

Good question, but it came across as more of a demand.

"Ceré, that's no place to be alone."

"Thought it wasn't haunted," I scoffed.

"That's not what I mean! There's an escapee on the loose!" Bishop was referring to Mackee Coleman, Sheriff David Russell's postulated scapegoat.

"Sheriff says he's in Louisiana. This is Texas. Anyway, I'm going to do this."

"Why?" Bishop demanded. Because I was mad at him?

"Analyze your behavior Ceré. Analyze my behavior. What does that tell you?"

I thought about his behavior and felt another flash of anger. "Your behavior was that of a first rate jackass," I retorted. We'd argued bitterly about the ghost after spending the previous night in Havelock loaded down with equipment, watched over by a deputy named Selma Willis, but at least Bishop had indulged my request to step foot into a church yard before dawn.

"You're right. And how often do you go out alone, Ceré?"

Once in a blue moon. I'm way afraid of people, but all I had to worry about right now were dead people, and they're almost never a problem.

"There's something else Ceré…"

The cell phone beeped and went dead. Convenient. I was about to hang up on him anyway. I pressed the power button. Nothing happened. Either the battery was dead, or the ghost had got it.

I shivered. November nights aren't made for wearing torn jeans, tee shirts, and light jackets. I shoved my cell phone in a pocket. I'd have killed for a Starbucks. On that note I turned and faced Havelock.

As cemeteries went, it wasn't large, sixty four graves spread unevenly among eight weed-choked rows. I heard and saw nothing. I flipped open the Ducati's saddle bag and took stock of my technological ghost hunting arsenal: electromagnetic field (EMF) meter, micro recorder, digital camera, laser thermometer, couple of small motion detectors, and a good, no-tech guarantee–a small plastic bottle of holy water. Scrounging about for one of the motion detectors, I placed it on a stone near the entrance and pressed the arm button. Its little light blinked reassuringly. Blink. Blink. Blink. I shoved the other gadgets and bottle into empty pockets, leaving my hands free for other things, like fending off any serial murderers that happened by. I flicked the Maglite beam around again. Desolation. I heard and saw nothing.

I took a temperature reading. Fifty degrees. I could solve the mystery and catch pneumonia at the same time. I checked the EMF meter. Normal. No significant EMF, which wasn't surprising for a cemetery in the middle of nowhere. Some investigators, like me, believe EMF and temperature variances indicate the presence of paranormal activity. Others, such as Bishop, do not.

I walked a little further back between the gravestones, a pretentious lot, big, tall, weathered, many covered in moss or lichen. Dry weeds scraped against my jeans and a few twigs snapped when I stepped on them. I heard something moving in the brush off to my right and froze.

Not a breath of wind stirred. Imagination? Had to be in overdrive.

I wondered about Bishop. What would he do? Would he race up here to rescue me? Did I need rescuing? Probably. Suddenly home seemed very cozy. Instead I was alone with a bunch of dead people stuck way under the ground.

A hiss, "Ceré."

I flashed the Maglite beam crazily.

Nothing.

I swallowed my heart. Wind. Had to be. My hyperactive imagination was getting the better of me.

Now a slight breeze stirred the branches. Their rasp sounded like old bones, and out of the corner of my eye I caught movement. I licked my lips again. My eyes were playing tricks, I knew it. I walked towards the back of the cemetery and found a freshly dug grave. Havelock hadn't seen a burial in decades.

Okay. Got it. Equation just changed. The ghost and I might not be alone.

It wasn't a very good grave. Four feet deep, uneven sides and bottom, shattered roots along the sides like claws. Good thing I didn't know about it before talking to Bishop. No need to complicate matters.

I set the second motion detector on the top of a decrepit stone obelisk. I returned to middle ground, found another tombstone, put the micro recorder down and switched it on. If I was lucky, I could capture some electronic voice phenomena— sounds resembling speech but not the result of an intentional voice recording. Ghost talk. Bishop claims it's a combination of static and stray radio transmissions, and a desire to find significance in insignificant phenomena. He didn't take kindly to my suggestion that he had a desire to find insignificance in significant phenomena. Maybe whatever whispered a few moments earlier would say something.

I took a bunch of pictures and shot several minutes of video, keeping my mind busy. My knees felt like ice.

The first motion detector went off. I recovered my composure, steeled myself, and turned. Through trees and tombstones, the red light blinked madly. Heart pummeling in my chest, I cautiously picked my way toward the light, looking frantically right and left. When I turned off the alarm silence clamped down.

My Ducati was only a few feet away, but I wasn't going to prove Bishop wrong by running around like a rabbit. I gathered my nerve to go back into the cemetery.

Für Elise again. I flipped my cell phone open.

"Ceré ..."

A hoarse whisper, long and drawn out. Not Bishop. Not the phone. So much for nerve. I jumped on the Ducati and booted the kickstand back. The Maglite beam danced circles in the dirt as I shoved the key into the ignition and cranked.

Nothing happened. Yikes!

I booted the kickstand down and swung my leg over the Ducati so that the motorcycle was between me and the cemetery. I gulped nervously and squeaked, "Who's there?"

Stupid question. If someone was out there he was deliberately stalking me. He wasn't likely to pipe up and say, "It's me, the random serial killer your imagination warned you about!"

Something scurried along the ground. I stabbed my light at it. Raccoon, stiff with fear, a lot like me. Small animals were setting off the motion detectors. Okay Ceré, I told myself firmly, get a grip. You're alone after all, just you and the local wildlife. Yeah? Who dug the grave?

I stepped around the Ducati and strained my eyes to see any sign of movement. I saw squat. Bishop's words came back to me, the ones about analyzing our behavior. I had it. We were both behaving out of character. Whatever it was about Havelock, something had manipulated us.

I remounted the Ducati and prayed. When I turned the ignition, the engine roared to life. I nearly jumped out of my skin. The noise was unexpected in the silence that gripped the cemetery. But it was a welcome sound. I felt a huge surge of relief. Escape was at hand.

Except for the fact that there were two motion detectors, a camera, micro recorder and an EMF meter back in the cemetery.

Damn!

I couldn't leave them.

Yes, I could.

No, I couldn't.

This argument went on for about four iterations. I lost.

Leaving the Ducati's engine running, its roar comforting, I collected the first motion detector, threaded my way through the gravestones and trees, snatched up the camera and recorder and EMF meter, and continued until I reached the second motion detector. Across the back wall more trees stared at me. Something about those trees unnerved me. There was darkness there, deeper than shadow.

I grabbed the motion detector and slowly backed away, but something glinted among the trees. I corralled my remaining nerve and cautiously stepped over the crumbling wall, a moth drawn to flame. I pulled aside branches. A sheriff's deputy's patrol car was parked there, the driver's side window shattered, something dark and dried staining the door jamb.

The Ducati's engine died.

Shit! Double and triple shit!

I ran for the Ducati, but a shadowy figure blocked the way. I jumped backwards, stumbled over a root, scrambled to my feet. I think my heart may have quit. Disoriented, I swung back towards the motorcycle and came face-to-face with a man in torn pants and shirt, the top three buttons missing, his hair straggling limply over forehead and vacant eyes.

I screamed. That, I'm certain about. His hands came up, grabbed my throat, and lifted me off my feet. Not a ghost, but Mackee Coleman. He shook me, stars exploded behind my eyes, and my sight dissolved into inky black patches that expanded until I was blind. I felt movement; walking. His grip released, and I twisted through space, landing on my back, sprawled, in mud and water.

I don't know how long I was out. I was cold and felt something pressing down on me. I heard a grating sound and seconds later dirt hit me in the face. I lay frozen, terrified Coleman would realize I was awake, equally scared of being buried alive. I heard footsteps walking away. I sat up with difficulty, heaving pounds of dirt off my legs and torso. I was in the open grave. No surprise there.

My face and hair were covered in mud, and I was barefoot. I felt my jeans. Thank goodness they were still buttoned, my belt snug around my waist. My jacket was open, my tee shirt torn, and I couldn't tell if the wetness on my torso was water, mud, or blood, but thank God my jeans were firmly buttoned around my waist. My chest burned with pain, and I had two pairs of feet and twenty toes.

Twenty toes?

I felt nauseous. I put my hand down to steady myself, got to my knees and faced the ground, and dug. I found myself staring at the face of a woman, a face I recognized. Deputy Willis, and her right eye and part of her skull crushed.

Scared shitless and shaking, vision patchy, mind numb, I pulled myself to my feet. My boots and socks were missing, but I didn't have time to put them on anyway. Placing my foot on a broken root, I reached up, and pushed and pulled myself out. Unsure whether I'd been seen, I darted for the back of the cemetery, stifling gasps of pain as rocks and twigs bit into the soles of my bare feet.

Something crashed towards me.

Panic ruled. I ran out of the cemetery, kept running, branches tearing at what remained of my clothes, ripping my feet. My jacket snagged. As I struggled I saw Coleman coming for me, but my jacket was stuck and wouldn't come free so I just slipped out of it, and off I went, running for all I was worth, and fell into a ditch!

Coleman jumped in after me, shoving my face down into the muddy water. Choking, I twisted sideways and felt cold, clammy hands clamp around my throat again and squeeze as they pushed my head under water. I kicked blindly, and the hands loosened. Coleman struck me across the face. I kicked again, he struck me again, but I came up out of the water. Gasping, I kicked again and again and again, sharp jabs of pain stabbing through my stubby toes, but I heard Coleman grunt. He lost his grip. I scrambled to my feet while the rational side of my mind struggled to regain control.

I flew. I had a stitch in my side and it was becoming harder to breathe, but as reason took hold, I slowed and turned back towards the cemetery. Nothing between me and the gravestones except trees and weeds. Quiet again, except for my labored breathing.

No, not quiet. I could hear the Ducati's motor, growling. The Ducati had stalled. Why was the motor running now? I doubled over, hands on my knees, breathing deeply, but my breaths came shorter. My feet were bloody.

I gagged and coughed. As I gasped for air I felt something in my mouth. Another labored cough and water sprayed out.

Water! I was coughing up water! That meant there was water in my lungs! It was bad enough Coleman was after me; I didn't need to deal with a ghost trying to drown me as well!

I ran blindly. I burst out onto the dirt road, my vision blurry. Everything was confusing. I had to get to hallowed ground, that's what the legend said. I needed a church.

No, another voice said, you swallowed water in the ditch. That sounds like Bishop I argued with myself. Quit panicking and acting irrational, the voice told me. It's Coleman you need to worry about. Run!

Ghosts 213

In the distance I could see my Ducati, eddies of bluish exhaust smoke suspended in the air as the engine continued to purr, the halo of my Maglite circling on the ground. I also saw a man. Coleman? Or the ghost?

I still couldn't breathe. I staggered. I would never reach the motorcycle. In blind panic, I dug down deep into my jeans pocket and pulled out the plastic vial of holy water. My vision was swimming, my thoughts incoherent. I sprinkled holy water on the ground. What little water was left I sprinkled on myself. The last thing I saw were three hellish lights racing down the road towards me. I stumbled, sprawled; gravel bit into my cheek, and I fell into a deep, deep well.

It was really deep. And black. Nothing seemed to be there. My thoughts echoed.

Lights. Flashing pulses in the darkness, red and blue and white. When people died, lights flashed inside their heads. I was dying. Water filled my lungs until I couldn't breathe. Or perhaps Coleman had killed me. I thought of Bishop.

The flashing became bright, pulsing orbs.

I coughed again. Coughed? Do dead people cough?

"Ceré?" Bishop's voice, a clarion call to life, dragging me back from the abyss, "Ceré, wake up. Please wake up."

My tired eyes opened. The pulsing lights were strobes from a sheriff's car. Bishop cradled my head in his arms.

I coughed again.

"Fucking hard way to prove me wrong," he rasped.

"Huh?"

"I hustled my ass up here as quickly as I could. I was already on my way when you finally answered your damn phone. Sheriff came with me."

"Willis..."

"They found her," he said, voice tight.

"I love you," I gasped, "I'm sorry."

"Ditto." About as much as I would get out of him.

"We can't leave hallowed ground."

"Of course we can," he told me.

"Not until morning."

"It is morning, five in the morning. You can leave now. You're safe."

"No, not safe...I saw..."

"Nothing," said Bishop firmly.

"No…"

"Yes," he repeated, "There's no ghost."

"Safe," I mumbled. I was safe in Bishop's arms. I didn't care if he believed me. There was a ghost. He'd filled my lungs with water.

I heard the sheriff walk up behind Bishop.

"Thought you'd like to know we found the sonofabitch who did this."

"Coleman?" Bishop asked.

"Yeah. Face down in a ditch near Willis' patrol unit. Looks like he drowned."

Live on Stage
by
Chris Rogers

Jake drummed his nails as the comic tossed another stale one-liner into the din. Nobody laughed. The audience had stopped listening two minutes after the clod opened his mouth.

"Tell you, Jake, you gonna love this girl coming on next." Silkie dredged a cherry from the depths of his Old Fashioned. "She don't look like much, but wait'll she goes on. Really comes alive in front of that mike."

Jake regarded the fat girl chewing her thumbnail and waiting her turn at the microphone. Silkie touted every client with the same enthusiasm, but he was right about one thing: she sure didn't look like much.

"I know what you're thinking, Jake, but give the girl a chance. She's a scream." The talent agent popped the cherry into his mouth, stem and all, and sucked his fingers. "Mark my words, she's the next Carol Burnett."

Sure, Jake thought. Carol Burnett, like the last one had been another Bill Cosby and the one before that another Seinfeld. The club needed a major draw, especially during the coming holidays. People could go anywhere to get drinks. They came to the Laff Club to be entertained. Lately, talent was lousy—clods with bad memories recycling old jokes. Wouldn't recognize good timing if it kicked 'em in the butt.

Halloween night. The place should be packed, and it wasn't half full. If he didn't find a decent talent soon, he might as well close the place down.

Across the room, a door opened. An old man shambled in. No one noticed. A few heard a faint creaking as he walked, like old bones scraping in dry joints. A dusty tuxedo hung limp on his shrunken frame, puddled around his shoes like shadows. Wisps of white hair defined his skull, pale eyes peered from the depths of his soul. The carnation in his lapel might have spent twenty years between the yellowed pages of a scrapbook.

He took a stool at the far side of the bar, laid a crumpled hat on the seat beside him, and watched the stage. He had waited a long time for this night.

When the bartender finally noticed him, the man ordered a beer. Paid for it with musty bills from a good leather wallet brittle with time.

The comic finished his routine and hurried offstage.

"She's next," Silkie muttered around his cherry stem. "Just watch how she comes alive when she hits that spotlight."

The fat girl slogged across the stage and picked up the mike. The audience hushed expectantly, hopeful of a better performance than they'd heard all night. As the emcee introduced her, Jake found himself holding his breath. Fat, skinny, young or old, he needed a winner.

Since the night he bought the club, almost three years ago, he'd been looking for a talent he could ride to the big time. A few good ones had come and gone; none were exceptional.

Now newer, fancier places packed in the crowds, while Jake's audience thinned out, his regular customers no longer so regular. What the heck, maybe this girl *would* be the next Carol Burnett.

"Good evening, ladies and gentlemen . . ."

She had a great voice. And she wasn't bad looking, once you got used to her size.

"My daughter had a friend over the other day. Showed her my new weight scale in the bathroom. The girl asks, 'What's it for?' and my daughter says, 'I don't know, but when you stand on it, it makes you say the 'f' word'."

The audience tittered. They wanted to like this woman. Her material was just a little stale, not bad at all, but her timing was jumpy.

"When I was a kid, I felt unwanted. Mama wrapped my lunch in road maps."

Naw! She tromped on her own punch line.

Background chatter rose a notch. The audience had given the fat girl her chance, and she muffed it.

Jake drummed his fingers.

"Honest," Silkie whined, the cherry stem wedged between a gap in his lower teeth. "She was better when she auditioned for me. She's nervous. You know how comics are, they don't come alive till they tune in to the audience. When she loosens up, she'll knock 'em dead."

Jake sighed and shook his head as people got up to leave.

"Dead is what she is now. Dead is what we've had around here for three years, Silkie. What we need is someone to shake things up."

218 Ghosts

The old man waited for the fat girl's routine to wind down, then he padded toward the stage. As he walked, his pace quickened, his suit filled out, the folds in his face smoothed and tightened. He spoke briefly to the band and strode backstage, his dark hair shining in the lights.

When the girl stepped down, the band broke into the opening strains of "Long Tall Texan," followed by a drum roll.

Jake lifted a brow. "Who's this? I thought you said the girl was the last one."

Silkie shrugged, forehead wrinkled quizzically.

A big man with bright black eyes, wearing a tailored tux and a sparkling white Stetson hat, burst onto the stage. His Texas drawl boomed across the room.

"Folks, I am *glad* to be here, but you know . . . getting here hasn't been easy. Took my car to the shop. Asked the mechanic how much to fix it, he's says, 'What's wrong with it?' I say, 'I don't know.' He says, 'In that case, twelve hundred, thirty nine dollars and seventy five cents.'"

The audience roared. Jake glanced around curiously. The joke wasn't all that funny, but the comic's delivery was superb.

"So, I got me a new car. This one's got a bell that reminds me to buckle my seat belt, a light that blinks when the gas is low, and a buzzer to tell me I'm going over sixty. My wife isn't bad enough, now my dashboard nags me."

The audience loved him. He had an expressive face—like Jack Benny or Nathan Lane—a face that could crack up an audience without a word said.

"Best thing about a little car, though: If you flood the engine, you can throw it over your shoulder and burp it."

For the first time in months, the dream awakened in Jake's mind. The short hairs on his arms and along the back of his neck stood at attention: This guy was good.

Silkie nudged him. "Say, doesn't he look like that old comedian, died fifteen, twenty years ago? Eddie Jackson? Meek as a mouse, but the minute he walked on stage he came alive."

"I don't care who he looks like. I want him. He can open tomorrow night and I want him booked straight through the holidays." Jake sensed the big time hovering on the other side of Christmas. This talent could put the Laff Club right up there with the best. Bulging with business. Recognized nationwide.

Ghosts 219

Frowning, Silkie tongued the cherry stem into a knot. "Maybe this guy's doing an imitation of Eddie Jackson. Sure sounds like him. Wears the same kind of hat and that white carnation to match. Eddie always wore a white carnation. And, man, he lived for the audience."

The comic started winding down.

"And remember, folks, if your teenager wants to learn to drive . . . don't stand in his way."

The audience howled with laughter.

He tipped his Stetson. "You've been a great bunch. Next time you're in Texas, stop on by the ranch."

"Yeah!" Silkie hammered his fist on the table top. "That's how Eddie Jackson always signed off."

But the audience wasn't ready to let the comic go.

"More. More. More," they chanted, until the big man strolled back on stage. Then they cheered for another minute before settling down to listen.

Jake felt like a gambler holding four aces on a million-dollar pot. He'd finally found his ticket to fame and fortune.

"Get over there, Silkie. I want him signed the minute he walks off."

Silkie waited beside the stairs leading from backstage. He had a strange feeling about this guy. Jake was right, the man was a topnotch comedian. He had the polish of someone who'd spent years on the circuit. He sure came alive on stage. So, what was he doing in a dive like the Laff Club?

And where was he, anyway? His final curtain call had ended two minutes ago. He oughta be out here by now.

An old man brushed past, so frail and thin Silkie almost didn't see him. He heard a faint creak as the man shambled by, like old bones turning in dry sockets. And something smelled sweet, sickly sweet, like dirt from a turned grave.

Now where the devil was that comic?

CPSIA information can be obtained at www.ICGtesting.com
Printed in the USA
BVOW071113281012

304135BV00005B/59/P